D1240834

Holiday Homicide

A University Mystery

Brenda Donelan

Holiday Homicide
©Copyright 2014 Brenda Donelan

All Rights Reserved

For Dan Donelan... we miss you. RIP.

Acknowledgements

Thank you to everyone who supported me during the preparation of *Holiday Homicide*. My beta readers, Audra Bonhorst Hawkinson and Clay Finck, provided wise and encouraging feedback on the first draft of my book. I credit my editor, Alastair Stephens, for finding my mistakes and helping me become a better writer.

Dr. Carol Donelan provided immeasurable assistance with the movie references for *Holiday Homicide*. Had it not been for her expertise, all of my media references would have come from obscure British programs and *The Hangover* trilogy.

I would like to give a big shout out to my friend Samantha Lund Hilmer on the design of the book cover. She spent numerous hours not only designing the cover, but also assisting me with my website and other technical endeavors associated with writing and publishing a book. Also I want to recognize fotohalo for the cover photography, courtesy of iStock.

Storytelling was not just a pastime in our family; it was a way of Oh, thelife. For that I thank my parents, Lawrence and Patricia Donelan.

My friend and fellow author, Johnny Bryan Ward, deserves a big "thank you" for enduring my long email rants about writing and encouraging me to keep writing.

Finally, the National Novel Writing Month (NaNoWriMo) program has helped me better my writing and commit to a writing schedule. It was during the NaNoWriMo writing program of 2013 that I started writing *Holiday Homicide*.

Contents

Generosity with money and possessions is not the same thing as generosity of spirit. Not the same thing at all. A person who donates to charity may be the same person who knifes you in the back. Such was the story of my life and my death.

Chapter 1

It was the Monday after Thanksgiving in 2005 and no one was in the mood to go back to classes. A five-day weekend which included at least one day of gluttony and one day of over the top power shopping, did not put professors, students, or staff at Midwestern State University in an academic mood. Marlee McCabe, in her third year of teaching at MSU, wore her fat pants. For her, the holidays for her started in early October, coincidentally about the time Halloween candy was on full display in the stores. By Thanksgiving she already felt like a bloated toad and after an overly-decadent holiday she resorted to wearing black yoga pants tucked inside her faux-fur-trimmed snow boots, hoping no one would notice.

A cold, biting wind whipped across the flat campus of Midwestern State University. If the weather forecasters on the news could be believed, there would be snow, preceded by freezing rain that night and into

Tuesday. From November through April, the town of Elmwood, set in the northeastern part of South Dakota, would be covered by inches and sometimes feet of snow. Everyone knew it was coming. The only mysteries were when the bad weather would strike, and just how bad it would be.

There were only two more weeks of regular classes until final exam week. Students stressed, fussed, and fretted over finals, but it was a time of relief for most professors. By that time, the failing students had either dropped the course or just stopped showing up. Most of the grades were already recorded and students would have a sense of where they stood in the class, unless they just started caring that week or were delusional. Marlee always had a student or two try to get an extra credit assignment on the last week of class to keep them from failing. Any extra credit she gave was always earlier in the semester and was usually used as a way to get students to attend a campus event such as Diversity Week or a speaker on a topic pertinent to the class. The students Marlee found to be the most irritating were those who would not drop the class and then tried with all their might to talk their way into a better grade at the end of the semester. They tended to be either athletes who were in danger of being cut from the team and losing scholarship money, or students who had been on academic probation repeatedly and were traveling down the same beaten path again. A few were high achieving students who insisted that they received straight As in high school and could not imagine why they were only earning a B in Marlee's class.

Marlee recalled the advice she had been given by the professor she replaced upon being hired at MSU. During her interview for the position, Dr. Arnott, who was retiring that semester, said, "Sometimes the best thing you can do for a student is to fail them." The more she thought about this over the past couple years, the more sense it made. If a student did not have at least a basic understanding of the material presented in class, then it was probably best that they withdraw or re-take the class so they could start again from scratch. Unfortunately, many students now felt entitled to a high grade in the class since they paid tuition. Professors, on the other hand, did not buy into this customer service model of higher education and assigned grades based on merit.

Students in the lower-level classes sometimes mistakenly believed they could significantly bring up their grade by the end of the semester. The reality was that if a student was struggling in the first few weeks of class, the rest of the semester did not bode well for them. Marlee had students re-take her classes after she failed them in previous semesters, even when they had the option to take the class with another professor, or online. She held strong to her principles and students received the grades they earned, regardless of how much she liked or disliked them.

Liking or disliking students was a topic that was off limits for formal faculty discussion. No one wanted to be accused of giving a high grade to a preferred student or a lower grade to one in disfavor. This conversation was saved for one's close friends on campus. Marlee's friends consisted of three professors and one director of a department on campus. "I'd like to punch that kid in the nose!" Marlee exclaimed once when she and her friends were at Marlee's home, discussing campus gossip. Her friends giggled nervously, glancing around as if to make sure no one was listening to their conversation in the private home. This was the only group Marlee felt comfortable enough to share her real feelings about certain students who got on her nerves.

Marlee's mood seemed to match that of the others she saw on campus that Monday morning. Professors were on autopilot, mentally pacing themselves to get through the rest of the semester. Remembering that the end of every semester was similar, and that she always prevailed unscathed, seemed to help. Other times, she needed a bit more encouragement. From mid-semester on, Marlee leaned on an old friend when grading papers at home. While sitting at her kitchen table in the evening she would rely on a frozen concoction she named Teacher's Little Helper. This drink consisted of putting a bunch of different types of alcohol in a bucket and mixing with juice or pop and then placing it in the chest freezer in her basement. A small glass or two of the frozen delight helped her cope with the mindlessness that was grading.

Some people are mean drunks. Not Marlee! She was a happy drunk and tended to get more lenient as the evening wore on. She was also more generous with her positive comments. "Good work", "great idea", "excellent point", and "outstanding" tended to grace more of the written papers as the clock ticked closer to midnight and more of Teacher's Little Helper was imbibed. She tried to go back and scan them quickly the next morning to ensure she did not assign a high grade with enthusiastic comments to a student who submitted less than stellar work.

Marlee's first stop upon reaching campus was to go to the bookstore. She already ordered her textbooks for the spring semester, but had received an email over the weekend stating that there was a problem with her order. She was concerned because a messed-up book order at this point would mean confusion from the campus bookstore employees and students. One thing Marlee learned about students in the short time she had been teaching: they will use any excuse to get out of an exam, a quiz, an assignment, or a term paper. If textbooks were late to arrive to the bookstore, Marlee would feel the backlash for weeks to come in the new semester. A few students would spend hours thinking up excuses as to why they should not have to take a quiz or test instead of spending the same amount of time reading and studying. She had to give them some credit, as she would not have had the balls or the level of creativity to pull this off with her Profs when she was a student.

Parking her Honda CR-V in the lot in front of the bookstore, Marlee shuffled toward the Student Union. This building, which was newly remodeled, looked like a factory in ruin. The motif was early Industrial Revolution with gray tones everywhere. She loved the color gray in clothing because it offset her pale complexion, green eyes, and auburn hair. In a building, however, gray was not the best choice, especially when the months of November through April tended to be gray and dreary. Marlee always thought Prozac should be handed out to everyone who entered this gloomy building, which housed the dining hall, Counseling Center, Disability Center, Campus Nurse, some administrative offices, several meeting rooms, and a host of other facilities. Therefore, it could not be avoided. Everyone had to enter the Student Union on a semi-regular, if not daily, basis.

Making her way downstairs to the bookstore, Marlee checked the time on the small timepiece in the shape of a ladybug that was clasped to her oversized book bag. It was 9:00 am, so she had an hour before her first class. She made her way to the back section of the bookstore, noting the new merchandise that had come in since her last visit. Marlee loved the new bright green and blue sweatshirts with the MSU logo. They were priced over sixty dollars, which no one could afford. No one except students with loans, that is.

As she fought the urge to shop as she walked, Marlee caught sight of Eva Gooding in her glass front office. Eva looked tired and worried, but it was the holiday season, so who wasn't tired and worried? Eva made eye contact and Marlee raised her eyebrows. It was then that she saw a woman in trouble.

Eva Gooding was in her early fifties and had worked at the MSU bookstore for fifteen years. She was well regarded on campus. When a student or professor had a concern about textbooks, they were often told, "just ask Eva, she'll help you." Eva's no-nonsense approach to problems and ability to make things happen made her a favorite at Midwestern State University. Marlee liked her from the first day she went into the bookstore because Eva mistook her for a student. She did this a few other times when Marlee came to buy red pens or notebooks, and for that, Marlee was forever grateful. Students assumed professors were old, regardless of age or appearance.

One thing Marlee came to realize was that if something was not vocalized to the individual, it was probably being discussed behind their back among faculty and staff. MSU was like a family. A large, gossipy, dysfunctional family. For the most part, people were able to work together to achieve the common goal of educating students and recruiting new bodies for future semesters. What went on behind the scenes was fodder for a television reality program. Undermining, back biting, and lying were all common practices on any campus and MSU was no exception. Marlee was used to confronting problems head on. Before she started teaching at MSU, she had worked in the Criminal Justice field for over ten years. She started as a Social Worker, then moved to a Probation Officer, and finally worked as an Investigator. She liked to bring her experience into the classroom, as it tended to enrich the material she was teaching. Working in various Criminal Justice professions gave Marlee the tools to confront negativity, manipulation, and unsavory behavior. Although she had these skills as a professional, she still struggled due to her upbringing, which was to avoid conflict at all costs.

"Hey, Eva. What's up?" Marlee said as she approached the buyer for the bookstore.

"You got the email I sent yesterday?" asked Eva, her eyes shifting from the floor to the ceiling to the shelves of books.

"Yeah. I can't imagine what went wrong with my order. I put it in early enough and I double checked all the book titles and ISBN numbers," Marlee said.

Eva waived her into her office and took her into a back room that did not have any windows, thus blocking off any outside view of them. "There really isn't a problem with your order. I just didn't want anyone to read your email and find out what I really wanted to discuss." The previous year, a professor was found dead on campus. The ensuing investigation brought to light the vulnerability of the campus communication systems. Since that time, the Computer Center had been under quite a bit of scrutiny. Many on campus still did not believe there was safety and confidentiality in inter-office emails.

"Okay, so what did you want to talk to me about if it's not my textbook order for next semester?" Marlee questioned. Eva was jumpy and worried, both out of character for her.

"You probably know we have a Christmas tree here every year that holds signs with the names of less fortunate children and the presents they want from Santa?" Eva asked, motioning to a large evergreen standing in the middle of the bookstore. It was an MSU tradition that faculty, staff, and students could choose one or more folded pieces of paper hanging from the Christmas tree inside the bookstore and buy gifts for that specific child. The first names of these children came from the local Department of Social Services. Some of the children were in foster homes, while others were placed in state-sponsored programs and group homes. The children were victims of abuse and neglect and some had landed in legal trouble due to alcohol, drugs, violence, or theft. Some of the children might be able to return home at some point, but most would remain in the custody of the State of South Dakota until they turned 18, which was legal age in the state. If it were not from the donations solicited by the Department of Social Services, many of these children would not receive any gifts during the holiday season.

Marlee nodded and Eva continued. "We've accepted donations of presents that various people from the whole Elmwood community dropped off to fulfill the wishes of these kids. The presents were all stored in the back room along with cash, gift cards to local businesses, and a few canned food donations people made. When I came in to get caught up on some paperwork yesterday afternoon, I noticed all the presents, the cash, and the food were gone. I asked Tia and Rob, the other two who work here full time, but they didn't know anything about the presents being moved. I know you helped out on that campus investigation last year, so I thought maybe you could help me with this."

"Did you call the police or tell anyone else on campus besides Tia and Rob?" asked Marlee.

"Everybody knows the Police Department doesn't have time for something like this and probably wouldn't put much effort into it anyway. I asked Tia and Rob if they knew where the presents and such were moved to, but later I told them the matter was handled," said Eva.

"Well, I have to say that there are still several problems with the police department, mainly in administration, but there are some great people working as patrol officers and detectives. At this point, maybe it's best that the police aren't brought into it. It could be just a miscommunication or a prank. Who has access to the bookstore when it's locked?" asked Marlee.

"Rob, Tia, me, the janitor, and Geneva Sanders," said Eva. Geneva Sanders was the Dean of Student Affairs and her office was upstairs in the Student Union.

"So it could only be one of five people?" asked Marlee. "No one else?"

"Well I didn't do it," said Eva, taken aback that she was being considered a suspect.

"No, Eva. I didn't mean that. I just meant that there could not be anyone else who works here that could access the bookstore. I wasn't accusing you." Marlee seriously didn't think Eva would steal presents and money from orphans and foster kids. It was hard to think who would do such a thing, especially at this time of year.

"Oh, okay. I guess I'm just being a little sensitive about it. The Christmas tree donations were my project and I feel responsible that they're missing," said Eva.

"Out of curiosity, why didn't you tell anyone in Administration what happened?" asked Marlee. Protocol at MSU, as well as most bureaucracies, was very clear. Everyone had someone to report to, and was required to inform his or her immediate supervisor when something was amiss.

"I'm not sure who to trust around here. Plus, I thought they might just lay the blame on me and fire me. I need this job. I can retire in ten years with full benefits and I don't want to lose that. You know how things go at MSU. You don't have to be guilty, just easy to blame. I was hoping you could help me figure out what happened and we could get everything back and no one else would ever need to know," said Eva.

Marlee nodded, knowing all too well that campus politics played a huge factor in remaining employed. How well you did your job was not the primary factor in determining who was retained. What mattered were your alliances and what they could do for you. Any amount of guilt could be overcome with the right connections, whereas complete innocence might result in termination without the right alliances. Marlee had run afoul of the Dean of Arts and Sciences, her supervisor, the previous year when he threatened her with non-renewal of her teaching contract because she disobeyed one of his directives. Marlee did not see herself as having connections at all, but was able to keep unemployment at bay since she was instrumental in bringing about a conclusion to a death investigation on campus.

"Can you show me the room where the items were kept?" asked Marlee.

"It's this room right here," Eva said spreading wide her arms to show that they were standing in the exact room. "We piled the presents up over here on this table." A long, barren table stretched along half the length of the wall.

"Were the presents wrapped?" asked Marlee.

"No, we asked that they remain unwrapped so we can make sure the kids are getting what they asked for. Sometimes someone will decide to give a gift other than what was requested. This might work out once in a while, but the kids are usually disappointed if they don't get at least one of their requested presents. When everything is unwrapped we can see what we're dealing with. Once in a while a donor really over-buys for a child and we might take some of the presents designated for them and distribute them to children that did not get as much. We just try to keep it all fair so as many kids as possible can have a nice Christmas," said Eva.

"Did any of the work-study students have keys, or access to the bookstore keys?" Marlee inquired.

"No, we're very careful about the keys. We know it would be too tempting for some students to come in and help themselves to textbooks, sweatshirts, and whatever else they might need," said Eva.

Marlee laughed. "It would be tempting for professors too. I have my eye on that lime green MSU sweatshirt out there." Switching gears, she asked, "How well do you know Tia and Rob?"

"Rob has worked here longer than I have. I get along fine with him. He's kind of strange, but I don't think he would steal the kids' presents," said Eva. "Tia just started here this year. She's a former MSU student. She graduated four years ago with a degree in Business Administration and was working in Minneapolis at a company. Tia wanted to move back to Elmwood to be closer to her parents after her divorce, so she applied with us and was hired. She was absolutely the best candidate we had for manager of the bookstore. Tia is a sweetheart and there's no way she would take presents intended for kids. She's a mom herself and knows how not having presents would crush many of these kids."

"Who's the janitor that cleans the book store?" Marlee asked. There were several janitors employed at the many MSU buildings on campus. At least one janitor, and sometimes more, was assigned to each building. Occasionally, a janitor was moved from one building to another and they frequently filled in for each other when sick or on vacation.

"Shane Seaboy," said Eva. "He just started here in August and I don't know him that well. He's really quiet and hardly ever talks. He kind of gives me the creeps," said Eva.

"Where did he work before MSU?" asked Marlee.

"I don't know for sure. He may have come from out of state. I've heard some rumors, but who knows?" said Eva.

"What did you hear?" Marlee enquired.

"I heard he's on parole and this is the only job he can get," said Eva.

"I don't think he would be able to get employment here on campus if he's still under court supervision," said Marlee, fairly certain of what she said since she used to supervise federal offenders in the community when she was a probation officer. Schools, even colleges, were very skittish about having anyone with a felony conviction on site. The possibilities for danger and subsequent lawsuits were just too high. It was possible that he could have had his felony conviction expunged from his record, which would make him much more employable. "It's just a rumor, or he's off parole now."

"Again, the rumor mill has it that somebody here on campus pulled some strings for Shane to get hired," said Eva.

"Any idea who?" asked Marlee.

"Geneva Sanders, the new Dean of Student Affairs," said Eva. "Apparently they knew each other before starting work here. They both started about the same time."

"What's their connection? Are they related?" asked Marlee.

"I don't know, but I'll do some more asking around," said Eva.

Marlee left the bookstore, wondering who would

take the presents donated for less privileged children. She assumed the motive was either greed or poverty. The person who stole the presents must have either intended to sell them for cash or give them to their own children and relatives. Since Mondays were Marlee's busiest days on campus, she knew she would not be able to do much until tomorrow.

Death for me was not one single, isolated event. I died a little each day until struck by the final blow. Truth be told, I was dead for a long time before I died.

Chapter 2

Marlee didn't have classes on Tuesdays, just three hours of office hours when students could stop by to meet with her. She left home around 8:30 am, even though her office hours did not begin until 10:00. The plan was to meet with Eva at the bookstore again to see if there were any new developments on the stolen presents. Although Marlee did not have time on Monday to do any investigation on the matter, she did think up several additional questions to ask Eva.

As Marlee pulled into the parking lot nearest to the Student Union, she saw police cars, a fire truck, an ambulance, and uniformed officers outside the building. She parked her car and made her way to the front entrance as quickly as she could. An officer she didn't recognize held up his hand as she approached and in a gruff voice said, "No one beyond this point but authorized personnel."

"What happened?" asked Marlee. She could not

fathom what had occurred that would generate this much fervor. She pulled out her MSU identification card to show that she was an employee of the university and not just a looky-loo.

The middle aged officer glanced around to see who might be listening. When he saw that none of his superiors were in earshot, he said in a low voice, "A body was found in the lower level of the Student Union. I can't tell you anything other than that. You can go to your building, but you'll have to go around the Student Union and not through it, since it is a crime scene."

Marlee nodded as if in agreement; however, the last thing she was going to do was go straight to her building. She needed to know who was hurt or dead and why. Glancing around, Marlee saw a friend of hers who was recently promoted to detective with the Elmwood Police Department. Her name was Bettina Crawford and she was a seasoned officer, although had only recently received the recognition she deserved for her law enforcement efforts.

"Bettina!" Marlee shouted across the din of the sirens and people talking. Bettina looked her way and motioned for her to wait until she was finished talking to a man in an EMT uniform.

"What's going on?" Marlee asked as Bettina approached her. "I heard there was a body found inside the Union."

"That's right. It was one of the janitors," said Bettina nodding her head with such vigor that her dark brown ponytail bobbed up and down. "Shane Seaboy was found dead this morning by another janitor."

"What happened?" Marlee asked.

"We're looking into that but don't know yet. Off the record, it looks like he was hit from behind with a heavy, blunt object. He has some cuts and bruising on his hands and face as well. We should know more after the coroner does the autopsy," said Bettina. "I have to go now, but I'll call you later if I have any other news."

Marlee stood around for a few more minutes until she reluctantly decided to go to her office. Just as she was getting ready to make the trek to Scobey Hall, the front doors of the Student Union were propped open. Two EMTs exited the building carrying a stretcher. Atop the gurney was a large black bag encasing the form of what she supposed was a human body. Marlee shuddered at the sight. This was not the first time she saw a person being carried out of a building in a body bag. She thought back to the previous incident, ten years ago, when she went to visit a college friend living in Rapid City with the intent of going to the annual Motorcycle Rally in Sturgis. It was to be Marlee's first trip to Sturgis and she had heard all the hype about active drug usage on the streets, sex in full view of everyone, and danger around every corner. She was prepared to see anything and was a bit disappointed when none of it came to fruition. The next morning as she was leaving her friend's apartment for home, she observed yellow crime scene tape around the building and police cars parked outside. She had waited half an hour before summoning the courage to go outside and see what was happening, then walked out to her car with some of her belongings and started up a chat with a man from the building who was walking his dog. The man had indicated there had been a murder. Just then, the back apartment entrance flew open and a black body bag on a stretcher was carried out by two EMTs and placed in the back of an ambulance.

Now the same feeling permeated Marlee's stomach as had ten years ago when she watched a person taken from a building. The finality of death hit her as she thought about an individual being pronounced dead and placed in a body bag. The black bag zipping closed over the victim's body and face was a vision Marlee relived over and over again. She turned as the ambulance doors were opened and the stretcher was slid inward. She knew what would happen next: the ambulance would leave without turning on lights or sirens and take the deceased to the morgue where the coroner would perform an autopsy.

Marlee made her way around the Student Union over to Scobey Hall where her office was located. As she trudged up the stairs, she made a quick stop in the secretary's office. Louise was at her desk talking on the phone in a hurried whisper. Marlee took her time thumbing through the documents in her mail slot, waiting for Louise to finish her phone conversation to see if she knew any details on the death. Secretaries always had the inside scoop on what was going on.

"Louise, hi. Do you know what's going on over at the Student Union? There are all kinds of cop cars and emergency vehicles over there," said Marlee, fishing for details.

"Somebody died, but I don't know who or what happened," said Louise with a little shudder. "I'll make some more calls to see what I can find out from the other secretaries on campus."

Marlee's relationship with the department secretary was a bit tricky. Louise had her obvious favorites in the department and, due to her gender, Marlee wasn't one of them. Louise was an older woman who held traditional beliefs about the roles of men and women. After working at MSU for a few months, Marlee observed a pattern in Louise's relationships with the other professors. For the men she had all the time in the world, but the women in the department were left largely to fend for themselves in terms of secretarial assistance. She even went so far as to bring home-baked treats to the office because she knew the male faculty enjoyed them so much. Of course, the men knew they were Louise's favorites and never missed an opportunity to praise her baking abilities, which gave Louise the maternal attention she craved.

Marlee went to her office. She had not volunteered the information she received from Bettina because the minute Marlee told Louise, she would blab it all over, attributing Marlee's name to the information. Since she was still in hot water with the dean over her involvement in a death investigation on campus last fall, Marlee did not want her name attached to this matter. The dean was still looking for an excuse not to renew her contract for the next year and Marlee was not going to give him any more ammunition than necessary.

Sorting through piles of term papers on her desk that still needed to be graded and returned, Marlee heard a commotion in the hallway. Della Halter, a colleague in her department, strode into Marlee's office without so much as a greeting or an invitation. She marched right up to the side of Marlee's desk and stood a bit closer to her than was comfortable. Della was from the South and tended to be a bit too familiar with everyone. Initially, Marlee found her a bit off putting, but soon learned to like Della even though she was like a bull in a china shop.

"*Heyyyyy*," Della drawled as she stood near Marlee's elbow. "What the fuck is going on over at the Student Union?" Della had a way with words.

"I don't know the details, but there are a bunch of police officers and fire trucks there," Marlee lied. Della was not the best at keeping information quiet or confidential, so Marlee decided to play dumb around her just as she had with Louise earlier.

"I don't know what's becoming of this place," Della stated, shaking her head in disbelief. "Just a year ago a professor died on campus and now we have police here again. I hope it's not another suspicious death."

"Me too," said Marlee looking down at her papers. She was using her body language to suggest to Della that she was busy and should leave. Della either did not read body language or chose to ignore it. She had tried this technique with Della in the past and it didn't work, so Marlee was not sure why she kept trying it. After Della became satisfied that Marlee did not have any news about the happenings in the Student Union, she marched down the hall in search of someone else to pester. Marlee got up from her chair and gently closed the door before calling Eva at the bookstore.

"Hi, Eva. I know there's a lot going on over at the Student Union right now, but if you could give me a call at my office as soon as possible, that would be great. Thanks," said Marlee, leaving a message on Eva's voice mail.

It wasn't two minutes later when Eva called back. "Marlee, the missing presents are the least of the problem now. Shane Seaboy was found dead early this morning and the police have been questioning all of us who work here. They asked me about a hundred questions before they told me I could go back to my office. Can you meet with me?"

"I don't think the police will let me come inside the Student Union. I was just over there and they shooed me away. Can you get out of the building without causing too much disturbance? Can you walk over to the library?" asked Marlee.

"I'll give it a try. If I can get out I'll meet you upstairs by the study carrels along the north wall," said Eva.

Before exiting her office, Marlee put a note on her

door stating that she was in the library and might be a few minutes late for her office hours. If someone really needed to talk to her they were advised to look for her in the library. A note on the office door was essential if a professor was going to be absent for all or part of their office hours. Marlee was good about keeping her office hours, but on the rare occasion when she had to miss them, she always left a note. Other professors were known to regularly blow off their office hours, even when they had scheduled appointments with students. This led to a fair amount of tension between those professors and some of their students who had been stood up. Most students didn't think much of missing an appointment with a professor if it was they who did the skipping. If the professor; however, was the one to bail on the appointment, then all hell broke loose and the matter was often brought to the attention of the department chair, resulting in a discussion with the offending faculty member.

As she left Scobey Hall, Marlee decided to enter the library through the back. It was normally locked, but she hoped it would be open today so she could gain access to the library without the police or anyone else seeing her. She did not want anyone to know she was asking around about the death in the Student Union. The library was located close to Scobey Hall so she made it to her destination in less than two minutes. It was her lucky day. The back door was unlocked and Marlee breezed right in, walking softly to minimize the click of her shoes against the tile floor. Once inside, she made her way to the stairwell and found the study carrel area in the back on second floor. Within moments, Eva joined her and they sat across from each other at a small metal table.

"Eva, what the hell happened over there?" asked Marlee, unable to get her mind around what little she already knew about Shane's Seaboy's death on campus.

"Shane Seaboy is dead and I think he was murdered. The police asked me all kinds of questions: did I know him, who did he hang out with, who might have a problem with him, who could benefit from his death, and on and on. My head is swimming from all the questions. I was so nervous that my voice and hands were shaking. I hope they don't think I'm guilty of killing him," Eva blurted out. She was clearly rattled, her normally calm demeanor replaced by panic.

"I'm sure they can tell that you were just upset and nervous. Do you know where in the Student Union Shane was found?" asked Marlee.

"He was found on the lower level. It wasn't in the bookstore, thank God, because I don't think I could go back there if that's where he died," said Eva, still shaken from the tragedy and subsequent questioning.

"Do you have any idea who might have killed Shane or wanted him dead?" asked Marlee.

"I don't have a clue. Like I said yesterday, he just started here and isn't much of a talker," stated Eva.

"Who found him dead?" Marlee inquired.

"Lindsey Gates. She's a janitor in the Student Union, but she usually doesn't clean the bookstore. I heard she found him and tried to revive him. When Lindsey realized he was dead, she called 911 around 7:00 am" reported Eva.

"What time does she usually get to work? What about Shane, what time did he come to work?" asked Marlee.

"Lindsey came in at 7:00 every morning, but Shane usually came in around 5:00 or 5:30 am. He could have been dead for a couple of hours before Lindsey discovered him," said Eva.

"What time did Shane leave work usually?" Marlee

asked.

"Mid-afternoon, I think. A student threw up in the bookstore two weeks ago and we called for him to come clean it up. Another janitor, Bruce I think was his name, came in about 3:30 and took care of the mess. He said Shane leaves by 3:00 or so every day," said Eva.

"So there's no chance Shane would have been working late and was killed last night and just discovered early this morning?" asked Marlee.

"I don't know about that. There was some sort of student activity held in the lower level last night, but I think they finished by 10:00. Unless Shane was working for someone else, I don't think he would have been there. You might double-check that with the Physical Plant. They do all the scheduling for the janitors," said Eva.

"What was the activity?" Marlee asked. Various types of student activities were held in the Caldwell Room, a multipurpose room that held tables and chairs as well as booths along the side walls. There was a DJ booth and a small stage on one end and a snack bar on the other end of the room. Dances, festival celebrations, and talent shows were but a few of the events held in the spacious Caldwell Room.

"I was told it was a banquet for the football players. I could smell something cooking as I walked by when I left last night around 5:00," said Eva. "I remember thinking that I wished I could grab some of it and take it home so I didn't have to fix supper."

"Anything new on the disappearance of the presents?" asked Marlee, switching topics since she was fresh out of questions about Shane's death.

"Not really, but I did tell the police when they were questioning me today about Shane's death. I didn't want them to think I had information I was holding back," said Eva.

"Given the circumstances, that's probably a good idea," said Marlee. "Did the officer who questioned you have any thoughts on it?"

"No, he just asked why I didn't report it on Sunday afternoon when I discovered the presents were gone. I didn't want to come right out and tell him that the police in this town don't have a very good reputation, so I said I was asking around to see if anyone moved them," said Eva. "I told him I asked around yesterday and planned on reporting the missing presents today if they weren't found."

"Did he believe you?" asked Marlee.

"Well, he seemed a bit skeptical, but since there's a death to contend with the missing presents seem like small potatoes," said Eva.

"Yesterday you said the presents were all unwrapped. Do you remember what some of them were?" asked Marlee, curious about the type of gifts people were giving to under privileged children in the area.

"There were a bunch of video games, a lot of DVDs, and a few clothes and toys," said Eva.

"What's the worth of the gifts each individual child would receive?"

"All of the donations hadn't arrived yet, so it's hard to tell. At this point, I would say each child would receive presents valued at around forty dollars," said Eva.

"Wow. I had no idea people were so generous," said Marlee.

"For some of the kids, this will be the only present they receive for Christmas, so most people who donate are really good about giving them plenty."

"That's great. I've never donated here at the bookstore, but I have at the gift tree out at the mall. I only gave gifts that cost around twenty dollars each.

Guess I was being cheap," Marlee said, feeling a bit sheepish.

"No, you shouldn't feel cheap at all. Some people only give five-dollar gifts. We get all kinds of donations and if there isn't enough for one child then we use donations from two or more donors or we use the cash that some give. Every little bit helps," Eva said with a smile, then noted the time and stood up. "I better get back to work before somebody notices I'm gone."

"Thanks, Eva. Please give me a call if you hear anything about Shane's death or the missing presents."

"I will. Thanks for meeting with me," said Eva as she strode through the stacks of books toward the stairs.

Marlee remained sitting at the table, thinking about the death of Shane Seaboy and how drastically the day had changed from one in which she would be sitting in her office grading papers and answering students' questions to a day of a death on campus. And not just any type of death. This was a murder!

Brenda Donelan

Every piece of a puzzle is important, but some pieces are much more valuable than others. It's the same way with people. Ask anyone.

32

Chapter 3

When Marlee arrived at her office shortly after 10:00, two students were standing in the hallway waiting to meet with her. "Sorry I'm a little late, guys," she called as she opened her office door, hanging her coat on the hook behind the door and motioning for the first student in line to enter.

"Actually, we wanted to talk to you together," said Jasper. Dominic Schmidt and Jasper Evans were both students in the Criminal Justice program and were advisees of Marlee's. They were also two of the three founding members of the Criminal Justice Club, an informal organization that met off campus to discuss matters related to law enforcement, the court system, and the correctional system in South Dakota. Mainly, their discussions revolved around incidents that occurred in Elmwood, primarily the death of Logan LeCroix on the MSU campus last fall.

"What's up?" asked Marlee.

"Donnie Stacks wanted to be here too, but she has Chemistry lab and couldn't skip it," said Jasper. Donnie was the third founding member of the Criminal Justice Club. She was a non-traditional student with short, curly red hair who always sat in the front of class and asked a lot of questions. What distinguished her from some of the other "Question Queens" in classes was that her inquiries were actually insightful and dealt with the deeper issues within Criminal Justice.

Dom looked at Marlee and began to talk. He was a shy kid until he warmed up to people. Then he talked and joked around continuously. "Dr. M. we heard about a janitor dying over at the Student Union. We wanted to talk to you about it."

Pulling the office door closed, Marlee began talking to the two students about the matter. The three shared the information they had, most of it Marlee already knew. She trusted Dom and Jasper and they had proven themselves to be very discreet in the past so she had no qualms about telling them what Bettina Crawford from the PD had shared with her about Shane Seaboy's death. After exchanging information, Dom started squirming in his chair. "Look, we might know something but we don't want to tell the police. Not yet."

Marlee raised her eyebrows wondering what information these two clean cut students would have about the death of an MSU janitor. Dom continued squirming and said, "A bunch of us were at a party last night at Collin Kolb's house. It's only a block from campus and he and his roommates were having a big house party since the semester is almost over."

"There are two weeks of classes and finals before the end of the semester," said Marlee, giving the students a knowing look. She really couldn't bring herself to be too irritated with them for not taking classes as seriously as they should right now. Twelve years ago she was their age and did the same type of thing when she should have been studying and putting extra effort into research papers. "Anyway, what you were gonna say?"

"It was about 9:30 last night and this guy walked into the party. I didn't know him, but he seemed a little drunk and started talking to someone else at the party we didn't know. They got into a shoving match and Collin yelled for them to break it up or take it outside. Somebody said he was a janitor at MSU but I never heard who the other guy was. They both went outside and Jasper, me, and some other people followed to watch the action. Anyway, they got into it pretty bad, with punching and even some kickboxing. The guy we didn't know picked up a bat leaning against the house and swung it at the janitor before some of us took it away from him and broke up the fight. We were afraid the cops would come because of the ruckus they were making, plus when the bat was brought into the fight it looked like it was going to get ugly real fast," said Dom.

"What happened then? Did the janitor leave the party?" asked Marlee.

"They both did. The janitor walked toward campus and the other guy walked west. That was the last we saw of either of them," said Jasper.

"What were they fighting about? Did you overhear anything that was said between them?" asked Marlee.

"The other guy said to the janitor, 'you shoulda kept your mouth shut,' and I couldn't understand what the janitor said," reported Jasper.

"Can you describe the other guy? Would you know him if you saw him again?"

"Oh, yeah. I'd know him in a heartbeat. He had short black hair, and a big scar that went from his mouth to his earlobe. I think he was Native American or maybe

Hispanic. He had a dark complexion and he was probably about five foot ten and medium build," Jasper said. Dom nodded his agreement.

"How old was he?" asked Marlee.

"Early to mid-twenties. I've never seen him in any classes or anywhere on campus," reported Jasper.

"Me neither. I think he knew one of Collin's roommates and that's why he was at the party," said Dom.

"Do you guys know Collin's roommates?" asked Marlee.

"I don't, but I'll see Collin in Criminal Law class today. Collin's a starter on the basketball team and his other roommates are all athletes too. I'll ask Collin about the fight and see if he knows who the guy is that fought with the janitor. I'll get the names of his roommates too," said Dom.

The three agreed to have an impromptu meeting of the Criminal Justice Club later that day to share any new information they gathered. Dom said he would be seeing Donnie Stacks in Criminal Law class, so he would mention it to her too. There were several other members of the club, but Donnie, Dom, and Jasper were the only students Marlee knew well enough to share information with, knowing what was said at their meetings would stay there. Other students from the club might be tempted to share their discussions with anyone and everyone.

After Jasper and Dom left, Marlee was pondering the death of Shane Seaboy when Diane Frasier, an assistant professor in the Speech department knocked on the doorframe. Marlee jumped when she heard the knock, unaware of how long she'd been thinking about the unfortunate events of that morning.

"Hey, wake up!" Diane said, her face stoic. "Haven't

you had your six cups of coffee yet today?" Marlee and Diane both started teaching at MSU at the same time. They had a number of things in common, mainly their love of wine, beer, coffee, food, and juvenile humor.

"Yeah, I'm awake. Just thinking. C'mon in," Marlee motioned for Diane to enter the cramped office and have a seat. "You heard about the death over at the Student Union this morning?"

"I heard somebody died and that much of the Student Union is considered a crime scene, but I don't know any details. That's why I stopped in to see you," Diane said, adjusting her dark framed glasses and settling in for a full report.

"It's a janitor named Shane Seaboy. Apparently, he just started working here in August. He was found in the lower level of the Student Union and Bettina Crawford from the police department said it appeared as though he was struck from behind with a blunt object. He also had cuts and contusions on his hands and face. Two of my students were just in here to talk to me about him. They were at a party at Collin Kolb's house last night and Shane Seaboy was there. Some guy they didn't know got into a screaming match with Shane and then Collin kicked them both out of the house. They went outside and a bunch of others from the party followed. The fight turned physical with punches and kickboxing. My students said the other guy picked up a bat and tried to hit Shane, but some of the other partiers took the bat away and broke up the fight. Shane walked toward campus and the other guy went in the opposite direction," Marlee reported in record speed.

"Wait, so the janitor was beaten up last night and found dead this morning? Maybe the guy he fought with came back to finish the job," said Diane.

"That's a strong possibility. I wish I knew what the

two were fighting about. Also, the party was at a house rented by a group of students. Doesn't it seem odd that a janitor would show up? My students said they didn't know Shane but some others at the party recognized him from campus. This all seems so weird," Marlee said, perplexed.

"Here we go again. Looking over our shoulders and suspecting everyone of being a killer. I feel like I just got over being scared when Logan LeCroix died on campus last year," said Diane, her normally cheerful face in a hangdog expression.

"Do you want to stay at my house again?" asked Marlee. Diane had been a guest at Marlee's house for nearly a week the year before when the whole town was worried about a killer on the loose. She knew Diane was fearful and didn't like to stay alone. Marlee wasn't scared, but she would welcome the company.

"Yes! That's the other reason I came down here to talk to you. Thanks. I'll grab my stuff and come over after my last class," Diane said, her face returning to its default cheerful expression. She jumped up from her chair and left the room with more spring in her step than when she entered.

No one else stopped by Marlee's office, so she took the opportunity to grade some papers. Students had submitted their project papers from Criminology class the previous evening and she was anxious to start reading them. After grading three of the papers, Marlee decided she was due for a break and went back to Louise's office to see if there were any new developments.

"Hey, Louise," Marlee called out as she swung around the corner into the secretary's office. It was only after she'd made her presence known that she realized Dean Ira Green stood near Louise's desk, with Louise talking to him in a somewhat hushed tone. The dean, who was known throughout campus as Mean Dean Green due to his lack of tact and willingness to sacrifice anyone under his supervision, looked up from his conversation and glared at her. Dean Green had threatened Marlee last year when she disobeyed his directive not to become involved in the Logan LeCroix death investigation. After Marlee was instrumental in working on the investigation, Dean Green backed off his threats and Marlee's teaching contract was renewed for another year. She was only in her third year of teaching at MSU and didn't have tenure, so she held no illusions about her job security at the university. If Dean Green could find a way to get rid of her, he would do so in an instant. And Marlee knew he was not above using dirty tricks to have her fired.

"Uh, hi Dean. Just stopping in to check my mail. Hope I'm not interrupting your conversation," Marlee stammered, hoping the expression on her face didn't reveal the real reason for the visit; to see if Louise had any new information on Shane Seaboy's death.

"McCabe, get your ass in my office right now!" shouted the dean as he stomped toward his office door.

Marlee entered the dean's well-organized office, noting a new bookshelf already stacked to capacity with books. Without waiting for an invitation to sit, she backed up to the dean's desk and parked one butt cheek on the edge. Although she was somewhat fearful of the dean and his power over her career, Marlee still enjoyed rattling his cage whenever she could. "So what's up?" she asked in a nonchalant tone.

"Don't get too comfortable," Dean Green growled. "I just want to make it crystal clear to you that I won't tolerate any involvement from you in the death investigation at the Student Union. We don't need any more negative publicity here at MSU. This is none of your business and I want you to keep out of it. You stick to teaching your classes and let the police handle criminal investigations. Is that understood?" he asked arching his left eyebrow as he stared through her.

Marlee nodded her head, at a loss for words and unable to think of anything to say that would not incriminate her since she fully intended to continue asking questions. She had all kinds of questions and exceptions that she wanted to bring up to the dean, but she'd learned a long time ago that sometimes it's best not to ask questions about what is and what isn't allowed. Better to plead ignorance after the fact than ask for permission in advance and be denied.

"Sure, you won't have any problem with me," Marlee said, fighting the urge to cross her fingers behind her back.

"Good. I'll see you at the campus meeting this afternoon," said the Dean, with a little less gruffness than before.

"What meeting?" Marlee inquired.

"It hasn't been announced yet, but we'll be having an all-campus meeting this afternoon with the Police Chief. He'll brief us on the investigation," the dean reported.

"Okey dokey, I'll be there," said Marlee as she stood up and walked toward the door.

"I mean it, McCabe! I'm not screwing around here. If you butt into this like you did the Logan LeCroix investigation, I'll see to it that your contract isn't renewed," snarled Dean Green as a small, evil smile crept to his lips. He was still stinging from the LeCroix investigation when Marlee made him look like a fool. She was sure about one thing: Mean Dean Green would do anything and everything he could to get her off campus... permanently! And Marlee knew he was not above undermining her or falsifying information to achieve his goal.

We all have a past. Most everybody is given a chance to overcome poor decisions and mistakes. I was allowed no such opportunity.

Chapter 4

As she returned to her office, Marlee was struck by the similarities between this death investigation and the one that happened on campus a year ago. Both involved a mysterious death on campus during the early morning hours, when the crimes could go largely undetected. The victims in each case were new to campus and had a number of unanswered questions about their backgrounds. The main difference at this point was that Shane Seaboy's death was being considered a homicide from the get-go, while that was not the case last year with Logan LeCroix. Marlee knew Logan, albeit superficially, so she had a connection to him, whereas she didn't recall ever seeing Shane Seaboy around the Student Union.

Marlee needed to keep a low profile in the dean's eyes, so she decided to stay in her office and see who came to her with information. To her surprise, no students came to her office for the next hour. Since it was so late in the semester, poorly performing students utilized this time frame to beg for time extensions, extra credit, or special treatment. Other students, often befallen by stress and a seasonal cold, came to visit their professors just for sympathy or comfort. Depending on where she was in her own personal stress and physical well-being at that point in the semester, she might offer up some soothing words and suggestions for time management. If she was in a foul mood or under the weather, then she didn't give them much sympathy. If she could be at work doing her job then they could just as well finish the required papers and projects for classes. Marlee resisted the urge to launch into tales of her own college years in which she had to complete all of her projects on time and without exception, even under the most dire of circumstances. Rose-colored glasses tend to work the best when looking in the rear view mirror. Still, she fought back the urge to yell, "Toughen up, Buttercup!" at the offending students.

In the absence of any whining students and complaining faculty members, Marlee broke out her green insulated lunch bag and looked inside at the protein bar, a small can of V-8 juice, and a sad little apple. With a sigh, she unwrapped the protein bar and took a bite, unenthused with her lunch selection. Constantly battling her weight, Marlee leapt between two extremes: dieting and gluttony. Currently, she was in the diet phase, not so much for long-term weight loss, but to be able to wrestle herself back into her normal size fourteen pants after a fall binge which had already lasted for more than eight weeks. Within two minutes, the lunch was consumed, but Marlee was still hungry. She knew the hunger wasn't from a lack of food, but rather the stress of the ending semester and the suspicious death on campus that morning. She threw away the trash and slung the insulated lunch bag into the corner near her book bag, ready to be taken home and filled with an equally unsatisfying lunch for tomorrow.

Marlee checked her email and discovered that, just as Dean Green had earlier indicated, there would be an all-campus meeting that afternoon at 2:00, so campus officials and the police department could address the death on campus. In the remaining time before the meeting, a slew of students, professors, and staff members stopped by Marlee's office to discuss the death of Shane Seaboy. None of them had any new information and Marlee was reluctant to share what she had uncovered that morning. She was willing to trade information, but she wasn't going to hand it out without getting something in return. Plus, she didn't want Dean Green hearing that she was asking questions again.

Just before the start of the campus-wide meeting, Marlee made her way to the Quinn Building. Ordinarily, campus meetings were held in the Caldwell Room, but that space was in the Student Union and currently sealed off as part of the crime scene. Marlee broke into a quick jog, attempting to catch up to her friend Kathleen Zens, an assistant professor in the Music department.

"Hey, Kathleen! Wait up!" called Marlee as she rushed down the sidewalk. The snow had been removed from the sidewalks, but patches of ice remained from a light rain the previous night. In a nanosecond Marlee found herself flat on her back, looking up at the sky. The fall happened so quickly she didn't even have time to react. Her coffee cup landed upright in a small pile of snow while her book bag and insulated lunch sack were strewn on the sidewalk before her. The worst thing about falling down was not the pain, nor the hassle of picking up all of one's belongings; the embarrassment was the worst. Marlee didn't like calling attention to herself for positive reasons and she really didn't like being the center of attention for falling down. Unfortunately, falling down in the middle of what seemed to be the whole campus on their way to the Quinn Building was not a way to fly under everyone's radar.

Leaping to her feet as fast as she could, Marlee grimaced both because of the stares and the shouts of, "are you okay?" from various onlookers. Two students walking directly behind Marlee witnessed the whole thing and attempted to help her to her feet.

"Are you hurt? Did you break a hip?" asked the tall athletic student with her blonde hair pulled back in a fluffy ponytail.

"No, I didn't break a hip," Marlee said crisply and rolling her eyes, wishing these students would just move along.

"Oh, good," said Ponytail. "My grandma slipped on her steps a few days ago and broke her hip." Marlee did a slow burn from the comparison to someone at least forty years her senior. Ponytail and her friend, satisfied that Marlee's fall had not resulted in a geriatric condition, continued on their way to the Quinn Building as Kathleen Zens walked over.

"I'm gonna give your routine an 8.0. You would've had a 10.0, but you didn't stick the landing," Kathleen said without cracking a smile. She grabbed Marlee's travel mug from the ground and held it up. "Lookie here...you didn't spill a drop of coffee!"

Well, that's one good thing, I guess." Marlee was not ready to smile yet, but Kathleen's humor was starting to lessen the embarrassment of the wipe out. Maybe not that many people witnessed the fall after all. As Marlee leaned over to pick up her book bag and lunch sack, she felt a twinge in her lower back. A couple over-the-counter pain relievers should help with that.

At Marlee's suggestion, the two seated themselves near the back of the meeting room so as to observe others in the audience. Someone knew much more about the death than they were telling. The murderer might even attend the campus-wide meeting. A microphone was near the stage, so Marlee knew they would be able to hear everything said by the speakers. Marlee scrutinized everyone carefully as they filed into the room. They all looked somewhat shifty, yet not overly suspicious.

Diane Frasier, along with Shelly McFarland and her partner, Gwen Gerken, entered the room and joined Marlee and Kathleen. The group of five women comprised an informal supper club, which initially started as a means to cook for one another in their own homes. As time went on, that goal quickly fell to the wayside and turned into a pizza-ordering, wine-guzzling, gossip-fest. This seemed to fit the spirit of the group much better, since the focus was now on the social aspect rather than food preparation. Shelly McFarland was a therapist at the campus counseling center and was held in high regard by students, faculty, and administration because of her dedication to those who sought her out for counseling. Gwen Gerken was an assistant professor in the Music department. She and Kathleen worked in the same department and managed to avoid the rivalry and animosity which tended to be present in many interdepartmental relationships across campus. Both were talented beyond belief, and Marlee wondered how MSU was able to hire such accomplished musicians. Kathleen was a concert pianist who taught piano, while Gwen was an opera singer and provided vocal instruction.

At five minutes after the appointed starting time, a group of administrators moved from the front row of the seating area to the stage. Kendra Rolland, Vice President of Student Affairs, turned on the microphone and tapped it lightly, her bracelets jangling as she ensured the microphone was in working order. Kendra was professionally dressed in a brown sweater and a complimentary black and brown skirt, accompanied with tall brown suede boots. Her multi-layered dark brown hair partially concealed her dangling earrings, which hung nearly to her shoulders. After ensuring the functionality of the microphone, she stepped back and John Ross, the President of MSU stepped forward.

"Good afternoon. Thank you for coming to this campus-wide meeting," said President Ross with a flat, robotic tone. The president had a somewhat stocky frame with wildly fluctuating weight. At present, he was stuffed into a black suit a size too small for him. His pink and blue necktie was cinched tightly around his neck and he tugged at it unconsciously as he spoke. "As most of you are aware, a body was found on campus this morning. I've asked Bill Langdon, Chief of the Elmwood Police Department to talk to us about the ongoing investigation."

Chief Langdon strode from the back of the group to the front of the stage. He was clad in khaki pants, a white dress shirt open at the collar, and a tan sports jacket. On his belt hung his cell phone encased in a faux leather pouch. The toes of Langdon's brown shoes were scuffed and covered in the street grunge that covered the footwear of most of Elmwood's residents this time of year. The Chief had a bad habit of staring at people, which was magnified by his big, googly glasses. His shaggy mustache covered his upper lip and the corners of his mouth, so his emotions were often difficult to read. Over his past three decades in law enforcement, Chief Langdon had developed a rather flat affect when dealing with the public. Other than being on the receiving end of

48

his anger on one occasion, Marlee had never seen the Chief display any type of emotion.

"Early this morning the Elmwood Police Department was notified that a body was found on the MSU campus," stated Chief Langdon without a bit of feeling to his voice. "Officers arrived and found the body of Shane Seaboy, an employee here at MSU. He was pronounced dead at the scene and his body was transported to the morgue for an autopsy. Cause of death has not been determined and the matter remains under investigation. For now, we're treating the death as a homicide. We're interviewing friends, relatives, coworkers, and associates to determine who might have wanted harm to come to Shane Seaboy. If anyone has information, talk to one of the officers here today or come down to the station immediately."

The chief backed away from the microphone and President Ross stepped forward to speak again. "Extra police officers will be patrolling the campus area, both during the day and at night, to ensure the safety of all who attend classes and work here. Classes and activities will continue as usual. You're all urged to stick to your regular schedules, but just exercise caution when doing so. Don't go anywhere alone. We suggest you walk in pairs or groups, especially at night. If you would like someone to walk with you, simply call the Student Union Help Line and a volunteer will meet you at your dorm, car, or classroom and escort you to where you need to go. Until the matter is resolved, we want everyone to rest assured that they are safe here at MSU." President Ross's words rang hollow. No one had felt completely safe at MSU since Logan LeCroix's death on campus last fall.

In the back of the stage party stood a woman shaking with sobs. Tears ran down her face and she covered her mouth with both hands. Her short dark hair made her light complexion appear ghostly pale. She wore a calf length blue print dress and a matching blue cardigan over the top. Although she wore work-appropriate clothing, the woman appeared rumpled, as if she had dressed in the dark. Marlee felt an elbow jab into her side. "Who's that in the back? The lady crying?" whispered Kathleen.

"I think it might be Geneva Sanders, the new Dean of Student Affairs. Apparently she and Shane Seaboy knew each other before working here. I was told she pulled some strings to help him get the job," Marlee replied, knowing the information she shared with her supper club friends would be kept confidential. "Eva from the library seemed to think Shane Seaboy had a prior record and Geneva helped him to get the janitorial job here at MSU, even though everyone is supposed to go through a background check before being hired."

Kathleen raised her eyebrows at the information. "So you're gonna ask around and find out more about Shane Seaboy and Geneva Sanders, right?"

"Yeppers. I have to be extra careful, though, because Mean Dean Green already hauled me into his office and threatened to have me fired if I did any nosing around. I told him he didn't have anything to worry about, and that I'd keep my nose in my own business," Marlee said with an impish grin which prompted Kathleen to roll her eyes and shake her head.

Kendra Rolland continued the announcements from administration by stepping up to the microphone once again. "Counselors are available at the campus Counseling Center. This service is free of charge and available to all students, faculty, and staff at MSU. We know this is a tough time and encourage you to talk to one of the therapists if you are struggling. There's no shame in talking to someone about things bothering you.

Mr. Seaboy's next of kin has been notified of his death and I know you all join me in sympathy for Mr. Seaboy's friends and family." Kendra gave a brief nod to show the meeting had come to an end.

Charles Wilmhurst, a long-time fixture in the Business School and frequent meeting grandstander, jumped to his feet before the administrators and police chief could leave the stage. "Wait! Do you have any suspects?"

Chief Langdon approached the microphone again and chewed at the corner of his mustache. "Uh, we do have a person of interest; however, we cannot divulge his or her name at this point. A person of interest doesn't mean they're a suspect, it's just someone we want to talk to."

Not finished with his line of questioning, Professor Wilmhurst asked, "Have you checked the campus security videos? Did they show the crime or any suspicious people on campus last night or this morning?"

"We're reviewing the security videos from the Student Union for the past twenty four hours. Other than that, there's not much else I can tell you at this point. Continue on with your regular activities, be cautious, and let us handle the investigation," the Chief said, looking straight at Marlee in the back of the room.

BRENDA DONELAN

Which is more deceptive–a lie or a half-truth?

Chapter 5

After exiting the meeting room, Marlee and her friends congregated in the hallway of the Quinn Building to discuss the developments. In trying to make sense of Shane Seaboy's death, they all had more questions than answers.

"Why was Geneva Sanders so upset?" asked Gwen, curious as to why an administrator would have such deep feelings for the janitor. Marlee filled her and the others in on the possible connection between Geneva and Shane.

"So are they related? What is their connection, other than knowing each other?" asked Diane, brow furrowed as she puzzled over the matter.

"I don't know, but I'm going to do some asking around," said Marlee with conviction, although she didn't have the first clue as to how she would find out the connection between the two people.

"Hey, that was a doozie of a fall you took outside

before the meeting. Are you okay?" asked Shelly McFarland.

"Yeah, I'm okay. I was hoping not that many people saw it," Marlee said with a sheepish grin, the embarrassment coming back.

"Everyone saw it!" Diane said. "I'm surprised you don't have a concussion!"

"It reminded me of the old Charlie Brown cartoon when Lucy holds the football for Charlie Brown and insists she won't move it before he can kick it. Of course she does, and he lands flat on his back," said Kathleen with a chuckle.

Marlee closed her eyes, trying to forget the spectacle she'd made of herself in front of a large portion of those on campus. After sitting for a half hour, she was becoming stiff and sore. She opened her book bag and rummaged around until she found a bottle of Motrin. Popping two in her mouth and washing them down with the remains of tepid coffee in her travel mug, she offered up a small smile. "Glad I could provide entertainment for everyone."

Dominic Schmidt and Jasper Evans, along with Donnie Stacks, made their way past Marlee and her group. "Whoa, Dr. M. That was some wipe out!" exclaimed Jasper.

"Yeah, everyone's talking about it," said Donnie with a level of excitement Marlee rarely saw in the petite redhead.

"You know what it reminded me of?" asked Dom. "Have you ever seen that show *Jackass*, where an actor does all these crazy stunts and has it filmed? That's what I thought of right away when I saw you fly into the air and crash down on the sidewalk."

"Uh, no, I've never seen that show. Is it on PBS?" Marlee asked with equal amounts bitterness and sarcasm, which amused Diane, Gwen, Kathleen, and Shelly. Comparing a professor to the actor on Jackass right to her face took some enormous *cojones*.

"No, it's on MTV," Dom replied, oblivious to the subtext of the conversation. Marlee knew Dom meant no harm by his comment. She also knew she would find it very funny in the retelling of the tale in a few days. Today, however, was a different story.

"Are you all free now?" Marlee asked Donnie, Dom, and Jasper. "Maybe we could meet for a bit to discuss this latest incident." As she made the comment she looked over her shoulder to ensure Dean Green was not in the vicinity.

They all nodded in unison and decided to meet at the Chit Chat for coffee and pie. After bidding her friends farewell, Marlee drove to the Chit Chat on the edge of Elmwood. It was a cozy, kitschy, little diner which served a host of local favorites, most of which were smothered in cream of mushroom soup. The café was populated with booths and tables while the walls were covered with old-fashioned sayings Mod-Podged onto wood and painted on old tin scraps. Marlee was the first to arrive and selected a table in a corner, out of the earshot of most of the other customers. She looked around as she waited for service and noticed a new addition to the signs above the window. This one read "Common sense isn't that common," and it featured a donkey kicking up its heels.

A waitress balancing a tray of steaming food breezed past Marlee. "Be right with ya, hun," she said over her shoulder as she pivoted on one foot to a nearby table and unloaded the tray of four plates in under ten seconds. Moving back toward Marlee's table with a dancer's precision, the waitress, whose nametag identified her as Norma, whipped a menu out of her apron waistband and plopped it down on the table. "Know what you want to drink?" she asked, her pen poised above her notepad.

After placing her drink order, the three students joined Marlee at the table and eventually decided on their drinks as well. The one menu was passed around so everyone could look at it, all finally deciding on pie. The students were more boisterous than usual, anticipating the conversation they were about to begin. Caffeine and sugar would only serve to enhance the level of excitement felt by everyone at the table.

"Hey, check it out," said Dom with delight, pointing to the common sense wall hanging with the donkey. "It's a jackass and we were just talking about that show, *Jackass*! Do you believe in signs?"

Marlee gave him a long stare, trying to maintain her composure. She finally decided to ignore the comment and move the conversation forward. "So, did any of you have a chance to talk with Collin Kolb about his house party, and how he knew Shane Seaboy and the guy Shane fought with?"

"Yeah," said Jasper. "Collin went to high school in Sisseton with Shane and the other guy. The other guy's name is Tony Red Day, Jr. Collin said he didn't really hang around with Shane or Tony in high school, but knew them fairly well."

"Did Collin invite them to the party?" Marlee enquired, wondering why else high school acquaintances would show up at a college party, especially if they were not college students.

"I don't know if he did or not. We never discussed that part. What Collin told me was that Shane and Tony were really great friends in high school but that something changed a bit before graduation. He didn't know what happened, but was aware there was some type of falling out between the two," reported Jasper.

"Did Collin know what the fight was about at his party?" Donnie asked, as she had not been privy to the conversation Jasper and Dom had with Collin.

"Collin didn't know why they were fighting, just that they haven't gotten along in the past few years," Jasper said.

"Did Collin think Tony could've killed Shane?" asked Marlee, turning in her chair to face Jasper.

"I didn't ask him outright," said Jasper, upset with himself for not asking about the obvious. "I did ask him if he knew anybody who would want Shane Seaboy dead and he just shrugged before he left the classroom. I got the feeling Collin might have some ideas on this that he just didn't want to share with Dom and me."

"I think the next step is that I'll talk to Collin Kolb myself and see what I can find out. You two already did a great job of gathering some initial information from him," Marlee said nodding at Dom and Jasper. "Do any of you know Collin's class schedule?"

"He has Cultural Anthropology with me tomorrow in the Quinn Building from 11:00 till noon," volunteered Donnie, anxious to take more of an active role in the foursome's unofficial investigation.

"Perfect," exclaimed Marlee. "I have class in the same building until noon. I know some of the classrooms are empty then, so I'll see if I can get him to talk to me in private."

Donnie, Jasper, and Dom all nodded, thinking the plan sounded solid.

"So what should we do in the meantime?" asked Dom.

"Keep your ears open and don't talk about any of this with anyone else. Dean Green is looking for a chance to fire me and I don't want him finding out that I've been asking questions about Shane's murder," advised Marlee.

"If you hear anyone talking about Shane Seaboy or Tony Red Day, Jr., take note of who is doing the talking and what they are saying. If you know the people well enough to insert yourself into the conversation, do so. Otherwise, just observe and make note of what you hear."

After finishing their pie and ordering multiple refills on their drinks, the group left the Chit Chat with plans to touch base the following day. Marlee drove home and parked in the detached garage. She carefully made her way up the sidewalk, careful not to slip on any hidden ice patches and put the key in the lock. The door was already unlocked, which was strange since Marlee nearly always locked her doors. Just as she was making her way inside the back door, a voice shrieked, "Stop right now or I'm calling the police!"

Life is not like a movie. A movie has to be believable. Life does not.

Chapter 6

"Diane, it's just me! Calm down!" shouted Marlee, wondering how her friend had accessed her house without a key.

Around the corner poked a head full of long, black waves. It was definitely not Diane. "What the hell?" exclaimed Marlee.

"Hey, cuz. Thought I'd pop in for a visit," said the dark haired woman.

Marlee took a deep breath and began to smile as she recognized the intruder in her home was none other than her cousin, Bridget McCabe. Bridget was five years Marlee's senior. She was a professor of film studies at a private college in Minnesota. Bridget was a few inches taller and much, much trimmer than Marlee could ever hope to be. She was dressed in jeans and a blue argyle sweater. Her shoes were kicked off by the back door and she stood sock footed as Marlee entered her own home.

"Bridget! What the hell! How did you get in here?"

Marlee was still reeling from the shock of having an uninvited relative in her house without any fore warning.

"I called your mom when I found out I was coming to Elmwood. She suggested I stay with you and told me where you hide your spare key. I found it on the nail under the dustpan in the garage, just like she said I would, so I let myself in. I hope that's OK," Bridget said.

"Of course it's OK. You're welcome here anytime," Marlee said and she meant it, although she was going to have to have a word with her mother about telling people to let themselves in with the spare key.

Marlee closed the back door behind her and set down her book bag and insulated lunch bag. She gave Bridget a hug and said, "So what brings you to Elmwood? It's kind of out of the way to just be passing through. Are you here for work?"

Bridget nodded. "Yes, I am giving a talk at Marymount College tomorrow." Marymount College was a private Catholic institution of higher learning in Elmwood. Although the population of Elmwood was only around 25,000, it easily accommodated Marymount College as well as Midwestern State University. The two institutions had different programs and curricula, so there was very little competition between the schools.

"Well, you're welcome to stay here as long as you like," Marlee said, excited to catch up with her cousin. Not only was Bridget one of her favorite cousins, she was also a great sounding board for all things academic. Bridget had been teaching for years and could warn Marlee of the academic pitfalls and land mines better than anyone. Plus, Bridget was someone she could trust. Marlee was learning fast that not everyone who purported to have her best interests at heart on her own campus actually did.

"Thanks. I was hoping you'd say that. I brought in

my bag and put it in the spare room," Bridget said.

"No problem. My friend, Diane from MSU, is going to be staying here tonight and maybe for a few days, but she'll sleep on the couch because she likes to stay up late and watch movies," reported Marlee.

"Well Diane and I will get along just fine since movies are my thing," Bridget said with a grin. "Why's she staying with you? Is she having repairs done at her place or something?"

"Oh, crap, I almost forgot! We had another death on campus. One of the janitors was found dead in the basement of the Student Union. It looked like he was beaten. The cops are considering it a homicide right now and they don't have any suspects. Diane is kind of skittish about being alone with a murderer on the loose, so I invited her to stay with me until the matter gets sorted out," said Marlee.

"Do you have a gun?" Bridget asked, her eyes getting larger with each second she thought about her cousin with a firearm.

"Nope, I don't like guns. I only had a gun when I was a probation officer and I never liked carrying it, so I always kept it hidden in my junk drawer at home," said Marlee.

"Whew, that's good. I don't want to get shot in the night when you forget I'm staying here and think it's an intruder," laughed Bridget, although the scenario she had just devised could be all too true. "It would be like that scene from *All the Rage* when Jeff Daniels shoots his wife's lover because he thinks he's an intruder."

"True," acknowledged Marlee. "We wouldn't want that to happen."

A sharp knock at the back door made Marlee and Bridget both jump. Marlee trotted to the back door and found Diane Frasier standing there with three tote bags, a duffel bag, her coffee pot, and an oversized orange pillow. "Hey, Diane. Are you moving in?" Marlee joked. She knew her friend wanted all the comforts of home while away from home. She didn't blame Diane one bit for bringing so much stuff, but had to give her a hard time about it.

Diane struggled to get herself and her belongings through the back door. Turning sideways to accommodate the multitude of bags, Diane laughed. "No, I have my book bag full of class materials, the duffel bag has clothes and toiletries, the blue tote bag is full of coffee and snacks, and the grey tote holds a few bottles of wine. It looks like a lot, but it's really not."

Marlee laughed, grabbing the grey tote bag and extricating three bottles of red wine from inside. "Awesome! Hey, I want you to meet my cousin, Bridget McCabe. She's staying here for a few days too."

Following the introductions, Diane and Bridget chatted about academic similarities between their institutions while Marlee retrieved three wine glasses from the top shelf of the cupboard over the sink. The trio adjourned to the living room and made themselves comfortable on the over-stuffed blue couch and love seat. Marlee placed their glasses on the wooden coffee table and began to pour from a bottle of Shiraz Diane had brought. Pouring the wine glasses to nearly the rim polished off the wine bottle and Marlee set it aside.

"So Marlee was just telling me about this murder on campus before you got here, Diane," said Bridget taking a sip of wine.

"Yeah, it's pretty upsetting," said Diane as she folded her legs beneath her on the couch and hugged her big orange pillow to her chest. "It's been just over a year since a professor was found dead right outside the building where Marlee and I work, and now a janitor was killed in the Student Union. The cops are saying it was murder."

"I found out a little bit of new information from some of my students from the Criminal Justice Club," reported Marlee, anxious to share her updates with Diane and Bridget. She updated them on the connection between Shane Seaboy, Tony Red Day, Jr., and Collin Kolb.

"So they all know each other from high school but really weren't that close any more?" asked Bridget, confirming that she was following the story.

"Collin was never that great of friends with Shane or Tony, but he knew them. Sisseton has a small high school, so everybody knows everybody even if they don't hang out together. Collin apparently told the students from the Criminal Justice Club that Tony and Shane used to be really good friends but had a falling out some time ago. Collin had a house party the night before Shane was found dead in the Student Union. I plan to track down Collin Kolb tomorrow after class and see what he'll tell me about Shane and Tony and the fight they had at the party," said Marlee, already anticipating her questions for Collin.

Diane grabbed her wine glass from the coffee table and took a substantial gulp. "I don't understand how someone could get into the Student Union to kill Shane Seaboy unless they had a key to the building. It's usually locked by 10:00 pm, isn't it?"

"Yeah, unless there's an event. Eva Gooding from the bookstore told me there was something going on in the Caldwell Room that night. She thought it might have been a banquet for the athletes. I'll need to check to see what was going on and what time it ended," said Marlee, mentally adding more to her to-do list for the following day. She wasn't entirely sure when she would be able to fit all of her investigating around teaching, advising, office hours, and flying under the dean's radar, but she was going to make it work somehow.

"People get into fights at parties all the time, but most don't turn into one person killing another," mused Bridget. "Why would someone want Shane Seaboy dead? Did he have some sort of vital information? Like in *Gladiator* when Joaquin Phoenix's character kills his father because he knew his father was going to name Russell Crowe's character as his successor."

"Or maybe it was payback for something Shane did to Tony?" said Diane.

"Oh, like Mandy Patinkin's character did in *Princess Bride* when he hunted down the six-fingered man who murdered his father," Bridget chirped, happy to use her knowledge of film to participate in the murder discussion. Marlee and Diane both nodded.

"My students who were at the party said Tony told Shane he 'shoulda kept his mouth shut' or something to that effect," Marlee recalled. "That implies that there was some type of secret Tony didn't want others to know about."

"Do we know anything else about Shane?" asked Diane, finishing off the last of her glass of wine.

Marlee sipped the remainder of her wine and thought for a moment. "Yes, I guess we do. Eva told me that Shane was really quiet and didn't talk much. She also thought he might be on parole. The other interesting thing she mentioned was that Geneva Sanders, the new Dean of Student Affairs, was instrumental in getting this job for Shane. She might even have covered up a past conviction so he could be hired at MSU."

The three academics pondered the last bit of information, trying to make sense of it but failing miserably. Diane went to the kitchen and returned with an opened bottle of cabernet sauvignon and poured it into the three empty glasses. "We may need more wine soon," she said as the last drop fell into Bridget's glass.

"Don't worry. I have three gallons of homemade wine in the basement!" exclaimed Marlee. She fancied herself a bit of a brewer and was excited to have people try out her concoctions.

"Oh, no! It's not that same gag berry wine you served me last month, is it?" Diane said, her face contorted in horror.

"Choke cherry, not gag berry," Marlee said, exasperated with Diane's defamation of her wine. "And it's really good if you like sweet wines. It's my Mom's recipe, although I cut down on the amount of sugar because hers was way too sweet."

"It's horrible," argued Diane.

"Um, I recall you drinking several glasses of it one night, Diane. You didn't seem to have too many complaints about it then," Marlee retorted.

"I was being polite," laughed Diane. "Actually, after you get the first glass down, it's not so bad," she assured Bridget. "But watch out for the hangover the next morning. It's a killer!"

The trio looked at each other, mouths agape and eyes wide. A wine hangover wasn't the only killer to be feared.

Friends become acquaintances, acquaintances become family, and family becomes the enemy.

Chapter 7

Diane's prophecy came to fruition the following morning. Marlee carefully extracted herself from her bed, hoping to avoid jarring her already throbbing head. She felt as if she'd taken a beating, the aches and pains from her slip on the ice the day prior flaring up. She shuffled into the kitchen to start the coffee brewing. Coffee was probably the only good thing that would happen that day. As Marlee dragged herself toward the shower, she observed Diane in the living room. She was lying in a precarious balancing act with one arm and one leg thrust off the side of the couch. The remainder of her body was on the couch under three blankets and what appeared to be a rug from the kitchen. Diane's snoring sounded as if she were gasping for air while drowning. The snoring sputters were occasionally interrupted by a low gargling sound. Marlee had no idea how Diane was able to sleep through her own snoring.

On her way to the shower, Marlee glanced toward

the spare room, hoping Bridget was not feeling as rough as she did this morning. The door to the guest room was ajar and Marlee saw that no one was sleeping on the fold out sofa sleeper. Just then, she heard the front door open and in bounced Bridget bundled in padded athletic gear.

"Hey, Marlee!" Bridget chirped, removing her gloves and throwing them near the door. "Whew, glad I could get a morning run in before I needed to leave for my talk at Marymount."

"What the hell!" shouted Marlee, realizing that shouting was not conducive to eradicating her headache. "You're out running? With a hangover? In November?"

"Yeah, I like to get in my exercise a few days a week and I've been slacking off. I woke up an hour ago and decided to go for a run," Bridget reported as she disentangled herself from her crocheted scarf, insulated coat, running shoes, and knit cap.

Marlee considered that her cousin might be suffering from some type of alcohol-induced psychosis. "How are you able to run with a hangover? You drank as much as Diane and I did. If I didn't have to teach today I'd go back to bed for a few hours."

"I have a method for avoiding hangovers," Bridget said with a mischievous smile, not offering any details.

"Well, what is it?" groaned Diane from the couch. "If there's a way to prevent the way I'm feeling right now, I'd love to hear it."

"If I know I'm going to be drinking quite a bit, I eat a whole stick of butter first. It prevents me from getting drunk and counteracts the effects of a hangover. In fact, I have more energy this morning that I've had all week," Bridget said, jumping from one foot to the other to demonstrate her level of spryness.

"When did you eat a stick of butter?" questioned Marlee, her stomach lurching at the very thought of eating that much fat—unless it was combined with carbs, preferably in some type of pasta or potato recipe.

"Right before you got here yesterday. I figured we'd be drinking, so I rustled around in your fridge and found some butter and ate it," said Bridget.

Marlee and Diane looked at each other, a mixture of thoughts running through their minds. On one hand, if it prevented a hangover, eating butter was certainly worth a try. On the other hand, what if it didn't work and diarrhea had to be added to the list of symptoms the next morning? Diane shuddered and they looked away from each other.

After the trio rotated through the showers, they sat at the kitchen table consuming coffee as quickly as Marlee could make it. Choking down a piece of toast, without butter since Bridget had eaten it all the previous night, Marlee gathered her belongings and made her way to campus. It was going to be one hell of a long day. She promised herself she would not ever engage in this level of drinking again. And especially not on a school night.

Marlee didn't have enough time to go to her office before classes, so she drove straight to the Quinn Building for her two back-to-back classes. She intended on talking to Collin Kolb following his 11:00 am class, but she was fortunate enough to spy him walking into the building before 10:00 am. Although he hadn't taken any classes with her yet, Marlee recognized Collin since he was a Criminal Justice major and a star on the basketball team. Marlee quickly jumped from her Honda CR-V and ran toward the Quinn Building, slowing a bit as she remembered her fall from the previous day.

"Collin! Hey, Collin!" Marlee called as she followed him inside the Quinn Building. He turned and gave her a blank look.

Marlee introduced herself and gave her reason for

wanting to speak with Collin. He shrugged, making a face that communicated neither cooperation nor resistance. Collin nonchalantly followed her into an unoccupied classroom and slung his backpack atop a desk. He stood six and a half feet tall and was a formidable combination of muscle and bulk. His pale blonde hair was fashioned into a Caesar cut with the thinning bangs plastered across his forehead. He wore small, dark-framed glasses which Marlee suspected were more for show than visual necessity. Collin was dressed in jeans, an MSU sports jersey, and a Columbia down-filled coat.

Shutting the door behind her and flipping on the overhead lights, Marlee motioned for Collin to sit in one of the student desks and she did the same. "I was wondering what you could tell me about Shane Seaboy. I understand you knew him from high school," said Marlee, easing into the questioning.

"Yeah, I knew him. He lived in Sisseton, where I'm from. We weren't friends or anything like that," Collin stated matter-of-factly, obviously not going to offer up any additional information without prodding.

"Do you know if he had a criminal record?" Marlee queried.

"He did some time for selling eagle feathers," Collin briefly stated.

"Selling eagle feathers? That's a federal offense. He must have been in federal prison," said Marlee.

"I guess. I don't know much about it. He and some other guys were making money selling eagle feathers and some Indian artifacts," Collin said.

"Was Tony Red Day, Jr. involved in it too?" asked Marlee.

"I don't know. He didn't do any time, if he was involved," said Collin.

"Did you know Tony very well? Do you know what happened between Tony and Shane? I heard there was a fight at your party on Monday night," said Marlee.

"I knew Tony about as well as I knew Shane. Not very well. One of my roommates knows them both quite a bit better than I do. He invited Shane to the party since he knew Shane was living here now. I'm not sure how Tony found out about the party," Collin stated.

"Who are your roommates?" asked Marlee.

"Baxter Mohr, Ashton Dumarce, and Deshawn Jones," Collin stated. "Ashton is from Sisseton, so he knows Tony and Shane. Baxter is from West River somewhere and Deshawn comes from California."

"Why did Tony and Shane get into a fight at your party?" Marlee sensed Collin could provide helpful information on the matter.

"There's been bad blood between them for a few years now. They used to be friends in high school, but around senior year they got into a big fight at school and have hated each other since then. I think the fight at my party was just a continuation of that. Those two can't be in the same room together without fighting. Shane usually tries to stay away from Tony, but Tony flies into a rage every time he sees Shane," said Collin.

"Why did Tony show up at your party?" asked Marlee. "Was it to confront Shane?"

Collin shrugged. "Not sure. Maybe Tony knew Shane would be there."

Collin glanced at the clock, registering his readiness to leave the room and get to his class. Marlee picked up on the body language and squeezed in one last question before he could leave. "Collin, who do you think killed Shane Seaboy?"

"Well, that's easy. Tony Red Day, Jr. did it," said Collin as he stood up from the desk, grabbed his backpack and strode into the hallway of the Quinn Building.

Murder isn't the worst crime one can commit. Society portrays the intentional killing of another person as the ultimate sin. I know for a fact this is not true.

Chapter 8

After giving two surprisingly inspiring lectures despite a hangover from hell, Marlee returned to her office and placed a call to her friend, Aleece Jorgenson, at the Federal Probation Office in town. She knew from working there for five years herself, that the Elmwood Probation Office covered the Sisseton area. Probation officers from Elmwood traveled to Sisseton on a regular basis to check up on people under court supervision, which fell into two types: probation and supervised release. Probation was a sentence imposed instead of prison and carried a variety of conditions such as no alcohol consumption and no contact with the victim. Supervised release was another type of court supervision. It followed a prison term and also carried a variety of conditions tailored to the specific individual's needs and areas of concern, such as mandatory drug treatment or full financial disclosure. Even though the federal court system no longer imposed parole, most people outside the court system referred to supervised release as parole since the court-imposed sentences were very similar.

After exchanging pleasantries and catching up on the news in each other's lives, Marlee asked, "Aleece, can you tell me if Shane Seaboy from Sisseton was on supervision with you guys? I think it might have been for selling eagle feathers and Native American artifacts."

Aleece didn't respond, but Marlee could hear her nimble fingers typing at a break-neck speed. She was a probation officer assistant and handled all of the clerical work. Although she didn't supervise people on probation or supervised release, Aleece met with nearly all the defendants handled by the Elmwood office when they were initially charged with federal offenses.

"Yeah, here it is. I remembered his name and some of the details, but not all of them. Do you have a pen handy?" Aleece paused before launching into the details. "Shane Seaboy pleaded guilty to one count of Illegal Sale of Migratory Bird Feathers in January of 2001. He received a sentence of eight months in prison to be followed by one year of supervised release. The judge gave him credit for the time he spent in county jail awaiting trial, so he only had to serve six months in prison. Shane earned early release from supervision because he paid off his restitution early and he had no violations of his conditions. Shane was officially released from supervision of our office in March of 2002."

"Wow, sounds like the stories I heard were fairly accurate," said Marlee, thinking of what else to ask about Shane's case. "Wait, did he have any codefendants?"

"Yes, there were three codefendants: Chris Long Hollow from Sisseton; Warren Keoke from Sisseton; and Ryan Campbell from Minneapolis, Minnesota. Looks like Ryan Campbell was the ringleader because he got the most prison time. Shane received the lightest sentence of all of them, so he either was the least involved or had the best attorney," Aleece said with a laugh. They both knew that the representation a client had often resulted in an addition or subtraction of time the client spent in prison, depending upon the attorney's competence and diligence.

"Who supervised him from your office?" asked Marlee. Since leaving Federal Probation a few years prior, she hadn't kept up on the new hires in the Elmwood office.

"Lisa Abernathy was his Probation Officer, but she's gone now. She found true love and moved to Las Vegas. She's married now and they have a baby. Speaking of true love, did you know Vince Chipperton was just hired on in our office?" Aleece knew Marlee had a long-standing crush on Vince Chipperton, who previously worked at the state probation office in Elmwood. His move to federal probation was a career coup since it meant higher status and more money.

"Ooooh, maybe I should put on my best outfit and come up to your office so I can see him," Marlee said, her head in the clouds as she thought about Vince Chipperton and his dreamy blue eyes.

"You'll have to save that for another day. He's at the Federal Law Enforcement Training Center for the next two weeks. It's training for the new probation officers in Glynco, Georgia. It's like the one you went to in Baltimore when you worked here, but it's longer and more intense. They actually have to go through physical fitness challenges now," Aleece said matter-of-factly.

"Ugh... I got out just in time then," Marlee joked. She had enjoyed her time working as a probation officer, but she knew it had been time to move on to a new adventure after a few years. She still considered several of the people working for Federal Probation among her best friends. And now she had a good excuse to see Vince Chipperton!

After finishing her conversation with Aleece and pondering it a bit, Marlee reached beside her desk for her insulated lunch sack. She looked around and realized she hadn't brought her lunch with her that day. Leaving a note on her office door stating she would return shortly, Marlee walked over to the Student Union to grab a quick meal. It was also a good opportunity to nose around the crime scene and ask questions.

Marlee's hope for investigating the crime scene was dashed upon observing a section of the basement in the Student Union was roped off with bright yellow police tape. A uniformed officer from the Elmwood Police Department was sitting in a chair near the crime scene area to ensure that everyone understood the meaning of POLICE LINE DO NOT CROSS. *Frack!* Walking over to the cafeteria, she ladled up a bowl of chili and grabbed a diet Pepsi from the cooler. As she stood in line to pay for her meal, she plotted her next move. Since she was in the vicinity, she decided to stop in to the bookstore to see Eva Gooding. Perhaps Eva had more information on Shane Seaboy and the murder investigation.

Sitting at an unoccupied table in the dining room, Marlee looked around and noticed a few of her students. Some of them waved or said, "Hi," while others ignored her. Two senior professors sat at a nearby table and were engaged in a heated discussion about the merits of student evaluations. Marlee addressed them both by their first names as she walked by, but neither spoke nor even looked at her. She set her small plastic bowl of chili on the table and proceeded to wolf it down. There was a time not that long ago that Marlee would have been too self-conscious to eat in a public place by herself.

Although it was not the most comfortable of situations, she still managed to enjoy her meal. The cafeteria chili was made from unsold hamburgers from the previous day or two, but it was still damn good. Just as she was getting up to leave, Eva walked up to the table and motioned with her eyes for Marlee to follow.

Acting as nonchalant as she could, Marlee disposed of her trash and ambled toward the bookstore. Once inside, she went to Eva's office and Eva closed the door behind them. "What's up? Anything new on Shane Seaboy or the investigation?" quizzed Marlee.

"No, I really don't have any news. I just wanted to see if you knew anything," Eva said.

Marlee relayed the information she had collected up to that point. The two sat in silence for a moment before Eva began to speak. "I have some information on the missing Christmas presents," she said. After Marlee raised her eyebrows, Eva continued. "Some of them were found in the supply closet with a note. The note was basically an apology. Isn't that weird?"

"Very weird!" Marlee agreed. "Some were found but not all of them? Who had access to the supply closet?"

"Not all of them were found. Just some of them. The same people who have access to the book store have access to the closet: me, Tia, Rob, Geneva, and the janitor, whoever that is now that Shane is dead. We keep it locked all the time."

"Do you have the note?" Marlee was now sitting on the edge of her chair.

"I do. I didn't turn it into the police because I think I know who wrote it," said Eva.

"Who?" shouted Marlee, tiring of the slow reveal of facts.

"I think Tia wrote it. The handwriting looks like it was disguised. Plus, she's been acting really strange since all of this happened. Also, the toys and clothes that were not returned to the supply closet are for the ages of her two kids. The money, gift cards, and food donations were not returned either," Eva reported, not at all happy about the discovery or her theory.

"Oh, no. Did you talk to her about it?" Marlee inquired.

"Not yet. I wanted to talk to see what you thought before I talked to her. If she admits to it and agrees to return the items then I'd rather not get the police involved. She's a single mom trying to make a living and I don't want her to get fired and sent to prison over something like this," said Eva.

Marlee nodded, agreeing to some point, but knowing that since the police had already been notified of this matter the previous day, that it would be difficult to protect Tia. "Is Tia around today?"

Eva nodded. "She'll back from her lunch break any minute. Can you wait around a bit so we can talk to her?"

"Sure," said Marlee, glad that she had the foresight to leave a note on her office door explaining her absence during office hours. While they waited for Tia, they looked at the apology note written on a torn sheet of yellow legal paper in large, loopy, cursive letters. It read: "I am so sorry. Here are the gifts."

Within ten minutes, Tia returned from lunch, stowed her purse and coat in the employee break room, and sat before a computer at her desk located in an open area near the back of the book store. Her long blonde hair was wind-blown and she had large, dark circles under her eyes announcing a lack of sleep or intense stress. Or both. Tia's expression was one of worry, although she offered up a quick smile when Eva approached her desk and asked her to come to her office.

Tia smiled at Marlee as they were introduced and

she sat in the only remaining chair in Eva's office. "Tia, what do you know about the missing presents that were collected here at the bookstore?" asked Marlee, launching right into the heart of the matter without any preamble.

"Uh, nothing. I know they were taken, probably stolen, a couple days ago," Tia said, looking neither guilty nor innocent as she shifted her gaze from Marlee to Eva and back again. "Why?"

"Did you know that some of the presents were returned along with an apology note?" Eva asked, looking Tia right in the eye.

"No, why would I? Who wrote the note? When were they returned?" Tia's questions came tumbling out and then she stopped. "Wait! You think I did it?" she asked, her eyebrows shooting to the top of her forehead and her mouth agape.

"It kinda looks that way, Tia," Marlee said. "You're one of only a handful of people with keys to the book store and the supply closet. All of the items were returned except for the clothes and toys for a two and four year old, which are the ages of your kids. The money, gift cards, and food were kept too. The apology note was probably written by a woman, although the handwriting was disguised. We just want you to come clean about the whole thing."

Tia remained silent, looking at the floor. Her face was blank and impossible to read. Marlee had more questions, but let the silence hang in the air for a full minute. People are generally uncomfortable with silence and will frequently say something they did not intend just to avoid the discomfort of not talking.

"I didn't take the presents. Just because I'm a single mom and having a hard time staying afloat, doesn't mean I'm a thief." Tia's voice was devoid of any emotion.

"We want to keep the cops out of this as much as possible, Tia," Eva said pleadingly. Confrontation was not Eva's strong suit and it showed.

"Look, just fess up and return the presents that are still missing. Even if the police do have to become involved, maybe we can help you work out some sort of deal with the court where you can be on probation and just pay a fine or do community service work. We're not looking to have you thrown in jail. We just want you to make this right," said Marlee, familiar with the court processes. If Tia was a first-time offender, she was likely to get probation.

"Screw you!" Tia shouted looking directly at Marlee, avoiding eye contact with Eva. With that pronouncement, she left the room, slamming the door behind her, and strode back to her work area.

"That didn't go so well," said Eva, looking miserable.

"No, it didn't, but it doesn't mean it was a waste of time. Keep an eye on Tia's behavior and see if you notice anything odd. If she did steal the presents she's feeling guilty already. We know that because of the apology note," Marlee stated and Eva nodded her agreement.

"What if she didn't do it?" asked Eva. "I mean, I still think she took the Christmas presents, but if she didn't, she's gonna hate me for accusing her."

"Well, then we'll have to apologize later," Marlee replied.

Look under rocks. Overturn stones. Don't take anyone's word at face value. You can't trust anyone – especially not yourself.

Chapter 9

After spending nearly two hours in her office that afternoon, Marlee decided to call it a day. Only three students had stopped by during her scheduled office hours and neither really needed anything. They just wanted to chat. Normally she enjoyed chatting with students about life, future plans, and their views on topics, but today her heart just wasn't in it. Her hangover had dissipated, thanks to several ibuprofen and generous amounts of caffeine. Her back still ached from her fall on the ice, and she started to think she might need to go to her chiropractor for an adjustment. She'd give it another day or two before she took extreme measures such as actual treatment. Plus, there just wasn't time to be sick or injured right now.

Before going home, Marlee swung by the Elmwood Police Department to talk to Bettina Crawford, her friend and detective on the force. She swung her Honda CR-V into the employees-only lot and eased herself out of the vehicle, careful not to aggravate her back any further. Making her way inside, she approached the front counter, which was currently staffed by Lois. Marlee's relationship with Lois was a strange one. They had been work acquaintances for years; however, Lois never once acknowledged that she knew Marlee.

Today was no different as Marlee asked to speak with Detective Crawford if she was in. Lois gave Marlee and long stare and said, "Can I let her know who's here to see her?"

"Yes, Lois, you can. You can tell her it's Marlee McCabe. I think she'll remember me since I've known her and been in here to talk to her countless times over the years. In fact, I would have a hard time believing she didn't know me." Marlee fixed Lois with a long stare of her own wondering if Lois picked up on this intentional barb.

"I'll let her know," said Lois, pressing a button and announcing, "A McCabe lady is here to see you," into the phone receiver.

Within moments, Bettina Crawford appeared behind the counter and motioned Marlee through the door as she depressed the unlock button.

As they made their way back toward Bettina's office, Marlee muttered, "Lois is an asshole."

"Hey, that's my best friend you're talking about," said Bettina as she glared at Marlee. They stared at each other for a few seconds and both broke out laughing. "She is kind of a dick," Bettina agreed. The two made small talk for a few minutes before getting down to business.

"I imagine you want info on the Shane Seaboy case." Bettina said matter- of-factly.

"Yep. Anything you can tell me?" asked Marlee looking around to see if they were being watched or overheard by fellow employees at the Police Department.

"Only a couple things. First, the autopsy came back. Seaboy had some internal injuries, as well as cuts and bruises to his face, hands, and ribs. The coroner determined that the blows to the back of his head were what killed him. His death has officially been ruled a homicide by the coroner. This is all pretty much what we thought right away at the scene. Second, we know he just got off supervised release three years ago." Bettina went on to relay the information on the sale of eagle feathers that Marlee had just learned about the previous day. "Plus, we interviewed Tony Red Day, Jr. We tracked him down here in Elmwood. He said he was staying with a friend for a few days. He admitted fighting with Shane at a party but denies killing him or even seeing him after the fight at the party. We didn't have enough to hold Tony, so we had to release him after questioning."

"So not really much new information, then?" Marlee asked after she reported already having the news about Shane Seaboy's record.

"Well, here's something you don't know, Miss Smarty Pants," said Bettina with a smug look. "Ivan Flute is Tony Red Day's uncle. On his Mom's side. Do you know him?"

"Sure, I used to talk to Ivan quite a bit when I was a probation officer and covered the Sisseton area. Last I knew, he was a chemical dependency counselor at Prairie Winds. Is he still there?" Marlee not only knew Ivan, but trusted him. He had provided quite a bit of information and insight into some of the people she supervised in Sisseton and the surrounding area. Early on, Ivan had his own struggles with addiction and brushes with the law, but when he was around thirty years old, he went to alcohol treatment, became certified as a chemical dependency counselor, began working at the tribal treatment facility, and now worked helping those who faced the same demons he had.

"He sure is!" said Bettina with an adamant shake to her head.

"Hmmm...I wonder if it would be worthwhile to run over to Sisseton and talk to Ivan? He could probably shed quite a bit of light on both Shane Seaboy and the eagle feather sales," said Marlee. "Speaking of that, what do you know about all of it? You lived there all your life until moving to Elmwood a few years ago."

"I knew of Shane Seaboy, but didn't really know him personally. He was about fifteen years younger than me, so we weren't in school at the same time. I wasn't around Sisseton when Shane's case was investigated. I was at a law enforcement training course in Artesia, New Mexico for two months and when I got back it was all wrapped up and waiting to go to federal court," Bettina replied.

"Do you know Tony Red Day, Jr.?" asked Marlee, anxious to find out more about the person who had allegedly fought with Seaboy the night before he was killed.

"Yeah, I know the Red Day family fairly well. Not so much Tony, Jr. but his dad and uncles. They were frequent customers at the tribal jail when I worked there," Bettina said.

"What were they in trouble for?" inquired Marlee.

"Mostly alcohol stuff. Some DUIs, public intoxication, a couple domestics. The kids were removed from Tony Red Day, Sr. and his wife a few times, usually due to drinking," said Bettina recalling the all-too-frequent situation of pulling crying children out of their homes when the parents were drinking or absent.

"How many kids in Tony Jr.'s family?" asked Marlee.

"Two older brothers and a younger sister," said

Bettina. "Plus there's a half-brother on his mother's side. He's older than Tony Jr. and the rest of the kids."

"Wow, you have an incredible memory. You're a really good historian," Marlee said with admiration.

"Like I said, I may not personally know everyone, but I know *of* them. I lived there over thirty years and was related to many people in Sisseton and the outlying communities. Those I wasn't related to, I still probably knew because it's a small area and people are really involved in each other's business. Then, when I started working at the tribal police department, I became even more familiar with some people and how they were related to others. Anybody from the area can probably give you just as good of an account as I just did, if not better," Bettina said humbly.

"I don't know about that," Marlee replied.

"I think you were on to something when you said Ivan might be able to give you some background on Seaboy, Red Day, and the whole eagle feather incident," said Bettina.

"Yeah, I think you're right. I don't have classes or office hours tomorrow, so maybe I'll run over there and see what I can find out. Wanna ride along?" asked Marlee.

"I have to work tomorrow, unlike some privileged professors who get all kinds of time off," said Bettina with a smile. "Plus, it probably wouldn't look so good if I'm hanging out with you while you do your own investigation."

"Got your reputation to think about, huh?" Marlee teased although she completely understood why a detective investigating a case could not be seen conducting her own independent investigation with an overly-curious college professor—especially a college professor who was already on the wrong side of the detective's boss.

On her drive home, Marlee heard the announcement on the radio that the coroner ruled Shane Seaboy's death a homicide. This wasn't exactly news, but it took Marlee's breath away all the same. Who would want this young man dead? And why? She pondered these questions for the next few minutes until she arrived at home. Diane's car was not parked in front of the house but there was a car with Minnesota license plates parked across the street. She assumed it belonged to Bridget and Marlee realized just how anxious she was to discuss the investigation with her.

Marlee parked in her garage and walked up the sidewalk to the back door, passing the enormous weeping willow tree in the back yard which had finally lost all its leaves due to several hard frosts in the past couple months. Upon entering the house she heard a calamity that she soon realized was the television turned up to a raucous level. Marlee made her way to the living room and found Bridget lying on the floor atop a stack of folded blankets and covered up with a fleece kitty cat blanket. Surrounding her were several pillows tossed at various angles.

"Hey, Bridge. Whatcha doing?" asked Marlee, stepping over two pillows and making her way to the couch.

"Just watching *The 39 Steps*. One of Hitchcock's greatest. I've seen it a thousand times but when I got back from Marymount College this afternoon I saw it was on the classic movie channel and I've been watching ever since," said Bridget, her eyes a bit droopy from sleep. She reached for the remote on the floor near her and pushed mute.

"How did your presentation go at Marymount?" asked Marlee. She had already forgotten that was what brought Bridget to Elmwood in the first place.

"It went well. It went really well. In fact, I think I might be offered a visiting professorship for one year," Bridget said, perking up.

"What? Really? I didn't know you were here for an interview!" shrieked Marlee.

"Well, I didn't want to jinx it, so I didn't tell you. Actually, I didn't tell anybody. I should be hearing from the dean at Marymount by tomorrow," said Bridget, now upright and springing back and forth between her left foot and her right.

"Oh my God! That's so awesome! It would be great having you here in Elmwood. Just think of all the mischief we could get in to!" exclaimed Marlee, also standing and gesturing wildly as she spoke.

"Oh, good. I was hoping you'd be okay with me being in Elmwood," said Bridget.

"Are you kidding? This is gonna be great!" Marlee said swinging her arms and her hips in an attempt at a happy dance. The two continued their celebration of the possibility that Bridget would be moving to Elmwood, albeit on a one-year basis.

"Wow, I forgot to ask you about the Seaboy investigation," said Bridget. "Did you find out anything new?"

Marlee gave Bridget the updates on her conversations with Collin Kolb and Detective Bettina Crawford. The two batted around some theories until there was an enormous clatter at the front door. Both jumped to their feet to see what was going on.

The front door popped open and Diane entered carrying her book bag, a grocery bag, two pizza pans, and an assortment of miscellaneous items that were too numerous for one person to carry. "We'll have to wash these pizza pans before we use them because I just dropped them on your step," said Diane, pushing up her fogged-over glasses with a mittened hand.

"Yes, we heard," said Bridget with a laugh as she and Marlee moved to help Diane with her load of items. Marlee grabbed the grocery bag and book bag while Bridget grasped the pizza pans and remaining items. Diane struggled out of her snow boots, coat, scarf, and cap leaving them all in a heap by the front door.

Diane came inside and the trio decided to sample the chocolate chip cookies she just purchased. They moved to the dining room table and Marlee made them each a cup of sugar-free hot chocolate. The three discussed the Seaboy case as well as Bridget's interview as they sipped and munched their late afternoon refreshments.

"Tomorrow I'm going to Sisseton to see what I can find out about Shane Seaboy and Tony Red Day, Jr. Do you want to go?" asked Marlee looking at Diane and then Bridget and then back to Diane again.

"Tuesdays and Thursdays are my big teaching days, so I can't go," said Diane. "Besides, it might be too scary finding out more about the victim and whoever killed him." Diane shuddered as she spoke. Her involvement in the investigation would take mostly a discussion rather than an active role. She was quite interested in Seaboy's death, but didn't want any involvement in asking questions.

"Sure, I can go!" exclaimed Bridget, excited to be included in an investigation. "When do we leave? What should I wear?"

"Dress casual. Jeans and a sweatshirt would be fine. We can leave right away in the morning. Oh, shit! We can't either. I don't have classes or office hours on Thursdays but I do have a meeting at 8:00 am tomorrow. Crap!" shouted Marlee, disappointed that the start to their big day was already being delayed.

"Who schedules a meeting at 8:00 am?" questioned Diane with disdain.

"Somebody who should be pistol whipped," Marlee retorted.

"What is the purpose of the meeting?" asked Bridget.

"The purpose is to have faculty input on the new building on campus. I tried my best to get off this committee but I was appointed by the dean. I suspect it's his way of getting back at me. He knows I hate meetings," grumbled Marlee. "I think we should be finished by 9:00, so I could just swing back and pick you up after the meeting." Marlee nodded in Bridget's direction.

"Or I could just go to campus with you and prowl around until you're done. I haven't seen much of the MSU campus. I'd like to check in on their library and take a look at the fine arts building," Bridget replied.

"Sure, that works," said Marlee. Diane sat at the table with a long face. "Don't worry, Diane, we'll give you the full run down tomorrow when we get back."

The trio, having learned their lesson the night before, decided to forego wine and stick with hot chocolate and brewed tea. They savored their drinks while making homemade pizza on the freshly washed pizza pans Diane provided.

"Diane, did you get these pans from your apartment?" asked Marlee, not believing Diane would be brave enough to go home just to retrieve cookware.

"Yeah, I needed to pick up my mail, so I ran in quickly and grabbed the pans and a couple boxes of pizza crust I had and ran out. I was in there less than a minute," Diane said, not caring who knew she was afraid to be by herself with a potential murder on the loose in

Elmwood. "Whatever you guys do tomorrow, just promise me you'll be safe," said Diane looking at Marlee and Bridget.

They promised they would, but deep down, Marlee knew the matter was coming closer and closer to revealing some information that could send someone to prison, maybe for the rest of their life.

A straight line is not always the quickest route to your destination.

Chapter 10

Marlee's hangover the next morning was due to the massive intake of food and not because of alcohol consumption. She, Diane, and Bridget constructed two enormous home-made pizzas, loaded with toppings they found in Marlee's refrigerator and cupboards. Her favorite was the ham, artichoke heart, and kalamata olive pizza and she showed her appreciation for it by devouring well over half of the pie.

"Hmmm...maybe I have a food allergy to artichoke hearts," Marlee thought as she burped her way toward the bathroom, not considering the vast amounts of pizza and cookies she consumed the night before had anything to do with her ill effects that morning.

After starting the coffee, she took a quick shower and dressed in jeans and an MSU sweatshirt. This was not her normal attire for campus meetings, but Marlee didn't care since this was technically a day she didn't need to be on campus, but for the stupid meeting. Plus, she had a long day ahead of her with the drive to Sisseton, talking to Ivan Flute, and asking around at other places about Seaboy and Red Day. In addition, this campus meeting was at eight frickin' o'clock. What did they expect? Professors, like most people, tended to fall into one of two groups: early birds or night owls. Try as she might to become an early bird, Marlee just could not master it. She was a night owl through and through. Holding a meeting at 8:00 am for her was akin to conducting a meeting at midnight for an early bird.

As Marlee sat down to enjoy her first cup of coffee and a bowl of oatmeal, Diane rose with a start and bounded into the bathroom carrying an armload of clothing. "I overslept!" she exclaimed. It was only 7:30 am, but Marlee knew Diane had to be on campus around 8:00 am for her first class of the day. She taught all four of her classes on Tuesdays and Thursdays, so she was busy teaching and holding office hours from 8:00 am until after 5:00 pm those days. An enormous amount of clanging and banging came from the bathroom along with sudden bursts of water from the sink. Two minutes later, Diane emerged looking remarkably presentable considering she hadn't showered or done anything with her hair.

"Wow, I'm impressed. If I don't shower and fix my hair in the morning I look like I've been dropped out of an airplane," said Marlee with more than a little bit of envy.

"It's because I have straight hair. That helps a lot," Diane replied as she ran her fingers through her mane.

Bridget stumbled out of the guest room and poured herself a cup of coffee. She was still clad in her pajamas and her long curly hair was pulled back in a low ponytail. The look on her face suggested she wasn't normally a morning person either and that the previous morning's jog had been an anomaly.

After taking a few sips of her coffee, Bridget high tailed it into the bathroom and was ready in a few short minutes as well. By 7:50, the trio departed the house, ready for big adventures. Diane drove off in her car, while Bridget rode with Marlee. Even though it was close to 8:00 am, Marlee found a prime parking spot in front of the building where her meeting would be held. She pointed out some of the surrounding buildings that Bridget might find to be of interest and they agreed to meet at the Student Union cafeteria around an hour later.

Marlee scurried to her meeting, always afraid she might be late. She bounded up the stairs in the Philmore building to the third floor and made her way to the meeting room. Upon entering the room, she realized that she needn't have pushed the panic button. Only four of the twelve committee members were present. Normally, there was equal representation from all of the colleges in the university: Arts and Sciences, Fine Arts, Business, and Education. Since this meeting dealt with a new building in which the Arts and Sciences faculty would be housed, the committee was comprised of mostly Arts and Sciences professors.

Professor Ashman sat at the head of the table. Marlee groaned inwardly as she saw him. He was a pompous little man with a giant need for attention. Today he wore a beret, cocked off to one side. His love of hats and his personality had earned him the nickname of Asshat throughout campus. Asshat was holding court, lecturing to the three other junior professors seated at the table. He either didn't notice her or pretended not to as Marlee placed a book bag on the table and seated herself at the far end.

The three junior professors all had a glazed over

look in their eyes. They were in the process of learning that it never paid to be too early for a meeting lest they get entangled listening to a monologue from a senior faculty member. Certain senior professors lived for pontificating to new professors as a way of indoctrinating them into their way of thinking. Others just liked the sound of their own voices and could not imagine that others wouldn't feel the same.

Marlee set down her travel mug of coffee a bit louder than she intended and all eyes turned to her. "Ah, look who we have here," said Asshat with a smirk. "It's our illustrious crime solver, Dr. McCabe. She also teaches a little on the side when she has time." Marlee winced at the comment, knowing that was exactly what he had intended.

Looking at the three junior professors, Marlee nodded toward them and offered up a quick smile. She had met all of them before and really had no opinion of any of them. Hopefully they did not take Asshat's proclamations as fact. By the looks in their eyes, it appeared all three were well on their way to understanding Asshat and his motives.

Within moments, more faculty members arrived and seated themselves around the table. It was a few minutes after the scheduled start time, but Marlee knew the meeting wouldn't get underway for a bit. It would be delayed while everyone made small talk, waiting for the late committee members to arrive. Once the latecomers arrived it would be a battle of one-upmanship between the showboats to garner the most attention.

Dr. Michael Blackstone entered the room and seated himself at the head of the table. He had been a professor in the Education Department for over fifteen years at MSU and had established himself as one of the higher functioning nerds and was thus eventually promoted to

Assistant Dean of the School of Education. Professor Blackstone was in his early fifties, although his baby face and athletic physique suggested he was closer to late thirties. He was considered a dreamboat by most of the female faculty members–and a few of the males–but Professor Blackstone was oblivious to the buzz he generated. He had three loves: his wife of 25 years, his three children, and his two parrots. If anyone hoped to garner a favor with Professor Blackstone, they would be well served to ask about his family and birds before launching into the specific reason for the conversation.

With a fling of his hand and a toss of his head, Professor Blackstone whooshed the graying blonde hair out of his eyes and smoothed it to the side. "Ahem," he said as an introduction and also a way to calm the chatterboxes in the group. "I suppose we should get started. We're missing a couple people, but they can catch up when they arrive. Thank you all for coming. This is our first meeting to discuss plans for the new building, which will house some faculty departments, a number of classrooms, and will also be the technology hub for our campus. Stage one of the process..."

Professor Blackstone's overview of the meeting's mission dwindled to a halt as Professor Virginia Winkler entered the room with her ankle-length, down-filled nylon coat swishing loudly against her book bag. She shuffled to the side of the table farthest from where she entered the room. Her book bag hit the backs of chairs and occasionally a fellow faculty member as she noisily made her way to an open chair. Marlee heard another faculty member whisper, "Oh, no." Dr. Winkler's reputation preceded her, and most disliked being on committees with her.

"So sorry I'm late, Mike" said Professor Winkler to Dr. Blackstone in her monotone voice. "I've had a rough morning. I couldn't find a place to park, but then when I did the high school called and said my daughter needed me to get her because she wasn't feeling well. So I drove over to the high school and picked her up and took her home to find out she just got her period. We'd talked about it and she knew what to expect, but she was crying and I didn't know what to do so..."

"Ah, yes, yes," Dr. Blackstone interrupted with more than a little discomfort as he attempted to steer the conversation back to the intended purpose. He knew, that if given the chance, Professor Winkler would natter on endlessly about unrelated topics. "Virginia, we were just getting started here, so you didn't miss anything."

Professor Winkler proceeded to sit down before taking off her long coat and then noisily tried to wrestle herself out of it while seated. Professor Blackstone paused until the commotion died down before proceeding with his talk. "As I was saying, stage one for the new building is..."

He was interrupted by Professor Winkler who, now settled, was ready to argue the merits of even constructing a new building. "I don't see why we need this building. Scobey Hall is just fine and needs to be brought up to code. When I started here twelve years ago we were told there would be no destruction of current buildings on campus due to the historical value and..."

Professor Blackstone cut off Dr. Winker's rant. "Well, I can't speak to what you were told, Virginia, but the fact of the matter is that we are getting a new building and that Scobey Hall will be demolished because it does not comply with the American Disabilities Act. It would simply cost too much to bring it up to code. So let's focus on the construction of the new building."

Asshat, sensing this was a good time to stir the pot

interjected, "Why does Scobey Hall have to be demolished? Let's use it for something else other than offices. Maybe we could host campus debates there or hold special lectures. The building has a lot of character and shouldn't be torn down just because a professor died there last year."

Blackstone took a deep breath. "Scobey Hall was already tapped for demolition before the incident involving Logan LeCroix last fall. The fact remains that it doesn't comply with the ADA and will cost too much to bring up to code so we can't use it for debates or special lectures."

"How about turning it into a spook house at Halloween? Or a paintball park?" pressed Asshat, enjoying the game.

"No! We can't do any of those things because MSU would be in violation of the ADA!" Professor Blackstone shouted, a fine mist of sweat appearing on his brow and upper lip.

"Could it be used for mock crime scenes for the Crime Scene Investigation class?" asked Professor Winkler. "Marlee, you teach CSI. You could have a room in Scobey set up to look like a burglary. Another room could have someone playing the part of a murder victim. Students could collect evidence and take pictures of the mock scene." Marlee looked at Virginia but did not acknowledge the comment, since it was obvious, at least to her, that Scobey Hall would not be used for such purposes.

"Please, people! Let's stay on target. We can't use Scobey Hall for any of these purposes," said Professor Blackstone, agitated at the committee's lack of comprehension and general waste of time.

"What about using it as storage for papers and files? The ADA shouldn't impact that," croaked Professor

Marcus Imberry as he limped into the room with a cane. He was the oldest living professor at MSU and still saw himself as a valuable member of the faculty. He held Emeritus status and maintained an office, although he did not teach any classes. Dr. Imberry entertained himself by coming to campus daily and showing up, usually uninvited, to many of the committee meetings.

"We already considered that," said Blackstone, his tone a bit less gruff. "With everything on computer and disk now, we just don't need large rooms or a whole building for storage."

"What are you going to do when the computers don't work? Has anyone ever considered that? If people can't use their computers they won't have anything saved. Nothing!" Professor Imberry waved his cane in the air for effect.

"That's why we save information daily to the server and professors are encouraged to back up their work," said Professor Blackstone. "Now, let's get back on track. We need to meet with the architects in January and I'd like to have a list of what we want in the new building. I think..."

"Why was this meeting moved to this room? I thought it was supposed to be held in the Student Union but then I asked one of the secretaries and she said it was moved here," grumbled Professor Imberry.

Not having the nerve to point out that Professor Imberry was not actually on the committee and therefore, should not be in attendance, Professor Blackstone said, "A campus-wide email was sent out earlier in the week announcing the change of location."

Professor Imberry growled, "Harrumph...I don't use email. I haven't turned my computer on since they gave it to me. See what I mean about computers! How do you expect regular faculty members to get information on meetings if you don't let them know?"

"Oh, good God," whispered Marlee, a bit louder than she intended.

The meeting continued on in this fashion for another forty minutes before Professor Blackstone stood up, his mouth ajar. The hour scheduled for the meeting was nearly over and nothing had been accomplished. He looked at the table and shook his head. "Well, we won't be meeting again until the week that classes begin. In the meantime, just email me with anything you would like to see in the new building. We're done for today." He quickly walked from the room toward his office. Marlee suspected he was going to hug one of his parrots that he frequently brought to campus.

"Yeah, like emailing him with suggestions will do any good. He's in administration, and they will decide among themselves what they want to do. They never take input from faculty seriously!" grumbled Professor Imberry as Asshat and Virginia Winkler nodded their heads in earnest agreement.

In order to understand a culture you have to be willing to let go of stereotypes and prejudices. It's harder than it sounds.

Chapter 11

"So how did your meeting go?" asked Bridget as she slid up a chair next to Marlee in the Student Union cafeteria. Marlee decided to reward herself with a plate of bacon and scrambled eggs for enduring the horrendous committee meeting she just departed.

"A colossal mind-fuck, as usual," Marlee said. She hated meetings, and she truly detested unproductive meetings like the one she attended that morning. This was only her third year on campus, yet nearly every committee meeting she attended went the same way. Why she ever expected or hoped it would be different, she didn't know. Part of her thought about skipping committee meetings, but the heads of the committees reported attendance–or lack thereof–to the deans. If the dean heard a faculty member was regularly skipping out on service duties to the university, he or she would have a talk with the offending faculty member. Then, when performance review time came around in the spring, the truant faculty member would receive a low score in the service category, which could impact pay for the upcoming year. Even worse, if the faculty member was untenured, it could be used as a means by which to deny the academic permanent employment. If a faculty member was untenured the university had you by the balls and everyone knew it.

"What did you do around campus while I lost an hour I'll never get back?" Marlee asked as she shoveled in a generous scoop of scrambled eggs and followed it with a whole slice of thick cut bacon. Grease was on the fingertips of her right hand and in a circle around her mouth. Bridget grabbed a handful of napkins from the dispenser on the table and thrust them at Marlee.

"It was all very exciting," Bridget said as she recounted her experiences in her usual animated fashion. "I checked out the art displays in a couple of the buildings and I toured your building and saw your office. And then I met your dean. I hate to say it, but I don't think he likes you very much," Bridget concluded.

"That would be correct," said Marlee wiping her hands and face on the stack of napkins Bridget procured. "Are you going to get something to eat?"

"No, I had some oatmeal at your house before we left," said Bridget. "I'll grab a coffee for the road, though." She jumped up from her chair and her tall, slim body moved across the dining area to the coffee bar. Marlee was envious of Bridget's trim figure. "Must be genetic. I bet we take after opposite sides of the family," Marlee thought.

Within minutes, Marlee and Bridget had coffee to go, and walked toward Marlee's CR-V. "Hey, I heard you had a big slip and fall the other day," said Bridget.

"How in the hell did you hear about that?" asked Marlee.

"Some students were talking about it in the Art

department when I stopped by. I heard it was spectacular! Were you hurt?" Bridget narrowed her eyes and scrunched up her nose in a grimace, sensitive to the fact that Marlee might actually be in pain.

"Just my pride," Marlee brushed off the matter even though she could still feel pain in her lower back much of the time.

The drive to Sisseton was largely uneventful. The snow-covered ground did little to provide any unique aspects to the countryside. One patch of ground was largely indistinguishable from any other for the one-hundred-mile journey. As they neared Sisseton, Marlee told Bridget a bit about the area. "The reservation here is called the Lake Traverse Reservation and the Indian tribe is called the Sisseton-Wahpeton Sioux Tribe. Reservation land in this area is actually what's called a checkerboard. Pieces and parcels of land are part of the reservation and then a few steps over and you're on non-reservation land. It gets really confusing, especially for law enforcement, since only tribal or federal law enforcement can make arrests on tribal land. Local police or the sheriff can't, so it becomes a complicated situation to figure out who can and can't arrest a suspected offender."

Bridget listened with keen interest as Marlee continued. "The Lake Traverse Reservation has the same types of social and economic problems as do other reservations in the country. It is basically a rural ghetto. The vast majority of people here are unemployed because there just aren't that many jobs here on the reservation. The casinos can only provide so many jobs and these establishments have brought with them a whole host of problems; crime, gambling addiction, you name it. Alcoholism and drug usage are high, which leads to domestic violence, child abuse, and criminal activity. New businesses and industries are hesitant to move into the area because it's so rural and because they believe they won't have a stable work force. Since there aren't jobs here, many of the kids drop out of school. There's also a high teen pregnancy rate. Basically, it's a viscous circle of problems."

"When you were a federal probation officer did you have special power to arrest people on the reservation?" Bridget asked.

"We didn't make arrests. If our offenders weren't in compliance with their terms of probation or supervised release then we would petition the federal judge to issue a warrant for their arrest. Then they would be taken into custody by tribal police or federal agents if they were on the reservation or by city police or the county sheriff if they were off the reservation," Marlee replied. "If one of the people I had under supervision committed a new crime then that would be handled by law enforcement just like any other crime."

"Wow, that is complicated," said Bridget, taking a long swig from her cooled coffee and placing it back in one of the vehicle's two cup holders.

"Yeppers," Marlee agreed. "We'll be there in a few minutes. I think that instead of going into the town of Sisseton first, we'll go to Agency Village, a housing area outside of town. Most of the tribal offices are located there. Law enforcement is in one building, social services in another, and so on. Plus, the treatment facility where Ivan Flute works is in Agency Village. Since he's the main person I want to see, I think we should talk to him first."

"Ivan is a counselor?" asked Bridget after she polished off the last drop of coffee in the Styrofoam cup.

"Yeah, he's been a chemical dependency counselor at Prairie Winds for several years. He's a great guy and a really good source of community information. I've known him since the mid-90s and he's always been a big help when I'm trying to locate someone around the area or figure out who is related to who." Marlee wheeled the CR-V into the treatment facility's parking lot and the two McCabe women entered the building.

Prairie Winds was housed in a large, two-story building which had previously been one of the oldest residences in the area. It was an old farm building that had been remodeled and moved to Agency Village. Inside, it was divided into a lounge area, a dining area, counselor offices, and meeting rooms. In addition, those attending inpatient treatment lived there for 28 days and shared a room with one other person. Males were housed on one side of the facility while females were located on the opposite end. Those attending treatment on an outpatient basis were not housed at Prairie Winds, but came to treatment meetings daily and were able to return to their homes.

The facility provided treatment for alcohol and drug addiction while basing the treatment on the Native American culture, and thus utilized the sweat lodge, smudging, and other forms of traditional healing as a part of the regime. People were receiving treatment for a variety of reasons: they hit rock bottom and knew it was time to get help, they were coerced by family or friends, or they were required to complete treatment by the criminal justice system. Sometimes it was a combination of all three reasons that propelled them into treatment. Upon completion of the program, one graduated from treatment and a ceremony was held in which family and friends were encouraged to attend.

Aftercare was critical to one's success following treatment. Most aftercare plans included regular attendance at a support group such as Alcoholics

Anonymous. Aftercare classes were also held at the facility, which allowed participants to receive ongoing support in their battle with addiction.

Marlee approached the front desk, which was unstaffed, and waited for someone to help them. Within a minute, a young, energetic man appeared from one of the back offices and greeted them. "Can I help you folks?"

The young man guided Marlee and Bridget to an unoccupied office to wait while Ivan Flute finished the group session he was leading. The walls were decorated with paintings and crafts made by local artists. Within a few minutes, Ivan entered the room. He was a tall, slim man and wore his long graying hair in a ponytail tied with a leather fastener. Ivan was dressed casually in faded jeans, a long sleeved flannel shirt in a dark green tone, and a well-worn brown fleece vest over the top. As he walked into the office, he appeared stoic, almost menacing, but once he caught sight of Marlee, he smiled broadly.

Rising to greet Ivan, Marlee was embraced in a hug by the tall man. "It's been a long time! Why don't you stop by more often?" Ivan asked as he released Marlee from the bear hug.

"You know I don't work for probation anymore, right? I teach now at Midwestern State University," Marlee said smiling at Ivan.

"MSU is located in Elmwood, is it not?" asked Ivan looking her squarely in the eyes.

"Yeah."

"And that's where you lived when you were a probation officer and stopped by to see me at least once a month, is that right?" Ivan continued.

"Okay, okay, I get it. I should be coming out here more often even though I'm not here for work," Marlee said, realizing she hadn't been back to the Lake Traverse reservation in a few years.

Marlee introduced Bridget to Ivan and the three made small talk for half an hour before finally getting around to the main reason for the visit. "Ivan, I suppose you've heard about Shane Seaboy being killed in Elmwood this week, but..."

"Yeah, I heard. We have TV, radio, and even that new-fangled Internet out here," he said with a small smile. "Plus we have the rez telegraph."

"Of course. I guess there wouldn't be any reason you wouldn't know about it. Did you know Shane Seaboy very well?" Marlee asked.

"I knew his parents and grandparents better," Ivan said. "You know that if someone's been here at Prairie Winds as a patient, either inpatient or outpatient, I can't tell you, or disclose anything they may have said during their treatment."

"Yeah, I know. I'm not trying to get confidential information or anything, I just want to make sense of why someone would want to hurt Shane Seaboy. Any ideas?" Marlee asked.

"Shane didn't have many friends around here lately. He used to be a good kid, but then got mixed up with some renegades and some people off the reservation. His last year or so of high school was when it all started. He and some others were involved in selling eagle feathers and Indian artifacts. They got caught and he did some time. I heard he was living in Elmwood now, but didn't know what he was doing for work."

"He used to be friends with Tony Red Day, Jr., who's your nephew, is that right?" Marlee continued.

"Used to be friends. They were tight until Shane got involved with the eagle feather business, then Tony didn't have time for him anymore. He respected our

culture too much to profit from selling eagle feathers,"
said Ivan with an air of pride. He turned to Bridget and
continued, "Eagle feathers can only be owned by us
Indians for use in ceremonial purposes. It's illegal to sell
eagle feathers or anything that is considered a Native
American artifact like ancient tools, cookware, or human
bones."

"Human bones?" Bridget shouted in disbelief. "You
mean like grave robbing? Who on earth would dig up
human bones? Who would want to buy human bones?"

"Yeah, grave robbers. There's a huge market for the
bones of our ancestors, especially if they were a chief of
the tribe or did something especially noteworthy. Some
individuals will buy them, but there are also some
unscrupulous museums, both in the U.S. and overseas,
that will purchase the bones of Native Americans to use
in a display," Ivan said.

"As far as you know, has anyone been involved
around here in digging up human remains?" Marlee
asked.

"It's happened, but no one's been caught. I don't
know for sure who was involved, but of course there are
rumors. You can't live in a small place like this without
there being rumors about everything and everyone," Ivan
said.

"Has it happened recently?" asked Bridget, on the
edge of her seat.

"It was going on a few years ago and stopped. Then
it started again this summer," said Ivan.

"Can you tell us who's been rumored to be
involved?" asked Marlee, anxious to find out more about
the illegal activity.

"Usually I don't pass on gossip, but since his name
has been mentioned already, I guess it won't hurt
anything. Shane Seaboy and the group he ran with were

involved a few years ago. As for the recent grave robbing, I haven't heard any new names, just Shane and his old cronies," Ivan replied.

"Ivan," Marlee began gently. "Shane and your nephew got into an argument that turned physical the night before Shane died. What can you tell me about that?"

"I don't know anything about it," Ivan said. "Guess I can't say it surprises me. Those two got into it every time they saw each other."

"Did it involve anything other than the sale of eagle feathers?" asked Marlee.

"I don't know what all happened between those two boys. Like I said, they had a falling out when they were still in high school about the same time Shane started hanging out with a bad crowd," reported Ivan. "Other than that, I can't tell you very much."

"Can you give me some ideas of who I could talk to around the area about Shane Seaboy?" Marlee inquired. "I'd like to find out as much as I can about this guy."

"Sure. You might check with his brother, Duane Seaboy. He lives in Sisseton a block down from the grocery store in the little yellow house. You could talk to Shep and Judy Sanders. They were his foster parents for a few years when he was in his early teen years. They live out in the country a few miles from Veblen," said Ivan.

"I didn't know Shane was in foster care," said Marlee. "How long did he stay with the Sanders family?"

"Off and on for a few years. Shane's mother wasn't around a lot. She would leave the reservation and go off to work in another state. She would leave Shane and his brother with relatives who neglected them. Child Protection Services investigated the relatives a few times and removed them from their care and placed Shane with the Sanders family. They were a foster family that took in kids who needed a place to stay temporarily. His brother was taken in by other relatives," Ivan said.

"The studies I've read," said Marlee, launching into her professorial mode, "indicate that, nationwide, neglect is much more prevalent than physical, sexual, or emotional abuse. Do you think that's true on this reservation too?"

"Oh, yeah," said Ivan. "Well, I should say, it's more visible than abuse and definitely more reported than any type of abuse. It's easier to spot a child who's unsupervised, dirty, or underfed than to witness an act of abuse taking place." Marlee and Bridget both nodded in somber agreement.

"Do you know where Tony Red Day, Jr. is at these days? Does he still live around here?" Marlee inquired.

"He's back and forth between the rez and Minneapolis quite a bit. I heard he was in Canada for a while last year, but don't know why or for how long. Last I heard he was staying with his girlfriend, Verla Renville, and their two kids at her house in Sisseton, but I don't keep up with that part of the family. Tony's mother is my sister, but we don't talk much. She's still drinking and doesn't seem inclined to quit. Her husband is the same way. I follow the Red Road, so there's not much for us to discuss," said Ivan. He turned to Bridget and said, "The Red Road is a path of sobriety and living a life in balance."

Bridget nodded, appreciative that Ivan Flute took the time to educate her on terms she was not familiar with. The conversation wound down and Ivan saw the McCabe cousins to the front door of the facility. Before they were allowed to leave, Ivan embraced them both in friendly bear hugs and reminded Marlee that she needed to visit more often.

As they drove to Sisseton, Bridget was positively

beaming. "That was one of the most interesting conversations I've ever had," she exclaimed. "This would be an excellent setting for a movie. Did you see *Thunderheart*? Val Kilmer played the main character. It was a drama filmed on the Pine Ridge Reservation nearly twenty years ago." Bridget yammered on about films made with Native American culture as the focus while Marlee replayed the conversation with Ivan in her head.

They arrived in the town of Sisseton a few minutes later, after bouncing along on a road full of potholes from Agency Village. Driving east through town, Marlee pointed out several businesses that were unique to the area and some that were parts of regional or national chains. Bridget soaked it all in, her head moving from right to left as if watching a fast-paced tennis tournament.

Marlee circled the block, looking at Verla Renville's ramshackle house, where Ivan told them Tony Red Day, Jr. might be living. "Why did you pass the house? Wasn't that it?" asked Bridget, looking at the ranch style home which was in a state of disrepair.

"Yeah, that's it. I always circle the area first before stopping. Guess that's left over from my old probation days. It gives me a chance to see if there are any dogs on the property that might attack. Plus, I can see if the residents of the house appear to be home and if they have company, based on the number of vehicles in the driveway. The other important thing I look for is to see if there are neighbors watching or outside. Sometimes neighbors can be really helpful in providing information, but they can also cause quite a bit of problems, especially if they've been drinking."

"Did you have problems with neighbors when you were a probation officer?" Bridget asked.

"A few times. Usually they were mad based on a

misunderstanding. One time they thought I was there to take someone's children away. After I explained I wasn't with Child Protection, they were much more cooperative. Unfortunately, when there's a white lady driving around the reservation it's assumed she works for some social service department and is there to mess with somebody's family," Marlee said.

"What do you do if the person you want to talk to is violent or drunk?" Bridget asked.

"Typically, it's not the person I want to talk with that's the problem. It's someone else in the home that tries to raise hell, like a relative or friend. If it appears that people are drinking I usually just leave and come back later when everyone either leaves or sobers up. If the person I want to talk to is sober, I would try to get them to come outside to visit away from the others. Sometimes that worked and sometimes it didn't," Marlee recalled. "Of course it's a different approach based on whether or not they are under court supervision. Someone on probation or supervised release has to talk to their probation officer. They may not tell the truth, but one of their conditions is to meet with the PO as directed. Someone who isn't under court supervision is under no obligation whatsoever to talk to the probation officer."

The Honda CR-V neared the house and parked along the street. Marlee approached the home and stood on the front step, off to the side of the door. This was an old trick she'd learned as a PO that she used during and after her stint as a probation officer. Never stand directly in front of an opening door because you could be shoved off the step if someone were so inclined. She'd never had it happen, but was still wary of the possibility.

After knocking for nearly two minutes, a young woman dressed in shorts and a tank top opened the door. Her hair was mussed as if she'd just awakened, but she held a cup of coffee in one hand suggesting she'd been up for a while. She sported a black eye, a split lower lip, and was missing a front tooth.

"Hi. I'm Marlee McCabe and this is Bridget McCabe. Are you Verla Renville?" After receiving a slight nod from the young woman, Marlee continued. "We're looking for Tony Red Day, Jr. and his uncle, Ivan Flute, told us he lived here," Marlee stated.

The Verla remained silent for several seconds before answering. "He used to. I kicked him out."

"Uh, do you know where he's at now?" Marlee asked.

"Last I heard he was with that bitch, Collette Many Lightnings," the young woman said with more than a touch of bitterness. "Are you the people with that movie?"

"Uh..." Marlee stammered, stalling for time while she decided how to answer the question. As it turned out, she didn't have to.

"I'm a professor of film studies and have a special interest in movies made in South Dakota," Bridget stated, stepping forward. Marlee looked at her. Technically, she had not lied, but Bridget was certainly misleading Verla Renville.

"You can probably find him in Agency Village at the bitch's house," Verla said. She then gave them directions on locating the house.

"Verla, do you know anything about the feud between Tony and Shane Seaboy? I heard they were friends until toward the end of high school and then they became enemies," Marlee said.

A small smile twitched at the corner of Verla's mouth. "Uh, that had to do with me. I was with Shane before Tony and I got together." With that newsflash, Verla backed up and closed the door to her house.

"Get a job," they said. How could I find work when there are minimal jobs to be had on the reservation? The few people who are hiring wouldn't employ somebody like me anyway. No one wanted to hire a man seen as a traitor to his culture.

Chapter 12

After a brief stop at a convenience store to use the facilities and purchase snacks and coffee, Marlee and Bridget made their way back to Agency Village on the same bumpy road they travelled less than a half hour earlier. "What do you make of the whole Shane-Tony-Verla love triangle?" asked Bridget as she munched and crunched her way through a bag of low sodium pretzels.

"Love, jealousy, and revenge are all viable motives for killing someone," Marlee said, abruptly swerving to miss a pothole. "Actually, it looks like we have two love triangles. One involves Shane, Tony, and Verla. The other involves Tony, Verla, and Collette. Maybe one or both factor into Shane's death."

"Or neither," Bridget continued eating the last of her big grab bag of pretzels and then funneled the remaining crumb dust and salt from the bottom of the bag into her mouth. Some of the crumbs and salt made their way into Bridget's mouth, but most landed on the front of her coat. With the back of her hand, she brushed them off. Pretzel crumbs flew onto the dash, the floor, and at Marlee.

"True," mused Marlee as she brushed Bridget's snack crumbs off of her own jacket. "Neither one of these relationship dilemmas may have anything to do with Shane Seaboy's death." She chomped on a string of red licorice as she pondered the case. "Although I'd be willing to bet the past friendship between Shane and Tony has a lot to do with it."

Marlee pulled her vehicle into the area where Collette Many Lightnings lived and made a circle around the neighborhood looking for dogs, neighbors, and anything else that might pose an impediment to locating Tony Red Day, Jr. Seeing none, she parked in the driveway of a newly built ranch style home with a wooden deck attached to the front. The McCabe cousins approached the front door and, while standing off to the side, Marlee knocked. The door was opened instantly by an elderly woman in a wheelchair.

"You the movie people?" the old woman croaked. She wore a flowered zip-front housedress and white athletic socks pushed down around her thick ankles, and crocheted slippers. Her hair was thick and gray, hanging to just above her shoulders. She wore dark sunglasses, the type people wear after having cataract surgery when they are especially sensitive to light.

"Uh, you heard about us?" Marlee asked, going along with what now seemed to be the role she and Bridget were deemed to play.

"Rez telegraph," she said in a deep, raspy voice as she backed up her wheelchair and motioned the two inside with a toss of her head. "Tony!" she hollered. "*Wasicu* here to see you. Movie people." The old lady wheeled her chair toward the back of the house and the sound of a closing door could be heard.

A commotion from a back room ensued and a young man in his early twenties appeared. He wore his dark hair short and was dressed in light gray sweatpants, sans shirt and socks. Rubbing his rounded stomach, he looked at Marlee and Bridget with wide eyes and raised eyebrows. A vivid scar snaked across the left side of his face from his ear to the corner of his mouth.

Marlee introduced herself and Bridget and asked if he was Tony Red Day, Jr. He nodded hesitantly, not at all bothered by the lack of communication. Finally he spoke. "You're working on the movie?"

"Well, we had a few background questions for you first before we talk about the movie," said Bridget, easing into the lie. "We wanted to know how you knew Shane Seaboy, the guy that was killed over in Elmwood on Monday night."

"I don't have nothing good to say about him," Tony said, crossing his arms in front of his chest and taking a wide, defensive stance with his feet.

"Weren't you friends at one time?" Marlee asked.

"As kids, yeah. But then I figured out what kind of person he was and haven't had any use for him since," Tony clenched his jaw causing the muscles in his cheek to pop out.

"What kind of person was he?" Marlee asked, curious as to the reply Tony would provide.

"Well, he sold eagle feathers and other things that belong to our people. He worked with some guys from off the rez and made his money by selling our culture to white people and their museums," Tony stated.

"Yes, I heard about that. Who else was involved?" Marlee asked.

"How would I know? I didn't have anything to do with it. What does all this have to do with the movie?"

Tony snapped.

"Well, we're not exactly here about filming a movie–" Marlee began.

"No!" Bridget interrupted. "We want to talk about some things that have been going on around Sisseton and the reservation before we talk about the movie."

Marlee gave Bridget a sideways look. She did not have a problem stretching the truth, but outright lies were outside her usual investigation tactics. Tony had no obligation to talk to them and might throw them out of the house if he believed they were asking questions for anything other than the movie which was apparently discussed with him previously by some unknown entity.

"Oh, I see. To get some background information on the rez?" Tony asked, satisfied with that justification before it was even confirmed.

"That's right. We're getting the lay of the land, as they say," said Marlee, joining in on the fraud. "So who else did you hear sold eagle feathers or other Native American artifacts?"

"I didn't have anything to do with it, but I heard Chris Long Hollow and Warren Keoke were involved along with Shane a few years back. The other guy wasn't from here. I don't think he was even Indian," Tony reported, becoming more comfortable with the line of questioning.

"Who do you think killed Shane?" Marlee asked.

"Could've been a lot of people. After he sold eagle feathers and other stuff he was blacklisted by most of the tribe. He went to prison. There might be some people from prison who wanted him dead," said Tony.

"You two fought when you saw each other, I heard," said Marlee.

"You seem to be getting a lot of information about me from someone," Tony said suspiciously, crossing his arms in front of his chest again.

"Somebody told me you were at a college party in Elmwood on Monday night and that you and Shane got into a big fight," Marlee said looking him straight in the eye.

"Well, yeah. We fought. We fight quite a bit when we see each other, especially if he's been drinking. Shane's no good at all when he's drinking," Tony said.

"Somebody who was at the party told me that you said to Shane, 'you shoulda kept your mouth shut.' What was that all about?" Marlee asked.

"I don't remember that being said. But like I said, Shane was drinking," Tony replied.

"Were you drinking?" Bridget interjected.

"No. I don't drink. Been sober for a few years now. I used to drink when I was younger, but stopped before my first baby was born. Verla, my girlfriend, said she wouldn't stay with me if I kept drinking, so I stopped," Tony replied.

"We talked to Verla this morning and she said she kicked you out and you were with a new girlfriend," Marlee stated.

"We argued, but Verla's still my girlfriend. We'll get back together. We always do. I'm just staying here with my friend Collette until Verla calms down. This is her grandma's house," Tony said gesturing toward the back of the house where elderly woman went earlier.

"Why did she kick you out? Did you beat her up?" Bridget asked, oblivious to the possibility that Tony might not want to talk about his domestic life with two complete strangers.

Tony shifted from one foot to the other, uncomfortable with the line of questioning. "It was just a misunderstanding. Nothing big. She has a hot temper and after she cools down I'll be able to go home again."

"You and Verla have two kids?" Marlee asked.

"Yeah, Little Tony and Lily," he said with a smile, proud to acknowledge his kids. "Little Tony is five and Lily is two. So let's talk about the movie now."

"Uh, Tony, I have to be honest with you. We weren't really here about a movie. Collette's grandma just assumed that when we came to the door and we didn't correct her. Then you assumed it too and we went along with it," said Marlee. "We're actually from Elmwood and are trying to find out more about Shane Seaboy and who might have wanted to hurt him. We know the police already talked to you about him and the fight you had on Monday night."

"Yeah," Tony said and paused. "You know what, I have to be going. I have to meet a guy in a few minutes." He strode toward the door and held it open for them to leave. Tony Red Day, Jr. glared at Bridget and Marlee as they exited the home. "And I wouldn't come back here if I were you." Tony's words alone were not overly harsh, but his facial expression and body language communicated a rage boiling within.

The two made their way down the sidewalk and toward Marlee's vehicle when Tony poked his head out the door and looked directly at Marlee. "Hey, I know you from somewhere, don't I? You with the feds, right?"

"I used to be a federal probation officer a few years ago, but not any more," Marlee said as she quickly retreated from the house, snow crunching lightly on her shoes. Tony shook his head in disgust, slammed the door shut, and went back inside the house.

Marlee and Bridget high tailed it to the CR-V, jumped in, and locked the doors. Tony just demonstrated that he had the ability to go from friendly to ferocious very quickly and Marlee didn't want him to come out to the vehicle to continue the conversation, given the mood he was in. As they drove away, Tony stared at them through the large picture window in the living room. Tony made note of the make, model, and license plate of the vehicle before they turned the corner.

At what point in time do people realize they're dealing with a wolf in sheep's clothing? Some people never figure it out.

Chapter 13

"What's this rez telegraph everyone keeps talking about?" asked Bridget as they drove north toward the tiny town of Veblen.

"Basically, it's a way of saying news spreads very quickly on the reservation because everyone knows or is related to everyone else. It's not that different from any other small town where information and gossip spread like wild fire," said Marlee. "When I was a probation officer it wasn't unusual for many of my people on supervision to know I was in the area to see them long before I went to their homes or places of work. Somebody who knew them saw me driving through town, at the convenience store, or somewhere else and reported it to my probationers. So much for the element of surprise."

"I imagine if someone didn't want to talk to you they could make themselves scarce fairly easily, especially with a little advance warning that you were in town,"

Bridget said.

"Yep. I'm sure some were hiding in their own homes and had a family member lie for them. But that happens everywhere, not just on the reservation," said Marlee, mindful not to perpetuate stereotypes about any particular group of people.

"What did the grandma say about us? It was a word I'd never heard before." Bridget said.

"She said *wasicu*. It means white people. It's one of the few Lakota words I know," Marlee said.

"Who are we going to see now?" asked Bridget helping herself to the red licorice strings.

"Ivan Flute said Shane Seaboy's foster family, Shep and Judy Sanders, live up by Veblen on a farm. They're still on the farm and one of their sons lives there too. Hopefully they can give us some information on Shane," Marlee reported as she swung off the highway and onto a gravel road. The CR-V bounced along the road for three miles before a small red barn and a white two-story house came into view. The road-side mailbox indicated that this was indeed the Sanders residence.

As they pulled into the yard, the sound of several dogs barking could be heard. Marlee and Bridget looked at each other with wide eyes and open mouths. "What do we do?" asked Bridget, fearful of getting out of the vehicle and being attacked by vicious dogs.

"We wait for a couple minutes. By that time maybe someone will come out of the house and get the dogs to settle down," said Marlee. Bridget nodded as she was knew that much of the barking done by farm dogs was just to scare people, not necessarily harm them. She was raised in a small town but was very familiar with farm life.

After waiting in the car for less than a minute, a side door to the house opened and a lady walked up to the car. She motioned for Marlee to roll down the window, looking at them with an air of curiosity rather than suspicion.

"Hey, are you lost?" asked the lady as she shooed the dogs away from her legs.

Marlee introduced herself and Bridget and stated their reason for wanting to talk with her. After the lady confirmed that she was Judy Sanders, she invited them in for coffee. Bridget and Marlee cautiously extricated themselves from the vehicle, looking in all directions for dogs that could attack.

"Don't worry about them," Judy said motioning at her dogs who were now docile and quietly following the trio toward the house. Judy appeared to be in her mid-sixties, although her weather worn skin could have added a few years to her actual age. She was of sturdy build and looked as if she would not put up with much nonsense. Her wavy gray hair was pulled back in a bun from which several wisps of hair had escaped. She welcomed them into the farm house and invited them to sit at the kitchen table.

The furnishings in the farm house were old and worn but still functional. The trio sat at the table and drank from mismatched coffee cups, all sporting logos from different area businesses. Judy placed a plate of cookies on the table and motioned for them to help themselves. Old country western music from the 1950s played on a radio on the kitchen counter and a kettle of soup simmered on the stove. "This could be right out of a Norman Rockwell painting," thought Marlee as she looked around the home, noticing how comfortable she felt.

"Judy, we wanted to talk to you and your husband about Shane Seaboy. I'm sure you've heard by now that he was found dead on the MSU campus in Elmwood on

Tuesday morning," said Marlee. Judy nodded and a cloud of grief crept over her face.

"Shane was a good boy. He was placed with us by social services a few times when he was younger. His mom wasn't around and the relatives that he was supposed to stay with didn't do a very good job of parenting him. We took in kids for thirty years, both Indian and white kids. It was just two years ago that we stopped fostering kids. Shep was having some health problems and it just got to be too much for us to handle along with the farm," Judy said.

"I know Shane got into trouble later on, but he was still a good boy. He was a follower, not a leader. I always suspected he might get in with a group and be led into trouble and that's exactly what happened. He got roped into helping out some guys who were up to no good and they pinned a bunch of the crime on him. I'm not saying Shane wasn't involved at all, because I'm sure he was. He just wasn't as guilty as the others. He didn't have much self-esteem and was easily pressured into doing things he knew weren't right," Judy recalled, still looking grim as she recalled the young man who stayed in their home and was raised along with her own kids and other foster children.

"Did Shane stay in contact with you and your husband?" asked Bridget, sipping her coffee.

"The last we saw him was before he went to prison. He came out and told us he was sorry for what he did and that he knew it was wrong. He was feeling a lot of shame for what he did. Shane hugged us both and then left in tears. We knew he was out of prison because he contacted our daughter, Geneva, about getting a job in Elmwood when she moved there," Judy said.

"Wait, what? Geneva Sanders that works at MSU is your daughter?" Marlee asked, upset that she hadn't made the connection of the surnames earlier.

"That's her," Judy said as she sat up a little straighter in her chair and a small smile of pride crept to her lips. "Geneva's worked really hard and we were so glad when she moved back to South Dakota. Now we can see her all the time."

"Geneva helped Shane get a job at MSU?" Marlee asked, helping herself to a second chocolate chip cookie from the plate Judy placed in front of them.

"She sure did. She and Shane were really tight. Geneva really took on a big sister role with Shane, much more than any other kids we had placed with us. She was a bit older than Shane, but always acted as his protector and confidante. She was crushed when he was sent to prison and she's been having such a hard time with his death. If she hadn't just started work at MSU, I think she might take a few days off just to deal with it. Since Geneva's new and doesn't have much vacation time built up, she has to be there. I think she might come here this weekend, so that should help her with her grief," Judy said.

Marlee nodded, recalling seeing Geneva on stage at the campus meeting when Shane's death was announced. Geneva had been in tears and looked a wreck. "A weekend with her mother to take care of her was probably just what she needed," thought Marlee.

"Where did Geneva work before she moved to Elmwood?" Bridget asked. Marlee nodded in her direction, impressed with Bridget's knack for questioning. Together, they were making a pretty impressive investigative team.

"She lived in Minneapolis. She worked in administration at one of the community colleges there after she finished her master's degree. When she got the job as Dean of Student Affairs at MSU, she was just thrilled. And her dad and I were too," said Judy.

"Is Geneva married? Does she have kids?" Marlee asked.

"No and no. She was engaged for a while to a guy from Minneapolis but they called it off. I never knew for sure what happened and she didn't want to talk about it. We met him once, but I can't say as I knew him very well," said Judy. "I'm hoping she finds a nice guy in Elmwood and settles down. Shep and I really want her to stay in the area."

"So getting back to Shane," Marlee transitioned, hoping to garner more information on the deceased janitor. "Who do you think might have wanted to hurt or kill him?"

"A lot of people around here, especially the Indians, were very disgusted with Shane. They thought he sold out their culture by profiting from the sale of eagle feathers, old bones, and tools. People have long memories and are not quick to forgive. I think in time he might have been able to move past his negative reputation if he stayed out of trouble, but it wouldn't have been easy for Shane. People talked about him and shunned him, but I can't think of anyone who would want to hurt him. Most people just ignored and excluded him, which is a pretty harsh punishment in itself," said Judy. Marlee nodded recalling that ostracism from a group was frequently one of the most severe of sanction not only in early human groups, but also today.

"Do you know why Shane and Tony Red Day, Jr. had a falling out? Was it because of Shane selling eagle feathers?" asked Marlee.

"That was part of it, but the feud between them went back further than that. In high school Shane used to date Verla Renville, who's now Tony Red Day's girlfriend. Rumor had it that Shane and Verla still got together on occasion, especially when Tony wasn't around. Tony was back and forth between the rez and Minneapolis, so there was plenty of opportunity for Shane and Verla to get together. I don't know. It really wasn't any of my business and I stayed out of it. I figured if there was something Shane wanted me to know he would tell me," Judy said.

"What was Tony doing in Minneapolis?" asked Bridget.

"I have no idea. Tony tries to act superior because he doesn't drink and hasn't been in trouble with the law. My guess is he's into a lot more shit than anyone knows about. But that's just my two cents," Judy said. Although she said she tried to stay out of the gossip fray, it was appeared that Shane's enemies were her enemies too.

"Did Shane have a wife or girlfriend? Where was he living before he went to prison?" asked Marlee.

"He had a few girlfriends off and on, but nothing serious. I think he was still holding on to the hope that he and Verla Renville would eventually get together permanently. He never really had a steady home after he turned 18 and was out of the foster care system. Shane mostly stayed on the reservation, but he moved from one house to another. Some were relatives and some were friends. He'd stay at one home for a while until they'd get tired of him and then he'd go live somewhere else. He bounced around the reservation until he was arrested on the eagle feather charges. Shane was held in jail after his arrest because he didn't have anyone who would take him in while he awaited trial. We still had foster kids placed here, so we couldn't take him in," Judy said.

"Judy, do you know anything about a funeral service for Shane? I know his body hasn't been released yet from the coroner's office, but I would imagine someone will be making arrangements for a funeral soon," said Marlee.

"Geneva's working on that. Like I said before, there aren't too many people here that are fans of Shane's. Not even what few family members still live around here. They all washed their hands of him," said Judy with a crestfallen look on her face.

As they finished up their conversation and prepared to leave, Marlee grabbed another cookie for the road. Judy marched out to the car with them, stating she needed to finish up a couple chores out at the barn before lunch. Judy asked that they keep her posted on any new developments and the McCabe cousins assured her they would. She gave them a hearty wave as she strode off toward the red barn.

"Wow, I can't believe that selling eagle feathers and Native American artifacts put Shane in so much trouble with the tribe, and even his own family," said Bridget, working to understand the intricacies of the reservation.

"Yep, the prison sentence was probably the least of his punishment. Being shunned by family and friends and essentially kicked out of your home would be the worst. People can get through about anything if they have the support of friends and loved ones. It sounds as though the only people Shane could count on were the Sanders family and he was too embarrassed by his actions to go see them very much," said Marlee.

"Poor Shane. I know he broke the law, but this isn't the worst thing he could've done. He didn't kill anyone or molest children. He must have lived a very lonely life these past few years," Bridget said, feeling what she believed Shane must have experienced due to his illegal actions. The women drove back to Sisseton in silence as they contemplated Shane's isolating life of being shunned by his community.

The bark and the bite can be equally vicious. Nobody can rip you apart quite like your relatives.

Chapter 14

"So we're going to drop by Shane's brother's house. Then I think we'll have seen everyone on our list in the area. At least for now," said Marlee.

"His brother, Duane, may not be very cooperative. According to Judy, he didn't seem to have much of a relationship with Shane," Bridget said.

"True. I'm wondering if he'll be able to shed some light on who could've killed Shane. I understand that he was disliked by most people in the tribe after what he did, but I can't imagine there would be very many people who would actually kill him," said Marlee. "I'd also like to get a bit more info on Tony Red Day, Jr. Judy seemed to think he was up to some illegal behavior even though he acts as if he's holier than thou. Plus, it sounds like Tony had a reason to kill Shane if he thought Shane and his girlfriend were still seeing each other behind his back."

"And we know that Tony and Shane fought on

Monday night at a party in front of a bunch of witnesses. He could have easily followed Shane back to campus and killed him," Bridget said.

"I'm also going to look up Geneva Sanders on campus to find out what she has to say and also to express my condolences. According to Geneva's mom, she was about the only friend Shane had any more. It will be too late by the time we get back to Elmwood to talk to her today, but I'll look her up tomorrow after my classes," said Marlee. Bridget looked at her cousin with a woeful expression. Catching on that Bridget didn't want to be left out, she finally said, "You can come too. We'll meet at my office after my last class at noon and talk over our strategy. Then we can go to the Student Union for lunch and find Geneva. Sound like a plan?" Bridget's vigorous nodding and broad grin confirmed her enthusiasm for the idea.

"OK, so now let's go find Duane Seaboy," Marlee said as she roared into the town of Sisseton, not watching the speed limit. As she approached the downtown area, she noticed a law enforcement SUV behind her. She glanced at her speedometer and noticed she was going at least ten miles over the posted speed limit. Bridget flew as far forward as her seat belt would allow when Marlee stomped on the brakes.

"What are you doing?" Bridget yelled, attempting to place her back against the seat again.

"Sorry, I was speeding and just noticed a cop behind us. Luckily he didn't pull us over. Must have some real crime to tend to," Marlee said, thankful that she wouldn't have to pay a hefty fine for exceeding the speed limit. She had a tendency to not pay attention to details like speed limits when she was deep in thought or engaged in conversation.

"That gives me another idea!" Marlee shouted. "We

should talk to law enforcement while we're here. I still know of a couple people from my old probation officer days. Maybe we can get some details that will help fill in the blanks about Shane Seaboy's life and his death."

Bridget didn't speak, but acknowledged her agreement with Marlee's idea with a vigorous nod. She was still arranging her coat and her seatbelt after the jackrabbit stop from a few minutes earlier. Marlee continued to drive until she located the house where Duane Seaboy lived. She circled the block, per usual, and in finding nothing out of order, she parked in the grocery store parking lot across the street.

Marlee and Bridget did their usual routine of approaching the house, knocking, and stepping to the side. Within a minute of the first knock, they heard someone walking with quick, short steps in the house. A curtain near the window was pulled back an inch and an eye peered out. Bridget noticed this and waved. The eye disappeared and there was nothing but silence in the house. Marlee knocked again and finally the front door was opened a crack.

"Hi," Marlee began talking tentatively to the eye. "We're here to see Duane Seaboy. It's about his brother, Shane." The eye continued to look at Marlee and then blinked once. The eye disappeared and the door was pulled inward to reveal the body of a pregnant girl who appeared to be in her mid-teens. She motioned for them to enter the house, which was filled with a haze of cigarette smoke and the smell of fried food. Bridget and Marlee stood in the foyer, unsure what to do as the pregnant teen walked away.

"Duane, some people here to talk to you about Shane," she yelled over her shoulder as she stepped into the nearby kitchen. Heavy footsteps were heard from upstairs and then there was a thunderous commotion as

Duane clattered down the steps in the old, rickety house.

Duane appeared from the stairwell and the scowl on his face indicated he was none too pleased to see the women in his house. He wore a red and black flannel shirt and baggy jeans with streaks of dirt and grime on both pant legs. His medium length hair hung out from his baseball cap with the logo of Native Pride on the front. "What's this about?" he asked in a gruff voice, lighting a cigarette as his eyes flitted around the room.

Marlee introduced herself and Bridget, offered her condolences at the loss of his brother, and then proceeded to tell a pack of lies in order to entice Duane to talk. "I work at MSU in Elmwood. Shane was working there as a janitor when he died. We were hoping to talk to you about having a memorial or some type of ceremony for him on campus. We would like to include the Native American culture into the ceremony."

Duane snorted, cigarette smoke billowing from his nostrils. A small, mean smile crept to his lips revealing crooked, yellow teeth. "Why talk to me? I didn't consider him my brother. Not after what he did by selling sacred items to white people."

"I thought you were his only close relative in the area, so I thought I would check with you and your input on the funeral," Marlee said, realizing she wasn't prepared to deal with the level of hostility Duane held for Shane.

"You thought wrong. I washed my hands of him years ago and I don't intend to have anything to do with him now. He brought enough disgrace on me." Duane let his cigarette ashes fall to the carpet and then stepping on them with a scuffed cowboy boot.

"Was the falling out between you two over him selling eagle feathers and other artifacts, or was there more to it?" Bridget asked.

144

"Nunya," Duane mumbled.

"Nunya? What's that mean? We don't speak Lakota," said Bridget with an air of naiveté.

"It means *none ya'* business. Now get out," Duane said pointing at the door.

The McCabe cousins retreated from yet another house that day and made their way to their vehicle. "Jeez, we're not doing so well, are we?" asked Bridget.

"Actually, we found out quite a lot. Not as much as I'd hoped, but still plenty of details that can help us paint a better picture of who Shane was and why someone killed him," Marlee said. "Now, let's go to the Sheriff's Office and see what we can find out."

Arriving at the county courthouse minutes later, Marlee and Bridget made their way inside the old brick building which housed a variety of county offices, including the Sheriff's Office. "I used to chat with the Sheriff on occasion when I was a probation officer. Mostly on the phone, so I'm not sure if he'll remember me. But if he does, I bet we can get him talking," said Marlee. "It might work best if I talk to him alone."

The Sheriff's Office felt dingy and dark even though several windows let in light from two directions. Marlee moved to the front counter while Bridget seated herself on the wooden bench outside the office. A middle aged white woman heaved herself up from a desk and ambled over to the counter to address Marlee's needs. After a brief conversation on the phone, with who Marlee assumed must have been the sheriff in the next room, she was advised Sheriff Parker was in and would be able to speak with her.

Marlee made her way into the Sheriff's office and saw him standing over his desk. He was in his early fifties and had a stocky frame. He wore a khaki uniform shirt with a star on the front labeled "Sheriff", and black jeans. His bald head reflected light from the setting sun peeking through the window behind him. Marlee knocked on the door frame and he looked up from a map he'd been studying. Upon seeing her, Marlee knew he recognized her. "Okay, sure, I remember you. I was trying to place the name when the deputy said you were here, but I couldn't figure out who you were until I saw your face. How's it going?" the Sheriff asked extending his hand.

The two engaged in a hearty handshake and made small talk for a few minutes before Marlee asked questions about Shane Seaboy and Tony Red Day, Jr. Sheriff Parker studied her for a moment before answering. He recapped the stories Marlee already heard about Shane selling eagle feathers and indigenous artifacts, his prison sentence, and his tumultuous childhood. Sheriff Parker acknowledged that Tony Red Day definitely had motive to kill Shane, since Shane was still running around with Tony's girlfriend.

"You know, a lot of people around here are saying Tony Red Day did it, but I just don't think so," said the sheriff as he leaned back in his swivel chair and crossed his right leg over his left knee. "Tony's a little shit, even though he pretends that he's following the Red Road. He's been up to a lot of shady stuff around here and probably in Minneapolis too. He's just been lucky enough not to get caught. We thought he might have been involved in selling artifacts too, but couldn't ever get anyone to point the finger at him. Even with all that, I really don't think he would kill someone, not even Shane Seaboy."

Marlee filled Sheriff Parker in on the details of Shane's death on campus and then asked, "So who do you think killed him if Tony didn't?"

"Dunno. But it looks to me like somebody set him

up," the sheriff said.

"Any idea who would have something to gain from Shane being dead and Tony arrested for it?" Marlee asked.

"Not a lot of people around here liked Shane after what he did, but Tony really doesn't have many fans either. Tony thinks he's putting on a big show, but he he's not fooling too many people. He likes to portray himself as a devout follower of Native traditions, but he'd sell out anyone if he thought he could benefit from it. He's been parading around lately telling everyone he's gonna be the star of a movie. Mostly, people just get tired of him running his mouth," Sheriff Parker said with more than a hint of disgust in his voice.

"Do you know anything about a movie being shot here? I talked to Tony earlier and he thought my cousin and I had something to do with a film," Marlee said, jerking her thumb toward the door where Bridget waited.

"From what I hear, it's some kind of a documentary. Not sure what it's all about. Folks around here just been calling it "the movie," said the sheriff. "Over the years we've had a number of people from Hollywood, New York City, and other big cities show up and talk about using the reservation as a backdrop for their movie. Nothing ever gets off the ground."

"Can you tell me anything about recent grave robbing in the area?" Marlee detailed part of her conversation with Ivan Flute earlier that day and his suspicions that Shane Seaboy might have been involved.

"No, I haven't heard of any. One family allowed the feds to exhume the body of their grandma. A year or so after she was buried some information came to light that she may have been murdered, so her body was dug up and examined. The feds are still investigating it and I haven't heard anything new on it since this summer," said the sheriff.

"What do you know about Duane Seaboy? We stopped over to offer our condolences about his brother and he kicked us out of the house," Marlee said, indignant that someone could be so hostile toward her.

"Why exactly are you asking all these questions?" Sheriff Parker asked. "You haven't been a probation officer for a few years but you're asking questions like you're still in that line of work."

"Uh, well, I didn't have to teach today and Shane was killed on the MSU campus. My cousin, Bridget, is visiting me and hadn't been to this part of the state, so..." Marlee's voice drifted off as she realized she didn't have any good explanation for conducting her own investigation. In truth, she still had some concerns about the Elmwood Police Department. It wasn't so much the quality of the work the detectives would do on the investigation, but what Chief Langdon with do with those findings. Still, she knew better than to bad mouth one law enforcement agency to another.

"Kind of hard to let go of the old work, isn't it?" Sheriff Parker said with a wink.

Marlee laughed. "Yeah, it is. Now, about Duane Seaboy?"

"He's an interesting character. Shane never really seemed to find his place, but Duane did. He has a house that he and his girlfriend rent and they have a baby on the way. He's worked as a farm hand for a local family and earns decent money. Duane is a pain in the ass because he's always upset and grumbling about something, but he never causes any trouble himself. As far as I know he isn't a big drinker and isn't into drugs. Other than being a grouch, he's actually a fairly good citizen. Duane's a proud man and my guess is that he's really embarrassed by his brother's actions," reported Sheriff Parker.

"I think we saw Duane's pregnant girlfriend when we went to his house. She looks like she's fourteen years old," said Marlee, concerned that a minor might be taken advantage of sexually by an adult.

"She's nineteen, but she looks a whole lot younger. We already checked it out after some complaints were made by Duane's neighbors."

"So how were Shane and the guys he worked with getting the Native American artifacts and eagle feathers?" Marlee asked.

"Some Native Americans have artifacts in their homes. Old tools, weapons, and such were found by a family member and it just stayed with the family. Over the years there have been a lot of break-ins at homes and these things get stolen," Sheriff Parker stated. "Eagle feathers can be illegally obtained by shooting eagles, which will get you a stiff penalty. Or Native Americans can apply to the U.S. Fish and Wildlife Service to get whole eagles, eagle parts, and eagle feathers for use in ceremonies and cultural purposes."

"How does Fish and Wildlife get the eagles if it's illegal to hunt them?" Marlee asked.

"They run the National Eagle Repository. When golden eagles or bald eagles are found dead, either due to natural causes or accidents, or are seized from hunters, the birds are shipped to the Repository. Then the feathers, talons, and other parts can be given to those enrolled in an Indian tribe. It's a complicated process and they have to fill out an application," the Sheriff said.

"Were Shane and his buddies applying for eagle feathers legally and then selling them?" Marlee asked.

The Sheriff scratched his bald head. "I don't think so. Sometimes it takes up to two years to get an eagle or feathers after submitting the application. That would take too long for them to make any profit in selling the feathers. Mainly, they just broke into people's homes or cars and stole them."

They finished up the conversation and the sheriff walked her to the front counter. Bridget poked her head in and she introduced them. "You ladies have a nice drive home. And watch the speed limit," Sheriff Parker said with another wink and a grin.

Friendship never came easy for me. Those who said they were my friends just wanted to use me. At least with my enemies I knew for sure where I stood.

Chapter 15

The life and death of Shane Seaboy was discussed the whole ride back to Elmwood. "I think the sheriff made a strong point when he said someone was setting up Tony Red Day for the murder. After all, you'd have to be pretty stupid to assault someone at a party full of witnesses and then kill him in the same night," said Bridget.

"Most homicides aren't planned or intentional. Much of the time, someone flies into a rage and just snaps. The classic example of that is the woman who comes home and finds her husband in bed with another woman. She grabs the gun on the nightstand and shoots them both in a fit of rage. Or a fight turns into one person dying, unintentionally, as the result of a physical altercation. Like if Bob and Tom get in a fist fight and as a result Bob kills Tom even though that was never the intention. Bob just wanted to beat the crap out of Tom," Marlee said, stopping when she realized she had just given a partial lecture on types of homicide.

"Wow, you should teach this for a living," Bridget teased, which earned her a slap on the side of the arm.

"Ha ha... just trying to dispel notions perpetuated by the television and movie industries," Marlee shot back.

"So who do you think killed Shane Seaboy and why?" Bridget ignored the slam to her field of film studies.

"I think Tony Red Day is a strong candidate, but so is Duane Seaboy. I have a bad feeling about both guys and it's not just because they kicked us out of their houses," Marlee said. "Still, Sheriff Parker seems like he's got a good read on most people, so I tend to give quite a bit of credence to his ideas that Duane is a fairly decent guy and Tony is a blowhard that's being set up."

"If not one of them, then who?" Bridget asked. "Do you think it's someone we haven't even thought of yet?"

"Could be. Might be somebody from Elmwood with no ties to the reservation who, for whatever reason, decided to kill Shane. Or it could be somebody from his prison days paying him back for something he did while he was serving time," said Marlee.

"Is it possible that he died later on from the injuries he sustained during the fight with Tony Red Day?" Bridget inquired.

"I suppose it's possible. We should check with Bettina Crawford from the Police Department back home to see what she thinks," Marlee said as she reached for her cell phone.

"Bettina, hey, it's Marlee. You feel like having a beer tonight?" Marlee paused. "Yeah, I need something. But I also have some information for you, so we can trade." After another pause, Marlee spoke again, "Yep, see you there."

Setting her phone down in a cup holder, Marlee

turned to Bridget and said, "Put on your party pants. We're going out on the town tonight!"

"What? I don't really feel like making it a big party night," Bridget's eyes were blood shot and her face reflected the wear and tear of the day.

"Just kidding. We're meeting Bettina at Limbo's for a beer. It's a little dive so you don't even have to brush your teeth before we go," Marlee said.

"Good to know I don't have to doll up. Do you think Bettina will have any new information?" asked Bridget.

"Probably. She's a really good detective, plus she does a lot of listening and not much talking when she's at work, so she gathers all kinds of info from other detectives and officers." Marlee grabbed her cell phone again and began dialing. "I'll see if Diane wants to go too."

Marlee and Bridget stopped at a convenience store and took orders of chicken strips to their vehicle to eat as they drove. They arrived home around 6:00 pm, and after a quick chance to freshen up, they hopped back into the CR-V with Diane in tow and made their way to the bar. Limbo's was not popular with any particular group in Elmwood, so there was always an open table or booth. Thursday night was no exception. As they entered the dim, dirty little bar, they observed Bettina in a back booth sipping a bottle of beer. After brief introductions, they all sat down and began to talk at once.

The bartender, who did double duty as a server, came over and asked for drink orders. "Do you have white wine?" Bridget asked. Marlee quickly whispered in her ear and Bridget then said, "Never mind. I'll have a Bud Light in a bottle." Bettina and Marlee ordered the same while Diane asked for a Heineken.

"Did she warn you about drinking out of a glass here?" Bettina asked Bridget.

"Yes, she did. And I always take good advice," Bridget said, happy to be avoiding any type of germs or diseases from unsanitary beer glasses.

"So what did you find out today?" Bettina asked after their beers arrived. "You said something about trading information."

Marlee and Bridget took turns recapping their interviews with Ivan Flute, Tony Red Day, Jr., Duane Seaboy, Verla Renville, Judy Sanders, and Sheriff Powell for Bettina and Diane. Bettina nodded along in silence while Diane gasped, *ooh*ed, and *aaah*ed at the stories. "Okay, spill. "What do you have to report?" Marlee asked Bettina.

Bettina finished off the last of the beer in her bottle and motioned for the bartender to bring each of them another beer. "The autopsy confirmed death due to a series of blows to the back of his head. So, no, I don't think Shane died of injuries from the fight with Tony on Monday night."

"Do you know Duane Seaboy, Shane's brother?" Bridget asked Bettina.

"Know of him and I could identify him, but don't know much about him other than he's a hired hand for a farmer near Sisseton. Since I don't know much about him, that means he must have a clean arrest record or else he's just lucky and hasn't gotten caught," Bettina reported.

"Sheriff Parker said about the same thing. Do you believe his antagonism toward Shane is all about Shane selling eagle feathers and artifacts or is there something else?" asked Marlee.

"They've never really gotten along that well, even when they were kids, from what I understand. When their mother left them with relatives they didn't supervise the boys very well and they were removed from

156

the home. What I never really understood was why Duane was placed with other relatives while Shane was put into foster care with people he didn't even know. Usually, kids would be kept together, especially if there were only two of them. The only thing I can think of is that they have different fathers," said Bettina, trying to make sense of the Seaboy family history.

"But they both have Seaboy as their surname," interjected Diane.

"Sure, but one may not be biologically related to Oscar Seaboy. He didn't stick around long, so I don't know much about him. I heard he died a few years ago. He'd been living in Pine Ridge. Guess he got married and had a whole other family down there after he left Shane and Duane's mom," said Bettina.

"I wonder if Shane and Duane knew they possibly had different fathers?" asked Bridget.

"Marlee, you might want to check with either Shane's foster family or Ivan Flute. They would both have some idea of the history from the time they were born. They might remember some of the scuttlebutt as to the boys' paternity," Bettina suggested.

"Grand idea. I'll give them a call tomorrow. Speaking of tomorrow, I think I need to head home soon and get to bed. It's been a long day and I have a bunch of stuff to do tomorrow. Oh, and I have to teach a couple classes too," Marlee said. The foursome agreed, but decided one more beer would be in everyone's best interest before they left.

Later, when Marlee got home, she pulled on her pajamas, washed her face, and brushed her teeth. She looked at her day planner to see if she had anything going on besides teaching and doing some additional investigation on the Seaboy death. Noticing there were no scheduled meetings, she smiled and went to bed.

Tomorrow would prove to be a very interesting day. She could already feel it in her bones.

A snake, when threatened, might strike. It won't bite every time, but it doesn't need to. The possibility of a snake bite is enough to keep most people away.

Chapter 16

Friday morning came way too early. When the alarm sounded at 7:00 am Marlee crawled out of bed and lumbered to the dresser across the room to hit the snooze button. She believed she would be less likely to hit the snooze button repeatedly if she placed the alarm clock out of arm's reach from the bed. In theory, this was a sound plan. In practice, Marlee had no trouble collapsing face first back into her warm bed for another nine minutes of sound slumber before the alarm sounded again. And Friday was no exception. The trip to the reservation the day before, poor eating habits, not enough sleep, too much alcohol, and the overall stress associated with the end of the semester all took a toll on Marlee's system. The physical exhaustion was bad enough, but the mental exhaustion was worse. She just didn't feel like teaching today and began her daily countdown of how many teaching days she had until finals week. Only one more week of classes, which translated into three teaching days, were left for Marlee after today. That was one week and one day too many.

Marlee's grumpiness extended into all areas of her life that morning. As much as she enjoyed having Bridget and Diane stay with her, she was ready to have her house back to herself. Little things about each of them were wearing on her nerves. At the top of the list were Bridget's never-ending movie references. Entertaining and apropos at first, the constant 'this is just like' and then the movie reference became old. If Marlee wasn't familiar with the reference or even the movie, Bridget took it upon herself to provide a full synopsis of the film, including a critique. Marlee loved movies, but Bridget was out of control when it came to motion picture films! Diane, on the other hand, had become a permanent fixture on the couch. Whether it was sleeping, reading, or conversing, Diane conducted 99% of her activities in Marlee's home from the blue, overstuffed couch.

After inhaling her first cup of brewed coffee, Marlee refilled her mug and went into the bathroom to shower and get ready for work. By the time she was showered, dressed, and caffeinated, Marlee's mood had turned from sour to apathetic. She just needed to get through two classes that morning and then she would have the weekend free. Or, as free as it could be when she had papers and quizzes to grade, final exams to write, and student problems to spearhead. As much as she needed to focus on students and classes, her mind kept returning to Shane Seaboy and his death. She replayed the conversations from the previous day in her mind and tried to make sense of what she had learned. Shaking her head as if to remove the cobwebs, Marlee bundled up in a heavy fall coat, as it was just too early to dig out the full winter apparel. She poured a travel mug full of coffee and left the house as Diane and Bridget slept.

Marlee arrived on campus a full hour and a half before her first class. Her first stop was the Student Union to get some breakfast and another mug of coffee. Even though she only lived a few blocks away, she had nearly drained her travel mug in the minutes it took her to drive to campus. The cafeteria was busy with students, professors, and staff grabbing a quick breakfast or cup of coffee. Her mind knew that a fatty, carb dense breakfast was not in her best interests, but her tummy disagreed. She was a comfort eater and made poor nutritional choices when she was tired, upset, happy, sad, stressed, angry, or experiencing any other emotional states. Making her way to an elevated table in the corner, Marlee set down her tray of scrambled eggs, bacon, hash browns, toast, and coffee and hopped up on one of the tall chairs. From her corner position, she was able to see everyone who moved in and out of the dining area.

For five minutes Marlee ate her breakfast and sipped coffee in silence. She was so busy feeling sorry for herself because of all she needed to do before the semester's end that Geneva Sanders walked by almost unobserved. After doing a double-take to make sure her eyes were not deceiving her, Marlee jumped down from her elevated chair and approached Geneva after she paid for her cup of coffee. She introduced herself, expressed her condolences at the loss of Shane Seaboy, and invited Geneva to sit with her while she drank her coffee.

"I can only sit for a couple minutes," Geneva said, looking over one shoulder and then the other. "I'm supposed to be at a meeting shortly."

"Sure, I understand. Always plenty of meetings to attend at MSU, aren't there?" Marlee was trying to put a nervous Geneva at ease through small talk. Geneva nodded and gave a grim smile, the type of smile one gives when they really aren't happy but just responding to social cues.

"My cousin and I were out to the reservation yesterday and met with your mother. She told us you were planning a memorial service for Shane. When is it?" Marlee asked.

"Yes, I'm one of the few people who knew him here in Elmwood. Shane was my foster brother. He was placed with our family off and on for a few years. My meeting this morning is about scheduling the memorial service on campus. I'm hoping we can have it on Wednesday of next week, but that isn't official yet." Geneva's eyes continued to flit around the room as she kept tabs on who entered and who left the dining area.

"Do you have any idea who killed Shane or who might have wanted him dead?" Marlee asked as she finished the last of her breakfast and pushed her empty plate toward the center of the table.

"No, I don't. Now if you'll excuse me, I really have to get ready for my meeting," Geneva said as she stood up abruptly, grabbed her coffee, and marched out of the dining room.

"That was odd. Geneva was on pins and needles the whole time we talked and then she takes off like the house is on fire when I ask her who might have wanted Shane dead," Marlee thought to herself. "Very strange," she said out loud to no one in particular as she bussed her table of the breakfast dishes.

Despite being groggy from lack of sleep and a heavy breakfast, Marlee was able to engage her students in both classes in lively discussions. Student participation was largely unheard of this late in the semester unless part of the grade was based on verbal activity in class. The students were burned out too, but the topic of ethical dilemmas in criminal justice coupled with a scenario and small group discussion engaged the students' interest.

Marlee previously arranged to meet with Bridget on campus for lunch after her last class ended. They planned to talk with Geneva Sanders after lunch, but since Marlee already spoke with her without much success, she didn't think trying to talk with her again within a few hours would yield any better results. Huffing and puffing after walking up the stairs carrying twenty pounds of books and papers, Marlee turned the corner to her office.

"Hey, Marlee!" shouted Bridget as she did her little dance of excitement by hopping from one foot to the other.

"Oh, that's right. We were going to meet for lunch before you left to go home," Marlee said, entering her key in the lock and pushing open her office door. "There's actually been a change in the plan." She replayed her brief conversation with Geneva Sanders from earlier that morning. "I don't think there's much point in talking to her again today, but I'll try again next week. Maybe on Monday. I can at least use the excuse of finding out more about Shane Seaboy's memorial as a reason to talk to her."

"Hey, I've got some changes to report too," Bridget continued to do a nerd dance until Marlee motioned for her to sit down. "First, I got the one year appointment as visiting professor at Marymount!"

"Oh my god! That's wonderful," Marlee exclaimed. She was truly happy her cousin was moving to Elmwood, especially since she would have her own apartment. "When do you start?"

"Next fall. So I have a few months to line up a place to live and all that good stuff. I'm so excited. I'm on sabbatical all next academic year, so my one year appointment at Marymount won't overlap at all with my teaching back home." Bridget squirmed in her seat with excitement.

"What'll you be doing as a visiting professor of film studies?" Marlee inquired, not at all sure what that field entailed.

"I'll teach one section of Intro to Film Studies and one seminar on an advanced topic that I select. I also get to organize film discussions not only at Marymount, but also for the whole community of Elmwood. Another thing I'm really pumped about is putting together a film series on diversity for the town, which is just so exciting. Basically, I get to do the fun stuff like teaching and organizing film showings and discussions without all the blah stuff like meetings and committees."

"Are you sure you want to spend your sabbatical teaching at a different university? Wouldn't you like to travel to another country to do some research?" Marlee asked. Although she was several years away from being granted a sabbatical, she already had visions of herself standing before a pyramid in Egypt and rafting down the Nile. No thought had been given yet to her research if she were to be granted a semester or a year of leave, but she knew she wanted to travel somewhere exotic.

"This is exactly what I want to do for my first sabbatical. Teaching a seminar on a topic of my choosing and directing a community film series are both so exciting for me. If I get another sabbatical later on in my career, then maybe I'll look at traveling abroad to do some research," Bridget stated.

"That's so great!" Marlee said, and she meant it. As much as Bridget had been getting on her nerves, she knew having her cousin in town would be fun and a source of academic and familial support for both of them. "Now, what's your other news item?"

"Well, I've decided I don't need to go back home

today after all! I'm really getting into this investigation and don't need to leave until Wednesday. Isn't that great?" Bridget could barely contain her enthusiasm and jumped out of her chair to resume hopping from one foot to the other.

"Wow... that is great," Marlee said not faking sincerity very well. She needed to figure out a way to mentally brace herself for the remainder of her cousin's visit. Bridget was oblivious and returned to the topic of teaching at Marymount the following year.

"There was one other thing I wanted to tell you. I met with Dean Green this morning," said Bridget.

"What the hell? Why would you meet with him? Dammit, Bridget!" Marlee was so upset she could barely form words. Although Bridget would not intentionally sabotage Marlee's career, she may have inadvertently mentioned something to the dean that Marlee preferred he not know.

"Don't worry, don't worry!" said Bridget, prepared to tell Marlee the story as she sat back down, excess energy burned from her previous happy dance.

"Please tell me you didn't mention anything about going to the reservation or the Shane Seaboy investigation," Marlee said, dreading and anticipating the response at the same time.

"Nope, I didn't mention anything at all about the people we've talked to or our interest in the case," Bridget assured Marlee. "I told him about my visiting professorship at Marymount next year and asked for his cooperation with the community diversity film series I was telling you about. I thought several of the departments in the College of Arts and Sciences might like to be involved in the community film series, especially since we will be touching on topics like racism, discrimination, prejudice, and tolerance."

"That's it? Whew!" Marlee was relieved. "I'm so glad you didn't mention me. Will Dean Green be involved in the film series?"

"Based on the preliminary ideas I told him I had, he said he would give it his support. I don't think he'll participate, but he'll allow advertising here on MSU's campus and may get some of the arts and sciences faculty involved. Oh, and he did mention you." Bridget was hesitant in the telling of the last bit of information.

Marlee stared at Bridget from beneath furrowed eyebrows. This would not be good. "So what did he say?"

"Uh, well, he wanted to know why you involved yourself in criminal investigations. He wanted to know if you were working as a private investigator in addition to being a professor," said Bridget.

"What? Huh, I wonder where he got the idea that I was a PI? What did you tell him?" asked Marlee. She stifled a giggle as she envisioned herself with a trench coat and a long range camera lurking outside seedy motel room windows hoping to snap a photo of a cheating spouse.

"I told him I was sure you weren't a PI," said Bridget. "He went on to tell me how you butted into the Logan LeCroix investigation last year and your contract almost wasn't renewed for this year. So I reminded him that you were the main reason Logan's death investigation was finally resolved."

"Oh, no. Then what did he say?" Marlee asked.

"He muttered a bit. I couldn't understand all of it, but there were some cuss words. Then he told me he had a meeting to attend and needed to go. That was my invitation to get the hell out, so I did," recalled Bridget. "As I left he told me to remind you that if you expect to ever get tenure at MSU, you need to forget about investigating and spend more time on your teaching, research, and service. What an ass!"

"Yep, that's Mean Dean Green, alright. He's always making sure that I know he can get rid of me. That's why it's so important that we keep the Shane Seaboy investigation to ourselves." Bridget nodded in agreement with Marlee's assertion.

"So, what are we doing this afternoon?" asked Bridget. She shared Marlee's sense of inquisitiveness and was anxious to delve into unraveling the puzzle of Shane Seaboy's death.

"I thought I'd talk to one of the FBI agents who investigated the eagle feather case that Shane was convicted of. I know one of the agents a little bit and he might be willing to talk to me. The thing is," said Marlee, bracing for Bridget's negative reaction, "since he's law enforcement it might go better if I talk to him by myself."

Bridget tried, unsuccessfully to hide her disappointment. "Can I at least ride along? I'll wait outside the office or in the car."

"You know what? I have another mission for you," Marlee said, hoping to engage Bridget in a task of her own. "Would you be willing to contact Ivan Flute from Prairie Winds treatment center to see what he knows about Shane and Duane Seaboy's paternity?"

"Well, it's not as good as talking to the FBI, but okay," said Bridget, warming to the idea.

"You know, you could also talk to Ivan a bit about your upcoming diversity film series. He might be able to suggest some films depicting Native American themes and even give you some ideas for speakers to introduce the films," Marlee said.

"Hey, that's a great idea!" Bridget said, fully on board with Marlee's proposal. "I'll run back to your house and use the phone there. I don't have a cell phone and I'm avoiding getting one."

"That's fine. I only got a cell last year when I was doing quite a bit of driving during the summer," Marlee stated. "I only turn it on when I want to make a call, which is not very often, so it doesn't get much use. If anyone needs to reach me, they can call my home or my office." The two chatted on about the pros and cons of cell phones before deciding it was time for lunch. Marlee really wasn't hungry since she snarfed down a huge breakfast just a few hours before, but being a believer in eating to prevent hunger, she agreed that lunch was in order. The two made their way to the Student Union and stood in the cafeteria line.

"Hey, Dr. M!" shouted Donnie Stacks. She was approaching the cashier with a tray of soup and a grilled cheese sandwich cut diagonally. "Are you eating here or going back to your office?"

"Eating here. Do you want to join us?" Marlee asked, gesturing toward Bridget. She was anxious to see what one of her Criminal Justice Club students might have uncovered about Shane Seaboy.

"Sure, I'll grab us a table," said Donnie as she fished some coins out of her coat pocket and presented them, along with some dollar bills, to the cashier. Donnie was clad in jeans, a hooded sweatshirt, and rust-colored Columbia jacket. The coat color was nearly a match for her short curly hair.

After selecting tacos, cilantro rice, and refried beans for her meal, Marlee paid the cashier and joined Donnie at a corner table with four chairs. When Bridget joined them, Marlee made the introductions. Small talk ensued for the first few minutes until Donnie said, "Well, I've found out a couple things about Shane Seaboy."

Marlee raised her eyebrows. "Do tell."

"With all this talk about Shane and his past, no one seemed to know where he lived in Elmwood. I met up with one of Collin Kolb's roommates, Ashton Dumarce. I really didn't know Ashton, but we worked on a group project together, so I kinda knew him. Anyway, he said Shane lived alone in an efficiency apartment a few blocks from campus. He didn't have a car, so he either walked, road a bike, or hitched a ride. Ashton said he'd given Shane a ride to the grocery store and back home to Sisseton a couple times." Donnie stuffed a corner of the grilled cheese in her mouth, pleased with the amount of information she had uncovered.

"That's not all. I have a friend who kind of knows Lindsey Gates, the janitor who found Shane Seaboy and called 911. I had my friend introduce me to Lindsey and she basically reported what we already knew. When she found Shane she tried to revive him, but when she realized he was dead, she called the police. Lindsey said he was lying on his stomach and there was blood around the back of his head that had dripped down onto the floor," Donnie reported. "She didn't see a weapon or anything."

"Good work, Donnie," Marlee said, impressed that her student had taken the initiative to question both Ashton Dumarce and Lindsey Gates. After updating Donnie on what she and Bridget knew about the Seaboy murder, Marlee pushed her tray away, only a few stray grains of rice left on the corner of the plate. Her mind was swimming with all the new and old information.

More than anything, Marlee wanted to go home and take a three-hour nap. She was exhausted even before the day began and the heavy meals and added stress just made her even more tired. Still, she knew she needed to talk to an agent at the FBI office in town to see what else she could find out about Shane Seaboy's conviction. She gave Bridget a ride back home before going to meet with the FBI.

Originally, the office for the Federal Bureau of Investigation was located in the old, brick Federal Courthouse in Elmwood. In 2002, the agency moved to private offices on the edge of town after being allotted more money for office space. Marlee parked in the employee only lot outside the federal office. The agency was located in what looked like a strip mall. Entering the newly-fashioned building, Marlee was met with a locked glass door and an intercom system. After buzzing in and identifying herself, the door lock clicked, allowing her to enter the FBI's inner sanctum.

When Marlee worked as a probation officer she came to know the two FBI agents, although the relationship was purely professional. Both agents were polite, but reserved, keeping their personal information private. Nicole Severson was a native of Minnesota and was a nine year veteran of the Elmwood branch of the FBI, while A.J. Simms, who hailed from Chicago, had spent five years in Elmwood as a special agent. A.J. Simms was the only agent in the office at the time and Marlee asked to speak with him. Since beginning her teaching career, Marlee had asked A.J. to come to her criminology class to discuss the work of an FBI agent and what it took to be selected for that line of work. He was young and energetic and both traits played well with the college students who were looking toward future careers in law enforcement.

Marlee sat in the waiting room which was barren except for six sturdy chairs, one table covered with an array of magazines, an over watered plant in the corner with yellowing leaves, and a display of pamphlets dealing with identify theft, domestic violence, and victim compensation programs. A reception desk was located just inside the security door and was behind a glass shield. The low pile carpet was a medium brown print, while the walls and the furniture were also colored in earth tones. Had it not been for the security door and the front desk enclosed in glass, the FBI waiting room could have passed for a reception area in any ordinary dentist's office.

A wooden door on the far side of the waiting room opened and a large African American man stepped out. A.J. Simms smiled when he saw Marlee sitting in the corner reading a magazine on hunting safety. He was dressed casually in khakis, a button down shirt, and tan hiking boots. It was Friday, and since there was no chance he would need to testify in court, it was completely acceptable to dress comfortably.

After an initial greeting and some chit-chat, A.J. motioned for Marlee to follow him back to his office. A.J.'s office was nondescript and devoid of any family photographs or personal information. Three of the walls were lined with bookcases, filled with thick procedural manuals and federal law books.

Getting right to the business at hand, Marlee said, "So, I'm wondering what you can tell me about the Shane Seaboy case from a few years ago. He and some others were arrested for selling eagle feathers and other cultural artifacts. I've talked to Aleece at probation and she told me who the codefendants were. I've also talked to Shane's former foster mother, the Roberts County Sheriff, Duane Seaboy, and some other people out in the Sisseton area who knew him fairly well to see what they had to say about him. There are a variety of opinions on who might have killed him."

"Well, you've been busy. Are you trying to get your old job back at probation?" A.J. teased as he slid his chair up closer to the computer monitor on his desk.

"No, I'm just curious. I didn't know him or anything, but since he was killed on campus, it makes it personal.

Plus, I don't want to see somebody commit a murder and get away with it," Marlee said, making a not so veiled reference to the Logan LeCroix case that the local police chief initially mistakenly ruled a suicide the previous year.

"OK, so here's the story," said A.J. as he skimmed the information on the desk top computer. "Shane Seaboy was a minor player in the whole operation. If he'd cooperated and told us what he knew, he probably would've just gotten placed on probation. He might not even have been charged if he agreed to testify against his codefendants. But he didn't do that. He kept his mouth shut and took the punishment, even though I personally think he was the least culpable of any of them."

"Who was the leader?" Marlee inquired.

"Of those we arrested, Ryan Campbell was the most culpable for the crimes. The thing is, we never got the main guy we thought was behind the whole operation. He was able to get everybody else to do his dirty work, so the sales of eagle feathers couldn't be connected to him. Of course, if Shane or the others had talked and testified against him, he would have been serving a nice long stretch in federal prison," reported A.J.

"Who was the main leader? Where was he from?" Questions tumbled out of Marlee's mouth as quickly as she thought of them.

"We don't know his real name, but we call him Diego. We think he's still involved in illegal sales of Native American artifacts and cultural items. Our sources tell us he lives around St. Paul, Minnesota and the FBI office there is keeping an eye out for him. We think his connections in Sisseton dried up when Shane Seaboy and that group went to prison. Shane was the first to be released and we think that's when the connection to the Lake Traverse rez was reestablished, even though Shane didn't stick around Sisseton for long. Diego's still in the business; there was just a bit of a hiatus from the activities on the Lake Traverse reservation. Eventually this guy will mess up and then we'll nab him!" A.J. loved being an FBI agent and it showed. He lived for bringing the bad guys to justice.

"Diego?" Marlee asked. "Where do you think he's doing most of his illegal buying and selling now?"

"With the Internet, it could be anywhere and everywhere. We think he's got connections all over the world. In the Seaboy investigation we found that Diego isn't above ripping off his customers either," said A.J.

Marlee raised her eyebrows. "How do you know that?"

"We were able to recover some of the pieces he was passing off as artifacts and they weren't nearly as old as he purported them to be. He's able to adapt his level of fraud with the level of sophistication he believes his client has. If he's dealing with an expert like a museum curator specializing in Native American history and artifacts, then he uses the real tools and bones. If it's someone who just wants to have some Indian artifacts in their home as decoration, then he'll rip them off thinking they don't know any better. And often times they don't. We know of at least one occasion in which he substituted bone fragments from a deer and claimed they were the bones of an Indian chief," said A.J.

"Why isn't anyone ratting this guy out? I assume several people have been offered plea agreements with reduced sentences if they rolled over," said Marlee.

"Yeah, some wouldn't have done any time at all if they'd cooperated. Diego has them scared so no one is talking," said A.J.

"Doesn't that seem a little extreme for someone trafficking in eagle feathers and artifacts? I mean, people roll over on murderers and high level drug dealers all the time. Why are people so afraid of Diego?"

"We've never been able to figure that out. He's got them all scared to death and we don't know why. We think there must be some kind of connection there besides just the eagle feather sales. Like maybe he's related to some people from the area or has so much dirt on them that they would go away for a much longer period of time if they talked to us," A.J. reported.

"So, Diego's been able to convince everyone he has working for him to do all the dirty work, keep quiet when questioned, and take the rap for him?" Marlee asked, still trying to get her mind around the whole situation.

"That's about right," said A.J. rubbing his temples with his forefingers. "We don't know how he does it. That's part of the reason he remains free and continues in the illegal artifacts trade."

"Are you sure he's the right guy? I mean, maybe there's no link to him because he either doesn't exist or someone else is the top dog," said Marlee.

"You know, we kicked that idea around before but our information keeps leading us back to him. We don't know his real name, but he is a real person," A.J. said.

"Has he killed anyone? Or had anyone killed by one of his cronies?" Marlee asked.

"We don't have a direct link yet. There are some unexplained deaths and a few people missing over the years, but we can't hook it on him. Not yet. Like I said, he's being monitored and we'll get him eventually," A.J. said with confidence. "The biggest fish take the longest time to reel in."

Marlee smiled as she pictured A.J. in a boat on one of the small lakes around Elmwood. He was a city boy through and through and the image of him reeling in a fish just didn't fit. "Maybe he was responsible for Shane

Seaboy's death. Shane and Tony Red Day, Jr., got into a fight at a college house party here in town and Tony said something to the effect of, 'you shoulda kept your mouth shut,' to Shane. Any connection between Tony Red Day and Diego?"

"Not that we know of. Tony's name has come up a few times during some of our investigations out there, but always low level stuff like dealing small amounts of marijuana and thefts from cars. It doesn't look like he has any connection to Diego," said A.J.

"One theory we've heard batted around is that somebody Shane was in prison with wanted revenge. Any credence to that idea?" Marlee asked.

"Not that I know of, but the Bureau of Prisons would have more information on that than the FBI would," reported A.J. referring to the federal agency which oversaw the custody, control, and care of individuals imprisoned in one of the country's federal institutions.

"I guess I'll check with Aleece at probation again to see what she can tell me," Marlee said, making a mental list of the people she had yet to talk to today. "I've got one more question and then I'll leave you alone. For today," Marlee said with a smile. Is selling eagle feathers and cultural artifacts such a horrible offense that it would normally get someone shunned by their family and friends?"

"It's definitely looked down upon by most Native Americans, but it's not an offense that someone couldn't overcome." A.J. said, scratching his head and peering out the window to the vacant lot behind the FBI offices.

"So why is it that nearly everyone I've talked to mentions how awful Shane Seaboy is based on his involvement in the eagle feather case?" Marlee asked.

"This all gets back to Diego. I'd say the people on the rez are afraid of Diego and what he can do, so they all use

Shane's illegal behavior as a way to distance themselves from him. They say they don't know much about Shane and selling eagle feathers because they disapproved and, therefore, don't know have anything to report. Much safer for them than to reveal what they know; especially if the information leads back to Diego."

"That makes sense," Marlee said. "I doubted the whole Native American community would exclude and demonize someone for selling eagle feathers. It just seemed too severe of a consequence for Shane Seaboy's actions."

"I talked with Sheriff Parker over in Sisseton and he said Shane and the others were getting the eagle feathers and artifacts by breaking into people's houses," Marlee said.

A.J. nodded. "Sounds about right."

After thanking A.J. for his time and expertise, Marlee walked to the parking lot. She wanted to stop at the Federal Probation Office before going home. As she fished her car keys out of her coat pocket, she noticed the front tire on the driver's side was flat. "Sonofabitch!" she yelled to no one in particular. She was exhausted and needed to talk to one other person before she could go home and call it a day. Now she had to deal with a flat tire on top of everything else.

Marlee made a huge production of unloading everything from the back of her CR-V to get to the spare tire and crowbar. In the past she had been fortunate enough to have someone, usually an older male, take pity on her and change the tire for her. This flew in the face of all her feminist ideals, but the truth of the matter was that she just didn't like doing car repairs and maintenance. Plus, the lug nuts were always on so tight that she had difficulty in loosening them to get the tire off. She silently cursed the nail, broken glass, or other sharp object that had flattened her tire.

After a few minutes of struggling with the crowbar, Marlee's back was killing her. It was still sensitive from her fall on the ice earlier in the week and attempting to remove the lug nuts from the flat tire was just making it worse. She went back inside the FBI office and asked A.J. to help her. Being a gentleman and someone who liked to help those in need, he agreed and had the tire changed within ten minutes.

"Don't forget, this is just a donut tire. Don't use it permanently. You'll need to get your old tire fixed. If it can't be fixed, then you'll need a new one. My bet is that a nail is lodged in there somewhere and it can be patched up fairly quickly," A.J. advised in a paternal tone before Marlee thanked him and drove away.

Looking at the clock in the CR-V dashboard, Marlee saw that it was nearing 4:00 pm. Not wanting to miss meeting with Aleece Jorgenson at the probation office, Marlee decided to wait on getting her tire fixed. Most tire repair shops would be open on the weekend, while the probation office would not. Not making contact with Aleece today would mean waiting through the weekend until Monday.

Marlee parked in front of the Federal Courthouse and walked inside. A left turn would land her in the Post Office, but a right turn required her to pass through security in order to reach the elevator and proceed to the probation office. There had been major changes in the security system since Marlee had worked in the building. During her years of employment in the Federal Courthouse in the mid to late 1990s, there were no security guards or screening devices. Anyone could walk in the front door and take the elevator directly to the probation office where the front door remained open during business hours. After the terrorist attacks on

September 11, 2001, security in all federal facilities was increased and the probation office in Elmwood was no exception.

Pulling her driver's license from her coat pocket, Marlee handed it to the portly security guard sitting at the front desk and told him she was going to the probation office. Any extra materials like purses and book bags would slow the screening process, so she wisely left all of those in the car. All she carried were her ID, keys, a pen, and a small notebook. She placed her keys, pen, and notebook on the conveyor belt for screening and walked through the magnetometer so the guard could be certain she was not carrying any weapons. After he nodded at her, Marlee smiled at the guard, grabbed her belongings, and took the elevator up to the third floor.

Installation of security in the old building had not included painting or decorating the walls in the hallway. They remained the same dingy blue as when Marlee worked there six years ago. She approached the end of the hallway and was met with a plexiglass window and an intercom system. Marlee saw Aleece inside the office and waved. Aleece automatically pushed the release button on the door and motioned her in.

The interior of the probation office had changed dramatically. In addition to the security window and intercom in the reception area, the walls were painted a deep burgundy and flowers in planters accented the corners of the room. Terry Redlin prints depicting scenes of fields, birds, and old buildings decorated the walls.

"Wow! You guys get fancier every time I come up here to visit," said Marlee taking in all the beautification that had replaced the drab yellow walls when she worked there.

Aleece smiled and nodded her head. "Lisa

Abernathy did a lot of this on her own time. She said she couldn't work in an icky office and asked if she could paint it. General Services Administration gave her permission and even provided her with the paint, but the chief probation officer said she had to do the decorating and painting on her own time. She took them up on it and this is what we have now." Aleece moved her hands in a flourish about the room, happy with the results. "So what brings you up to the federal probation office on a Friday afternoon?" Aleece asked with a gleam in her eye. She knew Marlee well enough to suspect she wanted something other than just chit-chat.

"Yeah, I wanted to follow up on something from the Shane Seaboy case," Marlee admitted, not even trying to pretend she came to see Aleece for any other reason. "Do you have any records from his time in prison that indicates he was in some kind of altercation with one or more inmates?" Marlee went on to detail her conversation with A.J. Simms from the FBI and the various individuals around Sisseton who suggested Shane may have been killed due to revenge.

Aleece spun around on her swivel chair toward her computer monitor and began typing in a rapid fashion. After several clicks on the keyboard, Aleece spun back around to face Marlee. "There's nothing here to indicate he was in danger or might be facing some sort of retaliation. He's been off supervision with us for a year now. Lisa was his probation officer, but like I said when we talked on Tuesday, she moved away and isn't with probation any more. I doubt she'd have any recollection of the details of Shane Seaboy's incarceration since she really didn't deal with people until they came out of prison."

Aleece then picked up the telephone and hit a speed dial button. After a moment's pause she identified herself and said, "Juan, I need some information." Two minutes later, Aleece hung up the phone and reported that Juan Hernandez with the Bureau of Prisons did not have a record of any altercations or problems with Shane Seaboy while he was in prison. According to Hernandez's records, Shane had been a model prisoner.

"Okay, well, it was worth a shot." Marlee was discouraged hearing Aleece's report. She was almost sure the files at the probation office would hold a clue as to the motive for Shane's death. Dejectedly, Marlee left the office with a promise to return for a visit another day. This had been a hell of a day, and Marlee was going nowhere else today but home.

Looking for an answer to a mystery can be a lot like looking for clouds in the fog. The solution is right before your eyes, yet you can't see it.

Chapter 17

Marlee arrived home to a big surprise: Diane and Bridget, who had been home unsupervised for a few hours, had decided it was time to celebrate the weekend. Loud '70s disco music hit Marlee as soon as she walked in the door. She no sooner set down her book bag brimming with books and papers than she was greeted by Bridget, who handed her a giant margarita. Marlee's mood instantly went from surly to upbeat.

"What's going on? Did you two have a party?" Marlee asked, gladly sipping the sweet elixir from the salt-rimmed glass.

Diane bounded toward the front door doing some sort of disco moves infused with polka steps. "No, we just thought we'd liven things up a bit around here tonight. We made margaritas and burritos are in the oven. Want some chips and salsa?"

"Do I!" exclaimed Marlee as she settled in at the table with drink in hand. Bridget and Diane had gone to the trouble of tidying up the house, washing the dishes, preparing supper, and making drinks. Her fatigue and general upset with the day went out the window as she enjoyed the pleasant ambiance set by her friend and cousin.

"This is awesome, you guys! What a great surprise." Marlee meant every word of it. When she left for work that morning she was getting tired of both of her guests and was ready for them to hit the road. There was an old saying about guests and fish starting to smell after three days. Tonight, Marlee didn't care if Diane and Bridget moved in permanently as long as they took care of the housework and cooking.

"Oh, there's more to the surprise!" Diane shouted, pausing for effect. "The rest of the supper club members are coming over too and they'll be here shortly. They're bringing dessert."

"Oh. My. God. I could just cry! There's going to be dessert too?" Marlee asked with a level of enthusiasm suggesting she rarely ate dessert.

"Yep. We're going to play board games after we eat. That should get everyone relaxed," Bridget said with a giant smile. Marlee was already feeling less tension than she had in days. She relayed the information she gained on the Seaboy investigation that day to Bridget and Diane.

The three sat at the dining room table drinking margaritas and eating chips with salsa until the doorbell rang. Kathleen Zens stood at the door holding a pre-packaged container of cupcakes fresh from the local grocery store. Making their way up the sidewalk behind her were Gwen Gerken and Shelly McFarland. Gwen was carrying a tray of decorated Christmas cookies. She smiled as she handed them to Diane and said, "We had a little party in my department today and these cookies were left over so I grabbed them."

"Good thinking, Gwen!" Marlee shouted. She was also of the opinion, "Why bake when someone else will and let you have their extras?"

The newcomers settled in around the dining room table, margaritas in hand. A quick update on how everyone was doing was trumped by Marlee and Bridget telling what they discovered while investigating Shane Seaboy's death. The McCabe cousins tag-teamed the account of what they discovered over the past week.

"I know what we should do!" Bridget shouted, jumping to her feet and nearly upsetting Shelly's margarita. "Let's put together one of those crime boards like they did in *The Naked City*. Except the main character, played by Barry Fitzgerald, wrote the murder facts on a chalkboard. I think we could update that by putting up pictures of everyone involved and then draw lines or connected strings to everyone that had some type of association!"

Marlee rolled her eyes. "Here we go again with the film references," she thought as she grabbed for more chips.

"Do you have pictures of everyone?" asked the ever-practical Kathleen.

"Well, no. I don't think we have any pictures, but we could do drawings," Bridget said, her voice hopeful that the idea would catch on with the others.

"Is anyone here an artist?" Kathleen inquired. The group looked around the table and everyone shook their head from side to side.

Marlee thought on the matter for a moment. "You know, Bridget, you might be on to something. We could use names instead of pictures. Maybe a visual representation of the players in this crime would help us see something we hadn't thought of before."

Bridget beamed. Although she would have preferred pictures, the word diagram was a satisfactory conciliation.

Marlee rummaged around and found a large poster board she had left over from some project on campus. She located a handful of markers and, moving the food and drinks out of the center of the table, splayed the materials out before them. Everyone grabbed a marker and took the cap off. Shelly began to sniff the tip of her purple marker. When she noticed the other four women looking at her, she swiftly put the cap back on with a sheepish grin. "I just wanted to see if it smelled like grape."

"OK, we don't have time to huff the markers. Let's get down to business," Marlee said. Black marker in hand, she wrote SHANE SEABOY in the middle of the poster board. Then the five academics all looked at each other.

"Should we draw out a diagram first on notebook paper," asked Gwen.

"I think we should use different colors to show different relationships between people. You know, like red for romantic, blue for blood relative, green for friend, yada yada yada," said Diane.

"I'm going to get another margarita before we make any big decisions," said Kathleen, walking toward the kitchen. The others looked at their nearly empty glasses and all slid back their chairs to get refills.

After settling back in with full drinks, the five academics again approached the task of preparing the crime chart, as Bridget had named it. Reaching for a chip, Kathleen's sweater sleeve brushed against Shelly's full glass, sloshing the light green alcohol on the tablecloth and the crime chart.

"Don't worry!" Kathleen yelled. She was famous for

spills and many of her items of clothing featured bits of food and drink by the end of the day. She ran to the kitchen, grabbed two hand towels and returned to mop up the excess liquid from the table and poster board. "This happens to me all the time," she said as she glanced at Bridget.

After the cleanup, the group again settled in to concentrate on the crime chart. "Maybe we should all sketch out our own chart first and compare them before we make a master copy," said Marlee.

"But I don't even know who all the people are that are involved. My sketch would have about three people on it and that's not much help," said Gwen, getting frustrated with what initially seemed like such an easy task.

Ding! The oven timer signaled that the burritos were done and the group hurriedly cleared the table and replaced the chart making supplies with plates and utensils. Bridget placed the enormous pan of burritos in the center of the table and announced that it was time to eat. Pippa, Marlee's Persian cat, peeked into the dining room to see what the fuss was all about. She didn't like people, but she didn't like being excluded either. Mostly Pippa liked to be in the middle of the action when guests were over, but showed her disapproval of them by snarling and hissing when they approached her personal space.

After savoring the burritos, Bridget and Marlee cleared the dirty dishes and pushed the pan of remaining burritos to the side of the table to cool while Kathleen put the crime chart back on the table. The group looked at it and no one spoke. Finally, Shelly said, "Do you think we should take a break from the chart for a few minutes? I mean, maybe if we took a little time for our food to digest, our brains might be more into it."

"Yeah!" Marlee and Diane shouted in unison.

"Let's go into the living room and play Cranium for a bit while we enjoy some of the cookies and cupcakes you guys brought," suggested Diane. The group adjourned to the living room and set up the Cranium game. For the next two hours, the five women laughed, drank, and enjoyed cookies and cupcakes as they created objects from clay, guessed at the identity of drawn pictures, spelled words, and demonstrated their knowledge of facts. After the final game, they begrudgingly went back to the table to work on the crime chart. Pippa had been on the table, as was evidenced by small paw prints in red burrito sauce moving from the bottom to the top of the crime chart, growing lighter in color as more of the crimson sauce was deposited on the poster board.

"Well, crap!" said Marlee. Not only was the crime chart damaged, but Pippa had strolled through the leftover burritos. By this time, everyone had lost their enthusiasm for the crime chart and Gwen, Shelly, and Kathleen left for home. Marlee looked in the baking dish at the burritos. She had planned on warming up the leftovers that weekend. Had it been only her there, she would have still eaten them, but didn't think Diane and Bridget would go for this level of unhygienic behavior.

"You know, I think Pippa just walked along this one side of the burritos," Diane said. "I think the rest are okay."

Marlee raised her eyebrows at Bridget, wondering how she would feel about eating food a cat walked through. "Sounds fine to me," she said with an air of nonchalance suggesting she had eaten food before that had been walked through by pets.

The three picked up the remaining glasses and dessert dishes. By this time, they were too tired, full, and tipsy to delve into theories about who killed Shane

Seaboy and why. The crime chart, smudged with burrito sauced paw prints and wrinkled with the spilled margarita that had now dried, was propped against the wall as they all retired to their respective sleep spots.

My family disowned me. My friends used me. My tribe shunned me. Consistency isn't all it's cracked up to be.

Chapter 18

It was a real treat to sleep in on Saturday morning and Marlee took full advantage of it. For the first time since her guests arrived, she woke to the smell of brewing coffee. Tumbling out of bed, she grabbed her glasses from the nightstand and made her way toward the coffee. Diane and Bridget were already sitting at the dining room table enjoying mugs of coffee and looking over the crime chart they started the night before. At this point, they only had the victim's name written in the center of the poster board, unless the food and drink stains were counted.

Diane and Bridget both looked up as Marlee passed through the dining room. "Guess we didn't make quite as much progress on this as I thought we did," said Bridget, rubbing her temples. She looked rough. Her hair, once pulled back in a loose ponytail now looked as if someone had run a balloon all over her hair, making it staticky.

"What's the matter, Bridget?" asked Marlee,

attempting not to smile but really not succeeding. "Did you forget to eat a stick of butter last night before you drank all those margaritas?"

"Yeah. You were out of butter. Remind me to pick some up at the store today. Not that I'm going to be doing any more drinking while I'm here," Bridget said with a grim look on her face. "Why do I feel so terrible and you two look fine?" She asked as she nodded toward Marlee and Diane.

"I only drank two margaritas. I think you have five or six," said Diane with a giggle.

"I only had two. You were slugging 'em down pretty hard last night, Bridg," Marlee said. She didn't like enjoying her cousin's agony, but was amused that Miss Perfect was suffering from a hangover when neither she nor Diane had that problem.

"Don't know what got into me," Bridget mumbled, her head in both of her hands.

"I think you were celebrating your visiting professorship appointment at Marymount, so that's completely understandable," said Diane.

Bridget mumbled something unintelligible and left for the bathroom. A good deal of rummaging around could be heard before she emerged and announced, "I just took some Motrin. I'm going back to bed."

Marlee and Diane smiled and nodded. After the door to the guest room was closed, they broke out into a fit of laughter which they tried to stifle so Bridget would not hear. "It's about time she suffered the way we did after that night of drinking when she first got here," said Diane.

Marlee nodded. She was in complete agreement. "So what have you got going on today?" she asked. She needed to get her tire fixed and hoped to meet with Donnie, Jasper, and Dom for a bit to touch base on the

Seaboy case.

"If Bridget feels better, we're going to a classic movie double-feature at the old theater downtown. It doesn't start until 2:00 this afternoon, so hopefully she feels better by then. Until that time, I'm going to laze around here and maybe write up some feedback on my students' speeches," said Diane.

After leaving the house, Marlee drove to campus to see if she could locate any of her three trusted criminal justice students. She hit gold when she went to the lower level of the Student Union. Donnie Stacks was working at the information desk and looked bored beyond words.

"Hey, Donnie!" Marlee called out as she approached a comatose looking Donnie. "Are you awake?"

"Hi, Dr. M. I'm barely awake. My neighbors were having a party last night and it didn't quiet down until after 3:00 am. And I had to be here to work at 7:00. What brings you here on a Saturday morning?" Donnie ran a hand through her short, red curls, as if to stimulate her foggy brain.

"I was wondering if you, Dom, and Jasper would be able to meet sometime today to talk about the Seaboy case."

"I sure can. I'll call the guys to see if they can make it. I know they're both in town this weekend, but I'm not sure of their work schedules. I could call you on your cell later to tell you," Donnie said, waking up.

"Uh, I don't have my cell on me. I left it at home. Can you just call my home number and leave a message?" Marlee knew she was behind the times technologically, especially when compared to her students. They all had cell phones and had them on their persons at all times. Marlee rather enjoyed not being able to be reached by anyone at any time. She'd spent enough time on call in her previous jobs that she was burned out from the constant need for someone to reach her immediately.

Donnie looked at her as though she were a space alien and then smiled. "Okay. I can do that." Marlee wasn't sure if the smile was one of amusement or pity, but she really didn't care. Since she hadn't eaten breakfast and it was nearly lunch time, Marlee decided to grab something quick at the cafeteria rather than return home. Going through the line, she realized it had been a few days since she'd eaten any vegetables. The artichoke hearts on her pizza the other night really didn't count and she was still pondering the possibility that she was allergic to them. Passing by the fried food, the pasta dishes, and a plethora of desserts, Marlee went to the soup stand and helped herself to a bowl of vegetable beef soup. "I hope my body doesn't go into shock," she thought as she settled down into a table in the corner.

The Student Union was not busy at this time. Students were hit and miss in the cafeteria on weekends. Some left town for the weekend and those who lived off campus either prepared meals at their homes or went elsewhere to eat. Professors, administration, and most of the staff were largely gone from the campus on weekends. Professors occasionally came in to do some grading or needed to meet with prospective students and their parents, but even then, they did not frequent the cafeteria in the Student Union that much. Marlee knew her chances of seeing anyone she could talk to or question about the Seaboy murder were slim and she was right. Finishing her bowl of soup and discarding the trash, she left campus, dejected that no one was there to interrogate.

Marlee left campus and located a small gas station called Chucky's that also fixed tires. She preferred to give her business to small local places with good reputations, rather than the large, corporate entities that seemed to be taking over the town of Elmwood. A few of Marlee's friends and colleagues had mentioned Chucky's as a place that did minor repairs quickly and cheaply. The garage portion of Chucky's did not have a waiting room, just two chairs off to the side of the vehicle where the work was being performed. She waited while the mechanic looked the tire over, hoping it could be fixed and she would not need to purchase a new one. Christmas was coming up and she didn't want a new tire cutting into her gift budget.

The mechanic, whose embroidered name on his striped overalls identified him as Ralph, looked at the tire he removed from the back of her CR-V and then walked around the vehicle to look at the other tires. When Marlee spotted him doing this she said, "Wait, I'm not looking to get all new tires. I just need this one fixed."

Ralph ignored her and continued to poke and prod around the tires, both those still on the vehicle and the one that was flat. "You might have a bigger problem here than just a flat tire, ma'am." Marlee hated when people called her ma'am. She was in her late 30s, not her 70s, which was the age acceptable for addressing someone as ma'am.

"What do you mean?" Marlee braced herself for a high-pressure sale about her tires being worn and needing to be replaced before winter hit full force.

"The flat wasn't because of a nail or a piece of glass. It was stabbed with a knife. Somebody intentionally gave you a flat tire," Ralph said, looking at her with concern.

"What? Why would somebody cut my tire?" Marlee shouted.

"Well, ma'am, that I don't know, but you have more problems than that. The front tire on the passenger side has the lug nuts loosened. They could've come off at any time and you'd a lost a wheel," Ralph said.

"Well, maybe they just loosened up on their own. You know, wear and tear from driving?" Marlee asked.

"Nope. Not like this. And the slash in the tire isn't from wear and tear either. Both were intentional. I'd bet a hundred bucks on it," Ralph said with a confidence that made his declaration all too believable.

"What?" Marlee repeated, trying to get her mind around the information Ralph just provided. "The tire was flat when I came out of the FBI office yesterday. Who would have the guts to slash my tire outside the FBI office? And then loosen the lug nuts? Wouldn't they be afraid of getting caught?"

"This may have happened yesterday or it may have been done a few days ago and the tire just went flat yesterday when the knife cut wore all the way through. Sometimes we see cars where the tires were vandalized days earlier but the flat doesn't occur until later on. It's hard to slash a tire with a regular knife, so sometimes the cut is only partial and has to work through with continued driving. Same with loosened lug nuts. The wheel might fall off the same day or it might take some driving over a few days to completely loosen it. Depends on how much they loosened it," said Ralph.

By the time Marlee purchased a new tire and Ralph installed it and tightened all the lug nuts, it was after 2:00. Marlee returned home and found Bridget and Diane gone, presumably at the classic movies showing downtown. Feeling confused, upset, and somewhat lonely without her cousin and her friend there to talk to, Marlee collapsed on the couch. She had a hard time believing someone wanted to hurt her, but slashing one tire and ensuring another would come loose, probably while she was driving, were disturbing. "Why would someone want to hurt me?" she thought to herself. "And who?"

A red, blinking light caught Marlee's attention and pulled her out of state of worry and self-pity. Someone had left a message on her answering machine and she hoped it was Donnie confirming a meeting for them later that day. Listening to the message, Marlee was excited to learn that was exactly who had called. Calling Donnie back, they decided everyone would meet at Marlee's home around 4:30 that afternoon. In the meantime, Marlee had two hours to kill and decided to work on the crime chart started the previous evening.

Placing the chart back on the table, Marlee thought about the suggestions bandied about last night about how to best devise the chart. She eventually concluded it really didn't matter what order people were listed because it was their relationship to Shane Seaboy and each other that was the most important. She wrote the names of Tony Red Day, Jr., Geneva Sanders, Judy and Shep Sanders, Duane Seaboy, Ivan Flute, Diego, and Collin Kolb. After another moment of consideration she added Ashton Dumarce, Collin's roommate from Sisseton, realizing she had not yet spoken with him. The names of Shane Seaboy's codefendants in the eagle feather case were added as well: Chris Long Hollow and Warren Keoke, both of Sisseton, and Ryan Campbell from Minneapolis. Verla Renville, ex-girlfriend of both Tony Red Day and Shane Seaboy was added to the list, as was Tony's alleged current girlfriend, Collette Many Lightnings. At this point, Marlee realized she had yet to speak with Collette to see if she had any information on the matter. It was doubtful that she would, but Marlee knew any little tidbit might be enough to point her in the right direction. Finally, Marlee wrote "Unknown" to account for the possibility that someone else was responsible for Shane's death.

Even though some of the people identified on the crime chart were not serious contenders for the label of murderer, Marlee still listed them in order to more clearly see the relationships between the people whose names were mentioned in connection with the investigation or that she had spoken with in the past few days. Before she drew any lines, she wanted to wait for Dom, Jasper, and Donnie to arrive so they could discuss the case. After talking over the matter, some people on the chart might increase or decrease in their level of suspicion.

Marlee dwelled on the chart for what seemed like half an hour, but then the doorbell rang and she realized more time had passed than she originally thought. Donnie, Dom, and Jasper all stood at the front door looking slightly uncomfortable. Even though they had been to her home before and that they held a special status as members of the Criminal Justice Club, they still felt a bit uneasy at first about going to a professor's home. She welcomed them in and motioned for them to throw their coats on the coach and to sit down at the table.

"Thanks for coming over guys. I wanted to discuss this chart and everything we know about the case but was afraid someone might overhear if we met at the Chit Chat," Marlee said. "I don't have a wide array of food and beverages to offer you, but how about hot chocolate and some cookies?" She felt like she moved into mom or grandma role whenever the students came over. At least she resisted the urge to call them kids to their face.

The three students ate the cookies with gusto. Marlee was thankful there were some left over from a previous night's pig out with Bridget, Diane, and the rest of the supper club. "These cookies are delicious!" Jasper exclaimed as he grabbed for a third one.

"Here's a little something I've discovered about food in my thirty-eight years on this planet. Food always tastes better if someone else made it or bought it." The three students nodded in unison but Marlee wasn't sure if it was because they agreed with her hypothesis or if they would nod along at anything said as long as the cookies were in good supply.

After everyone was full of cookies and hot chocolate, the conversation turned toward the Shane Seaboy murder. Marlee showed them the crime chart and updated them on the information she discovered on the trip to Sisseton, from the local FBI agent, and Bettina Crawford. Unfortunately, none of them had anything to add in the way of information. At the end of their discussion of Shane Seaboy, Marlee mentioned the slashed tire and loose lug nuts on her vehicle.

Donnie gasped and then covered her mouth. "Oh my god, Dr. M. You could've died!"

"Is this something students would do as a prank? Or if they were mad over a grade?" Although Marlee was pretty sure she knew the answer to the question, she asked it anyway.

"No way!" Jasper said, wiping cookie crumbs off his mouth with the back of his hand and shaking them to the floor. "Nobody I know would even consider doing that to a professor, or anyone else."

"Even if it was a professor they hated," chimed Dom. "Uh, not that I'm saying people hate you."

"Okay, I didn't think this fell into the acceptable prank category, but wanted to get your take on it since you'd have a much better idea of what goes on with the students than I ever would," Marlee said. She was relieved and scared at the same time. On one hand, she was glad this did not involve a disgruntled student. On the other hand, someone seriously wanted her injured or killed. Had the lug nuts come loose while driving on the highway, the vehicle may have crashed, killing her and anyone else who was riding with her. A shiver worked its way up her spine, settling at the base of her neck until the hairs located there stood straight up.

Donnie, who was the most sensitive of the students, noticed Marlee's discomfort and sought to calm her. "Did you call the police?" she asked.

"Wow, I never even thought about it. I guess I'm still trying to figure it out. Ralph at the gas station said it could have happened yesterday while I was at the FBI office or several days earlier. I'm still trying to piece together who would do this." Marlee said.

"Someone who either wants to hurt you, kill you, or scare you," said Dom. "Do you think it's associated with the Seaboy murder or something else?"

"Well, I really don't think I have any enemies that would do something like this. It's not as if this type of thing happens to me all the time," Marlee snapped. She bit her lip, realizing she was becoming a bit more flippant with her students than she intended. She preferred to maintain a relaxed, yet professional demeanor with those she taught, even outside the classroom. Just because her comments to her friends were usually laced with acid didn't mean she wanted to talk that way to her students.

Just as she was thinking of a way to smooth over her sarcastic remarks and move on to a new line of discussion, the front door flew open and Bridget jumped inside with a bottle of wine in each hand. "It's party time, bitches!" she yelled, not noticing the three slack jawed students sitting at the dining room table.

Secrets, like old bones, can be dug up. But not everyone wants the bones and secrets to see the light of day. In fact, some will kill to ensure the buried remain so.

Chapter 19

"Oh my god!" Bridget yelled as she placed the wine on the coffee table and covered her mouth with both hands. She was a professor and was even more adamant about maintaining professionalism between herself and students than Marlee. "Uh, I'm sorry. I didn't know you had company."

"That's okay," Marlee said, a bit embarrassed but really more entertained by her cousin's behavior. She introduced Bridget to Jasper and Dom and nodded toward Donnie whom she met at lunch the previous day. "Where's Diane? I thought she was with you?"

"We drove separately to the movies and she said she was coming right over when we left the theater." Bridget still could not make eye contact with Marlee's students.

Just then the door burst open again. This time it was Diane and she carried a liter of rum and a whole pineapple that she carried by the stem. "It's party time, mon!" she exclaimed in her best Jamaican accent.

"Students are here," Marlee interrupted before Diane could incriminate them further in the eyes of those they taught. She introduced Diane to the students and they nodded at her, eyes wide and mouths still agape.

"Uh, yeah. I had you for Speech last year," Dom said nodding toward Diane.

"I did too," said Jasper.

"I'm in your class this semester," said Donnie.

"Uh, yes. I remember you all," Diane said, dropping the pineapple to the floor and setting the bottle of rum around the corner in case the students hadn't already seen it. Diane also liked to maintain a professional demeanor with her students and was not happy about what just occurred.

"Um, I feel like maybe it's time for us to go," Donnie said perceptively. She pushed her chair back and stood up so quickly she nearly tipped the chair over backwards. Dom and Jasper were right behind her.

"Yeah, thanks for everything, Dr. M. I have to go too," said Jasper, basically running for the door. The three students grabbed their coats and were putting them on as they went out the door. Marlee shuddered at what they must think of their two professors and Bridget. She watched them walk down sidewalk toward a red car. The students stopped before getting inside and all three broke out into laughter, grabbing their stomachs as they doubled over.

The three academics rehashed the events involving the students for the next hour as they made punch from the rum and pineapple Diane provided. They oscillated between horror and humor, reliving the expressions on the faces of Dom, Jasper, and Donnie. "I'm so sorry, Marlee. I never would have said 'party time, bitches' if I knew your students were here. I don't even know why I said it to begin with. I don't talk like that." Bridget said. "It just reminded me of the movie *Wedding Crashers* when Vince Vaughn's character was gearing up for some fun."

"You know what? It's okay," said Marlee. "It doesn't hurt for students to see professors as people too. Plus, we didn't do anything really wrong or unethical."

"Yeah," said Diane. "It's not like we invited them to stay and drink with us. Although that would really liven things up, I bet. I can't believe I did a Jamaican accent." Diane smacked her head and all three of the women laughed off the whole incident.

"I thought you were suffering from a killer hangover," Marlee said to Bridget. "You must be feeling much better if you're drinking rum."

"Caffeine, Tylenol, and greasy junk food. It helps every time," Bridget said.

"Hey, guess what? I worked on the crime chart today!" Marlee exclaimed. "Before the students came over I wrote down as many people as I could think of who are connected to the case. Either they're suspects, knew Shane Seaboy, or provided us with information. I didn't include any of the law enforcement officers on here, just people who had a connection to Shane." Diane and Bridget looked over the crime chart and nodded in approval. Although it may not have been formatted in the way each of them would have chosen, at least it was done.

"Oh, and guess what else I found out today?" Marlee filled Bridget and Diane in on her slashed tire and loosened lug nuts, much to their surprise.

"So your car could've been vandalized here in town or when we were in Sisseton on Thursday," Bridget stated, wrapping her mind around the possibility that not just Marlee, but she, could have been severely injured or killed if a tire had blown out or jiggled loose while they were driving seventy-five miles per hour on the way home.

"Yep. I talked to the Criminal Justice Club students about it and they said it was definitely not a prank a student would pull, even if they were upset with me about their grades," Marlee reported.

"No, I definitely wouldn't think so," said Diane. "I can't imagine any of our students being that angry with any of us to do that. I don't think they would even do it to some of the awful professors on campus."

"Me neither," Bridget chimed in.

"So who do you think did it?" asked Diane.

"I've been thinking about it and the only people I can think of are those who have a connection to Shane Seaboy. It could've been Tony Red Day, Jr. or Duane Seaboy. Both saw what I was driving and it wouldn't have been hard to track my vehicle around the Sisseton area. Or it could be someone else altogether. Someone we haven't identified or even thought of," Marlee reported.

"Maybe the real killer," Bridget mused. Marlee was relieved when there was no movie reference to follow her cousin's comment.

"So why would they slash one of your tires and loosen the lug nuts on another one? What were they hoping to gain from all this?" Diane asked.

"It could have been to either hurt or kill me. But it might have been just to scare me enough that I would butt out and quit asking questions about Shane. If I had to choose a motive at this point, I think it was just to scare me. Bridget and I have been asking a lot of questions, not just about Shane Seaboy's death, but also his conviction in the eagle feather case, his codefendants, and other people involved in the sale of Indian artifacts.

There may be several people who don't want this information to come to light," Marlee stated.

"Plus, didn't you say the FBI is still trying to track down this Diego person who's apparently the ring leader in the whole artifact sales operation that got away?" inquired Diane.

"Yeah. Good point. Diego and his cronies have a definite need for the Indian artifact sales not to be discussed or further investigated," said Marlee. "Plus, A.J. from the FBI told me that people in the area know who Diego is and are afraid of him to the point that they won't reveal his identity or confirm any involvement in the eagle feather case Shane and some others were convicted of a few years ago."

"And Diego lives in the Cities?" Bridget asked.

"A.J. said the FBI office in St. Paul is looking out for him," Marlee said and then paused. "But what if that really isn't him? What if the guy in the Cities is a decoy or the FBI agents are mistaken? It seems to me that in order for so many people to be this fearful of him, he would be living closer to them. You know, living close enough to Sisseton that he would hear right away if anyone ratted him out and close enough to make good on his threats."

"That actually makes a lot of sense," Diane said. "If he's in Sisseton, he has his finger on the pulse of the reservation and the whole community. He would know right away who talked to the FBI or the sheriff."

"I think tomorrow might be a good day to run out to the rez again and do some follow up visits," said Marlee. "Who's going with me?"

"Me!" shouted Bridget, always ready for any new adventure.

"I can't. I have more grading to do and need to prep for student finals," said Diane, appearing relieved to get out of going on the investigative expedition.

"Um, actually we need you to go with us," said Marlee. "Bring your grading along. You can work on it in the car."

"Why do you need me if Bridget is going?" Diane whined.

"Because Bridget and I will go into the homes to ask questions, and I need you to stay in the car and make sure no one does any further vandalism to it," Marlee said.

"Well, okay," Bridget agreed with a great deal of reluctance. She was not at all enthused about the trip the following day, but could not think of an excuse fast enough to get out of it. "Will it be safe?"

"Probably," said Marlee, hoping she meant it. "You can keep the doors locked so no one can get in."

"All three of us have Ph.D.s, so we should be able to think our way out of any problems that might present themselves," said Bridget, sounding much more confident than Marlee felt. Their advanced degrees in criminology, speech, and film studies would not be of much help if someone decided to silence them once and for all.

HOLIDAY HOMICIDE

Before I went to prison, I made certain promises. We all did. I intended to stay true to my word. Then the rules of the game changed.

Chapter 20

Sunday morning, normally a time to take it easy and laze around the house before starting on class prep, took on a very different form for Marlee. She woke early, without the aid of an alarm clock, and was antsy to get on the road to Sisseton. Not only were there new people to talk to, but there were individuals Marlee wanted to re-interview. The only problem was getting people to talk.

It was nearing 8:00 am by the time Diane, Bridget, and Marlee left the house. They had travel mugs of coffee in hand and went through a McDonald's drive-thru to get breakfast. The steering wheel in the CR-V was adjusted low enough that Marlee could use her left knee to drive as she ate her egg McMuffin with one hand and held her travel mug with the other. Finally setting the mug in a cup holder, she returned her right hand to the steering wheel, much to the relief of Diane and Bridget.

The day was overcast and gloomy, like so many days

in November and December in northern South Dakota. The gray of the day, however, did not stop the excited chatter in the car as they made their way toward the Lake Traverse Reservation. "Where are we going first?" Diane asked, not wasting any time on her grading and class prep for the following week. She had her pen and notebook out and they were only ten miles out of town.

"We should probably track down Ivan Flute again to get his take on some of the information we found out since we met with him on Thursday. I don't know if he'll be at the treatment center since this is Sunday, but it's worth a try. If he's not there, then we can swing by his house," Marlee said. Bridget nodded in agreement and Diane was looking off into the distance, her question already forgotten as she pondered her last week of teaching before finals week.

Luck was on their side, as Ivan Flute was at Prairie Winds for prayer services that morning. He only had a few minutes before the ceremony was set to begin, so Marlee and Bridget chatted with him in the empty break room near the front door. Diane guarded their locked vehicle from further damage.

"What do you know about Chris Long Hollow, Warren Keoke, and Ryan Campbell?" Marlee asked Ivan. "They were Shane's codefendants in the eagle feather case."

"I don't know Ryan Campbell, but Chris and Warren are from here. The last I knew, Chris was still in prison. Last month his mom told me he served his sentence on the eagle feather case and was released. Before he made his way back home he got into some more trouble and was sent back to prison. I think he was arrested for drugs."

"How about Warren?" Bridget asked.

"Warren is a bad guy. A really bad guy. He's not

somebody you want to mess with. He's been back here for a while now, but I'm not telling you how to find him because he can be dangerous," said Ivan, worry crossing his face. "He got out a few weeks after Shane was released."

"Do you think Warren could've killed Shane Seaboy?" Bridget inquired.

"Possible, but I doubt it. Shane was killed by being hit in the back of the head. That doesn't sound like Warren's work. He would attack someone straight on rather than a sneak attack from the back," Ivan said.

"According to A.J. Simms from the FBI office, the ringleader of the eagle feather operation was never caught. They call him Diego but don't know for sure who he is. Any ideas on the identity of Diego?" Marlee asked. "He lives in the Cities somewhere but has connections over here."

Ivan looked Marlee squarely in the eye and said with a voice more stern than she had ever heard from him, "You don't want to get messed up in this. Just go home before you get into something you can't get out of. This isn't a game." Ivan abruptly left them standing in the break room as he walked away without saying another word. This time Ivan did not offer any hugs as they left.

Back in the CR-V, Marlee and Bridget updated Diane on Ivan's strange behavior. "He acted like he was just concerned for us, but I felt like there was something else going on," Bridget said.

"Me too," said Marlee. "Maybe he knows who Diego is. Or maybe he or his family has been threatened by Diego. Ivan was his usual friendly, helpful self until we brought up Diego and asked about his identity. Then Ivan shut down the whole conversation and walked away. That's not like him."

"So are we going home now?" Diane asked, hopeful

that if they returned to Elmwood now she would have plenty of time to finish preparing for the upcoming week's classes.

"No way. If anything, this just makes me want to dig in deeper," said Marlee. Bridget nodded her agreement.

"Diane, did you see anything suspicious out here when we were inside the treatment center?" asked Bridget. The McCabe women were only inside Prairie Winds for less than fifteen minutes, but that was ample time for someone to vandalize their vehicle.

"No, I just saw people going in and coming out. Nothing out of the ordinary. Nobody even approached the vehicle. At least, not that I noticed. I was deep into my class prep, but I'm sure I would notice if someone tried to take off one of the tires or something," Diane said.

Marlee and Bridget both sighed. Diane was definitely not cut out for detective work. She was laser focused on whatever she was doing at that moment. If Diane had her mind on her upcoming classes, then she might not initially notice if two total strangers got in the car and drove away with her.

"Hey, I forgot to tell you about my phone conversation with Ivan," Bridget said. "You asked me to find out if Duane and Shane Seaboy had the same father. Ivan believed they did. He didn't have any explanation why some relatives would take Duane into their home but not Shane, other than it may have been a space issue. You know, they only had room for one extra kid in their home when Duane and Shane were removed by Social Services."

Marlee nodded, letting the information sink into her brain. "Let's go to the convenience store. "We can take a restroom break, get more coffee, and ask around about Warren Keoke and where he lives."

"Who's Warren Keoke? I remember the name but I can't remember who he is or what he did," Diane said.

"He was a codefendant of Shane Seaboy's in the eagle feather case. One thing Ivan told us before he clammed up was that Warren was really dangerous," said Marlee. Diane's face revealed both worry and fear. Marlee and Bridget were fearful as well, but curiosity was a more powerful motivator.

After stocking up on coffee and snacks, the three academics approached the counter of the small convenience store located in the town of Sisseton. Marlee remembered stopping at the C-Stop when she traveled to the area for her work as a probation officer. At that time, one restroom was located outside the building and it required a key, attached to a hubcap so no one would absent-mindedly walk off with it, which had to be obtained from the counter attendant. The offerings inside had been slim: black coffee, candy, chips, gum, beef jerky, pop, and beer. The old structure remained but had been updated inside since Marlee's last visit. The C-Stop now accommodated separate restrooms for men and women inside, a variety of hot and cold foods that were made fresh on the premises, and a cappuccino machine.

A Native American woman in her thirties stood behind the counter and looked at them warily when Marlee asked about Warren Keoke. "Why do you wanna know?" She asked as she smoothed the unbraided ends of her long, dark hair.

"Well, we're from out of town and I'm a film expert..." Bridget let that information hang in the air hoping the clerk would take the bait. After what seemed like a day long wait, she finally made the leap that Bridget hoped for.

"Oh, you're the movie people," the clerk said, now

BRENDA DONELAN

smiling. "I heard you were around. Warren lives on the road toward Agency Village, about two miles from the turnoff. Take the gravel road to your left and follow it till you see a grove of trees. About half a mile. His dad has a trailer back there. That's where he stays."

Marlee cringed at Bridget's use of the film ploy again, but was relieved that it had elicited the information they wanted. Attempting to assess the threat level before they approached Warren's trailer house, Marlee said, "We hear Warren's a pretty tough character. Is that right?"

The clerk nodded, her face transformed from smiling to stoic. "He's really violent. He beat up my cousin so bad that he's still in the hospital in a coma. Everybody knows he did it, but the cops can't pin it on him, so he goes free." She finished ringing up each of the women's purchases and began bagging them

"We've been hearing the name Diego. Can you tell us about him?" Marlee asked.

The clerk looked nervously from one side to the other, surveying the C-Stop for customers who might overhear her. "I don't know anything about him," she said placing the last of the snacks into a plastic sack and turning her back toward them.

Diane, Bridget, and Marlee did not try to push their luck with the clerk. It was clear, just as it had been with Ivan Flute, that no further information would be forthcoming. They made their way back to the CR-V and got in. "We know one thing for sure: Diego is very well known around here and no one wants to get on his bad side," said Marlee, crunching on a Cool Ranch Dorito as she maneuvered the vehicle toward the street.

Diane was more than a little worried at this point. "I think we should go home. This is getting scary."

"Yeah, it is a little bit scary, but I want to talk to

218

Warren Keoke first before we head back. And I'd like to see if Tony Red Day, Jr. is willing to talk to us more today," Marlee said, hoping Diane didn't throw a hissy fit and insist they leave immediately, making the whole trip fruitless.

"Alright. Just those two stops," Diane said, "but then let's get out of here."

Marlee nodded her assent, even though she knew if another lead popped up she would follow it rather than return home early.

The trio followed the directions the C-Stop clerk provided them and were parked outside the trailer where Warren Keoke reportedly lived. It was an older structure with duct tape covering cracks in the windows. Pieces of tin skirted the bottom of the trailer, although it had come loose in the corner and blew back and forth in the wind. Wooden stairs with an accompanying wheel chair ramp abutted the front door. An apathetic dog with matted fur and a milky eye lay on the far side of the ramp, out of the biting wind.

Marlee did a quick assessment of the property. They were in a semi-remote location, off the road and out of sight from passing vehicles. No other trailers or houses were in sight. If they were to need assistance, no one would be able to see or hear them. This was not the first time Marlee encountered a situation like this. When she was a probation officer she frequently had to visit people on her caseload who lived in similarly isolated areas.

"The dog could be a problem. It's not chained up," Marlee said as she motioned for Bridget to open the glove compartment. She shuffled the vehicle care manual aside and located what she was looking for: a small canister of pepper spray. She had never used it as a probation officer, but her fellow officers at the time assured her it would subdue an attacking dog. Or an attacking person.

"Are you kidding?" Bridget asked in a belittling tone. Preparing to use pepper spray on the dog seemed akin to using a rifle to subdue a naughty four year old. "I don't think that old dog could even get to its feet if it had to. It looks like its days are numbered."

"It looks nearly dead, but it could be an act. I've been chased by seemingly docile and elderly dogs before. One of my former coworkers at probation was chased by a dog and had to climb on top of his car and sit there until the people came home and called the dog off. He didn't have any pepper spray. Man, he was mad when that happened," Marlee recalled with a chuckle. It was amusing only because it had not happened to her.

Handing the canister to Bridget, Marlee said, "You're in charge of pepper spray. I'm gonna do the questioning and you keep an eye on that dog. If he attacks, just pull this lever here and depress this button. That will release the spray into his eyes and mouth and render him incapable of attacking. It affects the nervous system so the eyes clamp shut and it's almost impossible to breathe. People and dogs will usually drop to the ground within a minute or so, which would give us time to get away."

"What should I do?" Diane asked, not at all happy about the predicament they were in.

"You come up front and get in the passenger seat. If somebody suspicious approaches the trailer while we're inside, blast the horn. Keep the doors unlocked in case we need to make a speedy exit," Marlee said. "Don't worry. It'll all be okay."

"What if Warren or somebody else in the house attacks us?" Bridget said.

"Then use the pepper spray in the same fashion. Aim it toward their face," Marlee said. With the brief tutorial over, she exited the CR-V, and approached the front door via the wheel chair ramp. Bridget was on her heels, looking from side to side in an effort to spot any potential threats before they were upon the McCabe cousins. They briskly walked past the dog, not giving it any acknowledgement. Marlee's past experience with dogs suggested that showing no fear toward them was the best course of action.

Standing at the top of the wheelchair ramp on the step, Marlee pounded on the door to the trailer. She could hear a children's television program inside, so she knew someone was home. After another round of loud knocking, the door finally inched open. As usual, Marlee stood to the side as the door opened. A girl of about four peeked out. She was clad in a Dora the Explorer t-shirt, pink pants, and dirty white socks. Wisps of dark hair were pulled out of her ponytail indicating her hair hadn't brushed since waking up.

"Ruby, who is it?" a gruff male voice shouted. The little girl turned around, shrugged, and walked away leaving the door ajar.

"Who's there?" said a man as he approached the door. He was wheelchair bound and appeared to be in his sixties. He pulled the door open as he rolled his chair backwards.

"Hi. I'm looking for Warren Keoke. I was told he lived here. I'm Marlee McCabe and this is my cousin Bridget. We're from Elmwood and need to speak with Warren right away. He's not in any trouble or anything," Marlee rattled off as much insignificant information as she could in the shortest amount of time, knowing she needed to put this elderly man at ease or else they may be invited to leave the premises.

The elderly man did not utter another word except to yell, "Warren!" He rolled his chair backward, leaving

Marlee to wonder if she should enter or wait for Warren to appear. Experience told her that any invitation into a home, even an uncertain one, should be accepted. As she entered the home, she realized Bridget was holding onto the back of her coat as she followed closely along.

The interior of the trailer was in the usual disarray that a four-year-old would create. Blankets, pillows, and toys were strewn about the living room floor in front of the television. An opened juice box and an overturned box of cereal were on an end table. A small table with two chairs was pushed against the wall in the small kitchen. A bowl, surrounded by milk droplets and several pieces of cereal sat atop the table, as did a pack of Marlboros and a lighter. Dirty dishes were on the stove, counter tops, and in the sink, suggesting it had been a couple days since they were last washed.

Warren came from a room in the back. He was in his late thirties and dressed in low-slung jeans and a red, long sleeved t-shirt. His straight, dark hair was medium length and he wore it slicked back. He was of wiry build and without an extra ounce of fat. "What's going on?" Warren asked, his tone of voice and body language suggesting nothing.

After introducing herself and Bridget, Marlee launched into a similar spiel she had given the man in the wheelchair. She noticed Bridget had her right hand in her coat pocket, her hand no doubt on the pepper spray in case things turned ugly.

"Yeah? What do you want with me?" Warren asked, still not revealing any emotion.

Marlee took a deep breath and explained the death of Shane Seaboy and her attempt to find out what happened. "We know you were a codefendant of Shane's in the eagle feather case a few years ago. That's why we came to see you. We wanted to know if you had any idea who would want Shane dead." She held her breath as she waited for his response.

"That was years ago. We weren't even in the same prison. After he was released Shane came back here for a while but couldn't make a go of it. By the time I got out a few weeks later he already moved to the Cities," Warren said, matter-of-factly.

"So you haven't seen him since before you went to prison?" Marlee asked.

"No, I've seen him around here a couple times since then. I'm not sure why he came back. His brother doesn't have anything to do with him and he doesn't have any other close family around," Warren reported. "Just distant relatives."

"Who do you think killed him?" Marlee asked.

"No idea," Warren said without providing additional detail.

"Why would anyone want him dead?" Marlee continued with her line of questioning.

"I guess because of his involvement in the eagle feather case. In case you hadn't heard, neither one of us are very popular around here," Warren said.

"But you stayed around Sisseton and have managed."

"Yeah, but it hasn't been easy. People look at me like a traitor. I don't have any friends and quite a few enemies," Warren said.

"What do you do for work?" Marlee asked.

Warren snorted. "Look around. There's not much to do. I can't get a job with the tribe or any other government because of my conviction. No one wants to hire me for non-government jobs either. I can't find any work here, so I make art to sell." He motioned to a dream catcher hanging on the paneled wall of the trailer's living room.

Marlee took in a deep breath and launched into the question she was dreading asking Warren. "We've been hearing about a guy named Diego who is the ring leader of the Indian artifact sales. Tell me about him."

To the surprise of both Marlee and Bridget, Warren threw his head back and laughed. "Don't tell me that story's still going around," he said after he stopped laughing. "That's bullshit. There's no Diego. The FBI made him up."

"Why would the FBI make up the existence of Diego? He's supposed to be the ring leader that was never caught in the eagle feather case," Marlee said.

"The FBI made him up because they're always looking for some huge conspiracy. The only people involved in selling eagle feathers were me, Shane, Chris Long Hollow, and a white guy named Ryan Campbell. Shane's dead, Ryan's still in prison, and Chris got sent back. None of us said anything about Diego because there's no such person," Warren stated.

"But when we asked about him around the community, everybody clammed up," Marlee said. "We're going over to talk to Tony Red Day next to see what he knows about Diego."

"Some people around here believe everything they hear. Just because they're dumb enough to buy the FBI's story about Diego doesn't mean it's real," Warren stated.

"But–" Marlee started.

"Look, I have to be going. I have to take Dad and Ruby out to Old Agency to see some relatives," Warren interrupted walking toward the door. "If I thought there was anything to this whole Diego story, I'd tell you, but there just isn't." He opened the door and stood waiting for Bridget and Marlee to leave. They stood outside on the step. As Marlee was preparing to ask another question, Warren gave them a quick nod and smile, pulling the door shut.

It was chilly when they entered the residence, but now it seemed down right frigid as Marlee and Bridget walked back toward the CR-V. Diane leaned over into the driver's seat, peering out the window for any sign of danger. "What happened?" she asked as Marlee crawled in the driver's seat and Bridget hopped in back.

"Let's drive a bit before we talk," Marlee said, starting the car and maneuvering out of the yard. She didn't want Warren to see them discussing the conversation they just had with him. In fact, the less Warren thought they were interested in the matter, the better. Marlee steered the vehicle back onto the highway and drove toward Sisseton. Once in town, she parked in the grocery store lot.

"I can tell you one thing for sure," Marlee said with an air of confidence. "We're getting very close to finding out Diego's identity."

"Why do you think that?" Bridget asked.

"Because when Diego's name was mentioned to Warren, he laughed it off and said the FBI was just trying to make a big name for themselves by inventing a conspiracy that reached much further than it really did. When we mentioned Diego to Ivan Flute and the clerk at the convenience store this morning, both got very serious and warned us away from asking any more questions about him. That leads me to believe that Warren knows not only the identity of Diego, but also the location. I bet if we were to follow Warren around we could find out where Diego lives. My guess is that the ring leader is right here in the area," Marlee stated.

"Right under our noses!" Bridget exclaimed. "Just like when Humphrey Bogart's character in *The Maltese Falcon* identifies the real culprit as Mary Astor's character, who initially approached him to investigate the case."

Marlee let the movie reference pass without rolling her eyes or engaging in a menacing thought. Something else held her attention. A strong, suffocating smell permeated the vehicle and Diane started gagging.

"Everybody out of the car!" Marlee yelled, covering her nose and mouth with her scarf and jumping out of the CR-V. Turning to Bridget she yelled, "Did you set off the pepper spray in the car?"

Bridget, coughing and gasping for air, nodded her head as she braced herself against the body of the vehicle. "I forgot I had my finger on the trigger," she sputtered.

"Dammit, Bridget! Give me that damn thing!" Marlee yelled, holding out her hand.

Bridget handed over the canister of pepper spray, carefully pointing it away from Marlee's face. "I'm sorry!" she shrieked as she coughed. "I had it in my coat pocket and ready to go in case Warren or his dog or somebody else tried to hurt us. I forgot to turn the safety back on when we got in the car and I accidentally pressed down on the nozzle."

"Well, at least it wasn't aimed at any of us. Bridget, make sure you don't touch your eyes or your face with your hands. If you get the pepper spray residue anywhere else on your body, you'll be very sorry," Marlee cautioned.

"Well, now what do we do?" Diane wailed.

Marlee used the automatic button to roll down the windows on all four doors. Then she shut the doors and said, "Now we wait until the car airs out. It shouldn't take too long. Maybe half an hour. Bridget, do you have pepper spray in your coat pocket or on you?"

"No, I'd taken it out of my coat pocket and held it in my hand when I accidentally pushed the button. None of it got on my coat. The pepper spray shot right into the air," Bridget stated.

"Good. At least you'll be able to keep your coat on while we wait. Let's stand up against the building out of the wind," Marlee suggested. The three stood in a line against the grocery store, watching the car so no further vandalism could occur and waiting for the interior to get aired out.

"I'm really sorry, you guys. I had no idea the trigger was that sensitive," said Bridget as she and the other two academics stood shivering in the late November weather.

"It's fine, Bridget," Diane said, tears no longer running down her face.

"Yeah, it's okay. At least no one was sprayed in the face," Marlee said, her anger over Bridget's folly dissipating. "You know, I heard about an FBI agent up in North Dakota who accidentally set off his pepper spray and got it on his hands, which really started to burn. He went to the bathroom to pee, so you can guess what else started to burn. Then he rubbed his eyes. Finally, he came out of the bathroom and said he was going home for the rest of the day. They still call him Hot Pants," Marlee said with a chuckle. The trio simultaneously cringed and laughed as they thought about Hot Pants' predicament.

Marlee suggested Bridget and Diane go inside the grocery store to warm up while she watched the car for the remaining few minutes. At first they both declined, but Diane's lack of love for winter and Bridget's lack of body fat soon made the offer too good to refuse.

As Marlee waited outside the grocery store by herself, she paced to keep warm. As she was facing toward the entrance from the highway, she observed a red, two-door Acura pull into the grocery store lot. "Wow, that's a snazzy car," she thought to herself. The car parked on the far side of the lot from where Marlee's vehicle was located.

The driver exited the Acura coupe. "Well, I'll be damned," Marlee said out loud, instantly recognizing the young man.

Those who wanted to help me couldn't. Those who could help me didn't. Those who should've helped me turned a blind eye. I wonder how they sleep at night.

Chapter 21

Collin Kolb bounded out of the white car and walked in quick steps toward the entrance of the grocery store. Marlee was itching to talk to him and debated whether she should stop Collin now or wait until he exited the store. She took the first opportunity and called to him from the side of the grocery store. "Collin! Hey, Collin!"

The young man looked past Marlee in attempting to determine who was calling his name. Marlee waved her arms over her head and took steps toward him. Collin's face was unreadable as he saw Marlee approach him.

"Hey, Collin. It's me, Professor McCabe, from MSU–" she began.

"I know who you are," Collin stated, neither his voice nor his facial expression revealing anything about what he was thinking.

"Um, yeah," she said, a bit uncomfortable in how to approach him with questions. Collin was inscrutable, leaving Marlee questioning whether she was dealing with someone who would cooperate or a person who would stonewall her. "I was asking around a bit about Shane Seaboy and his conviction in the eagle feather case a few years back. We keep hearing the name of Diego as the ringleader of the operation. What can you tell me about him?" Marlee held her breath, hoping the direct questions would elicit a direct answer.

For the first time since she met him, Collin's face revealed a recognizable emotion. Fear. "You better get out of here before the wrong person hears you asking these questions," Collin stated in a low voice, his eyes darting around the grocery store parking lot to see who might view him talking to Marlee.

"Why is everyone so afraid of Diego? Does he live here?" asked Marlee, not wanting to let the matter drop.

"I have to go. I'm on my way back to Elmwood," Collin said, turning so abruptly toward his car that he nearly tripped. He opened the door to his car, but before he got in, Collin looked back toward Marlee and mouthed the word, "Go!" As the car swung out of the parking lot, Marlee thought she caught a glimpse of a person in the passenger seat of Collin's car. Due to the dark tint of the windows, she could not be certain, but it appeared to be another person in the car with Collin.

Just then, Diane and Bridget came out of the grocery store, each clutching a steaming cup of liquid. Diane handed one to Marlee. "Hot chocolate. It'll warm you right up."

"I'm already warmed up," Marlee said, relating the brief but strange conversation she had with Collin Kolb. "He didn't even go into the store, which I'm sure was his purpose for coming here. He told me to get out of here and then he hopped in his car and took off. The car had darkened windows, but I think there may have been at least one other person in the vehicle."

"Whoa!" Bridget and Diane said in unison.

"So Collin knows who Diego is," Bridget stated.

"And he knows he's dangerous. Let's get out of here, you guys," Diane pleaded. She was becoming more fearful for their safety by the minute.

"We've got a couple more quick stops to make and then we'll go home," Marlee reassured Diane. "Don't worry. We'll be okay. We won't take any chances."

"Let's see if the car's aired out enough that we can get back in," Marlee suggested. All three surrounded the car, sticking their heads inside and sniffing. "I think it's okay. Let's go!"

The three women jumped into the car and Marlee activated the power windows. "Let's wait here for a couple minutes with the windows up before we start driving. I'd hate to have the smell reactivated once I'm driving down the road." They waited in the car, windows up and motor running for nearly a minute before Marlee said, "Well, that should be long enough. I think we're in the clear."

"Where to now?" Bridget asked.

"Let's go by Tony Red Day's new girlfriend's grandma's house," Marlee said.

"Wow, that's not confusing or anything," Bridget said.

"Let's see, the new girlfriend is Collette Many Lightnings, but I don't know the grandmother's name. Of course, remember Tony told us that he and Collette were just friends and that he and Verla Renville were having a fight and they'd be back together soon," Marlee said, recalling the conversation she and Bridget had with Tony on Thursday.

"Do you think he'll tell you anything?" Diane asked.

"Probably not," Bridget said. "He basically told us to get the hell out of there last time."

Marlee glanced in the rear view mirror and sent a piercing stare toward Bridget. Diane was already worried for their safety and Marlee did not want her upset further.

"Let's go home!" Diane wailed. "I didn't want to come on this trip anyway. You guys made me. Now we're going to get hurt or killed because you two won't stop asking questions. I want to go home *now!*"

"Diane, it really wasn't that bad when we talked to Tony last time. He asked us to leave, but he wasn't mean or threatening when he said it," Marlee said, only half-lying about the previous interaction.

Not looking at Marlee any more, Diane slumped against the passenger side door and pouted. She resigned herself to the fact that Marlee and Bridget's quest for information about Shane Seaboy out ranked her own need for safety.

The trio drove to Agency Village where Collette Many Lightnings' grandmother lived. As was usual, Marlee drove past the home to observe the activities going on around the residence and at the homes of the neighbors. Nothing seemed out of the ordinary, so she circled around and parked in front of the home in question.

Marlee and Bridget exited the CR-V, leaving Diane behind in the locked vehicle to watch for vandals. As before, Diane was instructed to sound the horn if she observed anything suspicious or if anyone attempted to damage the vehicle. She was not at all happy about remaining in the car alone, but was much more willing to do that than go inside the home and question Tony Red Day. With all four doors locked, Diane felt some sense of security. Still she could not wait until they finished up and went back to Elmwood. She was already fantasizing about a glass of wine and a homemade meal.

After pounding on the front door for more than a minute, Marlee could hear footsteps. She and Bridget waited another minute before the door was pulled open. Collette Many Lightnings' grandmother was in her wheelchair and stared at them without uttering a word.

"Hello, ma'am," Marlee began, unsure of the best way to start the conversation.

The elderly woman nodded but still did not speak. She wore the same housedress Marlee had seen her in on Thursday. Her gray hair was somewhat askew and Marlee realized for the first time the woman was wearing a wig. The giant cataract sunglasses were still perched on her nose, obscuring much of her face.

"We're here to see Tony Red Day," Marlee said, deciding direct was the way to go when dealing with people who were not all that anxious to see her. Normally, she liked to build rapport, but was afraid she and Bridget might be asked to leave at any moment. That left no time for conversations about the weather or the upcoming Christmas holiday.

The old woman shook her head from side to side. "Not here," she said in a husky voice.

"Where is he?" Marlee asked.

"Don't know," the elderly woman said.

"When will he be back?" Marlee did not believe for one minute that the old woman was telling the truth.

The old woman shrugged her shoulders. Marlee could tell by her apathetic responses to their questions that they would not be able to get much more information out of her. Giving the questioning one last hurrah, she asked, "Have you heard of Diego? He was involved in the eagle feather case and has a bunch of people around here scared."

The elderly woman threw her head back and laughed a deep, hearty cackle. Then she grew somber. It

235

was clear she would not be speaking on the topic of Diego.

Just as Marlee was getting ready to thank her for her time, Bridget broke the silence. "Ma'am, what is your name? Tony told us you were Collette Many Lightnings' grandmother. Is that right?"

She nodded and paused. "Delphine Many Lightnings," she said, right before she shut the door in Marlee's face.

Bridget and Marlee made their way back to the vehicle and drove off. About two blocks away, Marlee parked and turned to Bridget who was seated in the back. "Even though it doesn't look like we got much information with that stop, we really did."

"Well, we found out the name of Tony Red Day's new girlfriend's grandma. I don't think that's exactly earth shattering news," Bridget said.

"That's not all," Marlee said, barely stopping to catch her breath. "Before Delphine came to the door I heard footsteps. Tony Red Day was in the house and Delphine was making sure we didn't get to talk to him. He probably saw us when we drove up or knocked on the door and then he told Delphine to lie about his whereabouts while he hid in a back room."

"So he's there right now?" Diane asked.

"Most likely, but we can't force our way in to talk to him. We could wait outside until he comes out, but that could be hours or days. I don't think it's worth the time."

"I vote that we go home," Diane reiterated, as if no one was aware of what she wanted to do.

"Did you notice anything suspicious while we were on the step talking to Delphine?" Marlee asked Diane. Diane shook her head indicating that she had not.

"You know, there was something else about Delphine that bothered me. When I asked her about

Diego she laughed. Everyone else looked afraid when I mentioned his name. Delphine and Warren Keoke are the only two who laughed when I talked about the identity of Diego," Marlee mused.

"Since it's Sunday, I know the Sheriff won't be in his office, but I'd like to do a quick drive-by of the courthouse just to see if he or any of the deputies are there. I want to ask law enforcement in the area if they know about Diego," Marlee said.

They drove past the courthouse but no light was shining through the windows of the Sheriff's office. Both the Sheriff's car and the additional car driven by the deputy on call were gone. Marlee sighed. She felt like she had all the pieces of the puzzle, but now just needed to assemble them. The easiest way to do that was by talking to someone from the area who would be honest with her. Since the sheriff was not around, Marlee decided her best bet would be to contact Bettina once she got home.

Very few acts of kindness were ever extended to me. Most came with too many strings attached. What at first appears to be a flotation device can quickly turn into an anchor.

Chapter 22

"Bettina, it's Marlee," the phone conversation began. "Yes, I do need something, but that's not the only reason I called. Do you wanna come over for supper tonight?" Marlee added the last part on in a fit of desperation when she realized the only reason she had contacted Bettina was because, as usual, she needed information. "Yes, you can bring the kids if you can't find a babysitter." Marlee rolled her eyes and stuck out her tongue as if being tortured. If there was one thing she had little tolerance for, it was children. They were so needy.

When Marlee hung up the phone she turned to face two other horrified faces. Bridget and Diane were also childless by choice, and not prepared to put up with two youngsters racing around the house. The least impressed with children was Pippa. As a cat, she was somewhat anti-social by nature, but she would not be exiled in her own home. Pippa had a tendency to sit in the middle of the action when visitors were in the home and then hiss and strike at them when they moved anywhere near her. For young children, this was just too much to resist. The fluffy gray Persian sitting inches away was a source of both fear and enthrallment for little ones. Even though she was declawed and had only three teeth, Pippa's sixteen pound body, covered with an ample supply of long hair sent children and adults fleeing when she leaped toward them to reestablish her rights in the household.

"We might have to put up with Bettina's two kids. Let's keep our fingers crossed that she can get a babysitter," Marlee reported to Diane and Bridget who already surmised what was going on. "They aren't bad kids, but they're still kids. And they're loud."

Marlee and Bridget started assembling the meal while Diane resumed her usual spot on the couch and worked on her class prep for the upcoming week. She had been a trooper in going along on the trip to Sisseton and Marlee knew Diane probably needed a little time to herself now.

When the doorbell rang, Bridget and Marlee had supper ready. The baked ziti was nearly ready to come out of the oven, the salad was made, and the garlic bread just needed a few minutes of toasting. Answering the door, Marlee couldn't help but feel relieved when she saw Bettina standing alone on the step.

"You don't have to look so happy," Bettina grumbled good-naturedly as she took off her coat and threw it on the couch. She knew kids were not at the top of Marlee's list. "Lucky so many junior high kids need money for Christmas presents right now. I was able to get a sitter on my first phone call."

Bridget came out of the kitchen with a glass of red wine and handed it to Bettina. She asked Diane, who was hunched over a stack of papers piled on the coffee table, if she wanted a glass of wine.

"I do! That would be great," Diane said with the most positive enthusiasm Marlee had heard from her all day.

"Marlee? Do you want a glass of wine?" asked Bridget as she turned back toward the kitchen.

"Does a cat have an ass?" Marlee quipped.

"Huh?" Bridget and Diane said at the same time.

"Does a cat have an ass? It's like the saying, 'does a bear shit in the woods?'" Marlee said. "You know, it's saying yes to an obvious question." She sighed and continued, "Yes, of course I'd like a glass of wine."

Bettina, Bridget, and Diane were all unimpressed with Marlee's folksy turn of phrase. After a moment of uncomfortable silence, Bridget said, "Uh, I'll go get the wine." Returning with glasses of cabernet in hand, Bridget announced that the meal would be ready in less than ten minutes.

Taking the opportunity to chat with Bettina before Diane and Bridget joined the conversation, Marlee dove right into the questions she had been dying to ask. "Bettina, was anything ever found on the surveillance video in the Student Union?"

"No, not really. Shane came in around 10:00 pm. Otherwise, just students came and went. It was some type of athletic appreciation banquet downstairs that night," Bettina reported.

"We drove over to Sisseton today to ask some more questions."

Bettina sighed and took a sip from her wine glass. They sat at the dining room table, which was set with flowered dishes on a deep red tablecloth. "I figured you might go back there. What did you find out?"

Marlee relayed her conversations with Collin Kolb,

Ivan Flute, Warren Keoke, and Delphine Many Lightnings.

Hearing the names, Bettina took in a quick breath of air. "You actually went to Warren Keoke's home? Dammit, Marlee! He's dangerous. He'll break your legs and not even bat an eye. Warren just put somebody in the hospital and they're still there. What were you thinking?" Bettina's disgust, fear, and anger blended together in a show Marlee had not witnessed before. She banged down her wine glass with such force that a few droplets of cabernet jumped over the side and down onto the table.

"I knew he was one of Shane Seaboy's codefendants and thought he might have some ideas about who killed him." Marlee felt the need to defend her actions to her friend.

"What did he say?" asked Bettina, beginning to calm down a bit.

"Not much. Said it might have been because of the eagle feather case."

"Marlee, I know you think you're doing a good deed by investigating the Seaboy death, but you're doing some really stupid things. Going up to Warren Keoke's home and asking him questions about Shane's death could've gotten you killed. Do you realize that? And if you're not worried about your own safety, what about Diane and Bridget? Do they know what danger you put them in today?" Bettina was now on her feet.

"What makes him so dangerous? He didn't seem that scary to me," Marlee said.

"That's exactly why he is dangerous. If you don't know him you might think he's friendly and nice. He has a reputation around Sisseton and it isn't good. The police don't even go out there alone. They take back-up. Back-up with guns. You need to stay away from him. I mean it!" Bettina said.

"Okay, I get it," Marlee conceded.

"What did you want to ask me about Delphine Many Lightnings? She's been gone for a few years now," Bettina said, her tone returning to normal.

"No, that must be a different person you're thinking of. We just talked to Delphine Many Lightnings today at her house at Agency Village," Marlee said, hoping to jog Bettina's memory.

"Yeah, that's where she lived, but she moved back to Minneapolis. My grandma lives right across the street from Delphine's old house. They were friends and grandma was sad when she left the rez. I heard all about it. More than once," Bettina insisted.

"There must be more than one Delphine Many Lightnings in town," Marlee said, realizing after she said it that it would be quite a coincidence for another Delphine Many Lightnings to be living at a house whose previous occupant held the same name.

"Not that I know of. I think it was about three years ago when Delphine moved," Bettina recalled.

"Well who was the old lady in the wheelchair at that house who identified herself as Delphine Many Lightnings?"

"You're sure that's what she said? Maybe you didn't hear her correctly," Bettina said.

"Bridget and I were both there. Twice. The second time we were at the house Bridget asked her name and she said 'Delphine Many Lightnings'," Marlee insisted.

Bridget, having heard her name mentioned, poked her head out from the kitchen. Upon hearing the end of the conversation she nodded in agreement and said, "Yeah, Delphine Many Lightnings. Heard her say it, clear as day."

Bettina shook her head. "It doesn't make sense. I

know Delphine moved. As far as I know, her relatives took over her house. I don't know who's been living there, but it isn't Delphine. Somebody's been telling you a tall tale."

"We tracked down Tony Red Day, Jr. at that house. Tony's old girlfriend, Verla Renville, told us Tony was staying with his new girlfriend, Collette Many Lightnings. When we got there, the old lady who later told us she was Delphine Many Lightnings yelled for Tony and he came out of the back bedroom. He said he was staying there with his friend, Collette Many Lightnings and that the house belonged to her grandmother. We never did see Collette around there. When we were there today we think Tony was hiding from us because we heard footsteps before Delphine answered the door," Marlee reported.

"Delphine was Collette's grandma; that much is true. I don't know who would be using Delphine's name. Everybody around there knows she moved. This old lady, whoever she is, probably got a good chuckle giving the white people a false name," said Bettina.

"What is her motivation for doing that? And who is she?" Diane had set down her paperwork and joined the conversation when she realized it was a lot juicier than the class prep she was completing.

"Yeah, she had nothing to gain by giving us a false name. We hardly know anyone around there. So who is it?" Marlee asked.

Bettina walked over to her coat and retrieved her cell phone from the pocket. "Give me a minute," she said as she took the phone into the guest bedroom away from the other three women. When she returned she said, "My source tells me that it's just Collette Many Lightnings living there along with a sibling or two when they need a place to stay. She's the home's main occupant."

"Is your source your grandma?" Marlee asked with a grin.

"Yeah," Bettina said, looking a bit sheepish. "Grandma had a stroke earlier this year, so her memory can be a little faulty at times."

"Does Collette have another grandma living with her that's senile? Or an elderly aunt? Or maybe somebody who's not related at all but is considered her grandma?" Marlee asked, the questions tumbling out.

"Not that I know of," said Bettina. "She's single, doesn't have any kids, and lives there alone except when one of her brothers or sisters needs a place to stay. A couple of them live in The Cities and another lives at Old Agency but has been on and off with her boyfriend for years. I'm thinking the old lady is either suffering from dementia or is a prankster. Either way, it sounds harmless enough," Bettina concluded. Still, Marlee was not so sure.

"Oh, and another thing. My source—uh, I mean grandma—said Delphine Many Lightnings was never in a wheelchair. She walked on her own and never needed any assistance to get around," said Bettina.

"Hmmm...I thought it was kind of odd that there wasn't any wheelchair ramp on the house," said Marlee. "I mean, so many of the houses in the area have ramps to accommodate the elderly and disabled that it seemed kind of odd that an older woman in a wheelchair would be in a home without easier access."

Back at the table, Bridget set the salad, bread, and baked ziti before them. They all helped themselves to generous portions of each and a new bottle of wine was opened. The conversation was light and veered from the Shane Seaboy investigation for a few minutes until Marlee exclaimed, "Jeez, I can't believe I forgot to ask you the most important question of all." She looked at

Bettina and asked, "Do you know anything about a guy called Diego?"

Bettina grimaced and her body noticeably stiffened as she put down her fork. Her eyes bore into Marlee. "What do you mean?" she asked tersely.

"Diego is the name the FBI gave to the guy they think is the ring leader of the eagle feather case and is involved in other Indian artifact thefts and sales throughout the world. They think they located him in The Cities, but for some reason, he has a huge amount of control over the people around Sisseton. Every time I ask someone about him they clam up and urge me to go away. The only ones who didn't do that were Warren Keoke and the lady who said she was Delphine Many Lightnings. I was wondering what you've heard about Diego," Marlee asked.

"Look, I'm not advising you. I'm not warning you. I'm telling you not to go out to Sisseton again. This case is so much bigger than anything you can even comprehend right now. If I hear anything about you going out there again I'll personally arrest you for interfering in an ongoing case. Do you understand me?" Bettina said, rising to her feet, her eyes never leaving Marlee.

"I know it's serious, but come on. Just tell me what you know about him. It's obvious you know something or you wouldn't be acting like this. Sit down and finish your supper. Let's just talk about it and why Diego has everyone so scared," Marlee said. Bridget and Diane followed the conversation between Marlee and Bettina like it was a tennis match.

"I've lost my appetite," Bettina said, striding to the living room, grabbing her coat, and leaving the house. As the door slammed behind her, Marlee, Diane, and Bridget struggled to understand what just happened.

"Are you going back out to Sisseton?" Diane asked, hoping Bettina's tirade made an impression on Marlee.

"Does a cat have an ass?" asked Marlee.

I was warned more than once. My life didn't hold much value for me anymore, so the threats rang hollow.

Chapter 23

"You can't go back to Sisseton! You heard what Bettina said," Diane pleaded.

"Look, you're risking a lot just to go back there and nose around again. And for what? You didn't even know Shane Seaboy. You could be beaten up or shot. Plus, Bettina said she'd arrest you and I don't think she makes a lot of empty threats. If you get arrested for interfering with an investigation, you can probably say goodbye to your career here at MSU," Bridget, ticking off the list of reasons on her fingers.

Marlee started to argue and then paused. With a resigned sigh she said, "You're right. So was Bettina. This is getting too dangerous. I just wanted to find out who killed Shane and that kept leading to more and more puzzles and I wanted the answers to them too. It's hard to give up when there are so many unanswered questions. Especially when we're so close." She flopped down on the couch and muttered, "I hate giving up."

"You're not giving up. You're just taking a safe approach. Besides, who knows what you might uncover. Obviously one or more people want you out of the picture or they wouldn't have sabotaged your tires. Whatever went on with the eagle feather case or whatever is still going on is probably what got Shane killed. Let's go to the FBI office tomorrow and you can talk to the agent you know and tell him everything. Maybe he can use some of the information you have," said Bridget, still trying to smooth things over so Marlee wouldn't feel left out of the investigation.

Marlee nodded sullenly. "I guess we could do that. It would be better than nothing."

Diane and Bridget went back to the table to finish their now cold meal. Marlee grabbed her coat from the coat closet and said, "I guess I've lost my appetite too. I'm just going to walk around for a little bit and clear my head. A lot's gone on in the past few days. I'll be back in a little bit."

A quizzical look passed over the faces of Bridget and Diane, but neither said anything. They knew stopping Marlee from a return trip to Sisseton was a huge feat, so they let it pass that she wanted to go for a solo walk in the cold, dark night.

Once outside, Marlee walked toward campus. The walk was not totally a lie. She did need to clear her head and think over all the events of the past few days. That much was true. However, Marlee was not just going to walk aimlessly around town. She was going to the house Collin Kolb and his roommates rented. The students from her Criminal Justice Club had mentioned where the house was located, so she knew it would be easy to locate.

Arriving at the ramshackle single-story building, Marlee rubbed her hands together for warmth and also to summon her courage. Given his abrupt behavior in Sisseton earlier that day and urging her to leave the area, Marlee knew a discussion with Collin about Diego was in order. She rang the doorbell, but no one opened the door even though she could hear the blaring of a football game on the television and the sound of male voices cheering. Realizing the doorbell might not work, she pounded on the door.

A young, burly Native American man opened the door with cash in hand. "What're you doing here? We ordered pizza."

"I'm Dr. McCabe from MSU. I was just stopping by to see Collin. Are you one of his roommates?"

"Yeah, I'm Ashton," he replied.

"Actually, I have a couple questions for you too. Did you invite Shane Seaboy and Tony Red Day, Jr. to your party last Monday night?" Marlee inquired.

"Yeah, I might have mentioned something when I talked to both of them," Ashton said.

"You knew they didn't get along, right?" Marlee continued.

"I knew, but it's not my problem. All they had to do was stay away from each other at the party," Ashton said with an air of defiance.

"Who do you think killed Shane?" Marlee asked.

"How would I know? Probably somebody he pissed off in prison," Ashton said.

"What can you tell me about Diego?" Marlee asked, looking Ashton Dumarce directly in the eyes.

He stared at her for what seemed like hours before replying, "I don't know anything about somebody named Diego." With that statement, he backed away from the door and yelled, "Collin, somebody here to see you."

Collin appeared at the door with a frightened look on his face. "I need to talk to you Collin. Grab your coat and come on outside if you don't want to talk in front of your roommates," Marlee said. He was wearing an MSU t-shirt and plaid cotton shorts that hung to his knees. She noticed Collin had a black eye and a split lip, which were not there when she saw him earlier that day in Sisseton.

"I can't leave right now, but I have something to tell you," he whispered. "Can I meet you later?"

Marlee nodded. "When?" she asked.

"The game should be over by 9:00. I'll meet you at the library then. On the first floor over in the reference section," Collin said as he shut the door in her face.

Marlee realized Collin might have the missing piece of the puzzle. She walked back home and told Diane and Bridget nothing of her encounter with Collin or their upcoming meeting later that night. Bettina had said one thing earlier that really hit home with Marlee. She had been putting Bridget and Diane both in danger by involving them in the Shane Seaboy investigation. That would not happen anymore.

"Well, you timed that just right," Bridget said as Marlee walked through the door at her home. "We finished washing the dishes and were just going to have ice cream."

"My timing is perfect," Marlee said with forced cheerfulness. She wanted to sit and concentrate on her impending conversation with Collin Kolb, but for appearances sake, she knew she needed to sit and visit with Bridget and Diane. If she retired to her room too early, they would become suspicious. The three academics sat in the living room with bowls of moose tracks ice cream and hashed over the events of the day.

"So you're really not going back to Sisseton and you're dropping the whole thing?" Diane confirmed.

"That's right. I'm going to talk to the FBI tomorrow

and tell them what I know. Then I'll concentrate on the last week of classes and finals week. After I get the finals graded and the grades posted, I'll focus on Christmas and finishing my shopping," Marlee lied through her teeth. She did not relish lying, but had no qualms about doing so in this matter if it meant keeping Diane and Bridget safe.

At 8:15 Marlee took some papers and books out of her book bag and placed them on the now-cleared dining room table. She knew she would never be able to concentrate on preparing anything for class, but she needed to put on a good show for Bridget and Diane. Luckily, there was very little she needed to do for the following day's classes. She glanced across the table at the crime chart, which was propped against the wall. Something was bothering her, but she couldn't figure out what it was. The answer to the whole case was right in front of her. She just needed to figure it out.

At 8:45, Marlee made a big show of announcing that she had forgotten one of her most important books in her office and needed to go to campus to retrieve it. "If I don't have that book I can't get anything else done. If I wait until tomorrow I'll have to leave here before 6:00 am to get everything ready for my 10:00 am class," she lied.

"Want me to go with you? I'm really not all that tired yet," said Bridget, attempting to suppress a yawn.

"No, I'm just gonna make a quick run up there. I might stop at the grocery store on the way back and get a few things," Marlee said, hoping the grocery store ruse would keep Diane and Bridget from worrying when it took her longer than was necessary to retrieve a book from her campus office.

"See you in a bit," Diane said, smiling, as she looked up from the book she was reading while sitting on the couch. "Can you pick up more ice cream?"

"Sure," said Marlee, instantly pissed that she would now have to make an actual trip to the grocery store after her meeting with Collin.

Marlee parked in the lot nearest the campus library and made her way inside the newly-remodeled building. The library, normally vacant on Sunday night, was a hub of activity with students preparing end-of-term projects and studying for final exams. She walked over to the reference section as Collin had requested. Not sure what to do with herself, she pulled a folder from her book bag and caught up on grading. Glancing up several times a minute, Marlee looked for Collin to appear at the long table where she sat. After an hour, Marlee gave up. Collin had sent her on a wild goose chase. He never had any intention of meeting her and was probably at home with his roommates laughing at her right now.

With more than a little disgust, Marlee crammed the grading back in her bag and stomped out of the library. She drove home and parked in her garage before realizing she did not pick up ice cream at the grocery store as Diane had requested and would need some story to account for her hour long absence from home. When she unlocked the back door, she was relieved to see only the kitchen light on. Diane was asleep on the couch and the door to Bridget's bedroom was closed.

Marlee summoned her last ounce of energy and changed into pajamas before collapsing into bed, face unwashed and teeth unbrushed. She immediately sunk into a deep, dream-filled slumber. The sleep was so deep that she thought she was dreaming when she heard the explosion. It wasn't until she saw a flicker of flames coming from the living room that she knew she was experiencing a living nightmare.

HOLIDAY HOMICIDE

255

Sometimes a sacrifice is needed to drive home a point.

Chapter 24

"Diane!" Marlee yelled, running toward the flames in the living room. Her friend was wide awake and on her feet, stomping wildly at the ignited carpet. Bridget ran out of the guest room, flipping on the living room light, and joined Diane in suppressing the flames while Marlee fumbled for the fire extinguisher under the kitchen sink.

"Step back!" Marlee yelled as she depressed the trigger on the fire extinguisher, coating the carpet and surrounding furniture in a sea of white foam.

"What the hell happened?" Bridget screamed.

"I don't know! I just heard a loud pop and then saw flames!" Marlee shouted making sure the flames were fully doused before she took her hand off the extinguisher trigger.

"Diane, what happened?" Marlee asked.

"I... I don't know. I went to the bathroom and when I came back the floor was on fire," Diane said, still dazed from the blaze.

Although the furnace had kicked on, the room was getting colder by the second. Marlee wrapped her arms around herself as she peered at the floor. Beneath the foam from the extinguisher lay the charred carpet and shards of a green glass bottle. She turned toward the couch and noticed the blinds covering the windows behind the couch were in disarray, exposing a broken window. Small pieces of glass from the broken window lay on the couch where Diane had been sleeping just minutes before.

"Sonofabitch!" Marlee yelled. "We've been hit with a Molotov cocktail! Somebody was trying to burn down the house with us inside!"

"What?" Diane asked, now shaking from cold and shock.

"A flammable liquid is placed in a breakable glass container. Then a piece of cloth is put in the mouth of the container and lit on fire. When the glass container is thrown, it will break and flammable liquid will fly all over and start on fire," Marlee lectured, very familiar with this form of destruction that was used today in various forms of modern terrorism.

"I'm calling the police," Bridget said, grabbing the telephone and dialing.

"Don't move anything or touch anything. We need to keep everything as is for the police. We can't even do something to the window to block out the cold," Marlee advised as she went to the coat closet to retrieve blankets and heavy outerwear for the trio while they waited. Then she shooed Pippa into her bedroom and closed the door. The last thing she needed was for her cat to escape during the police investigation.

It was nearly an hour before the first officers arrived on the scene. "What the fuck took you so long? Were you at the donut shop?" Diane yelled in an uncharacteristic showing of anger.

"A body was found an hour ago and we were assisting with that investigation," said a young, weary police officer with dark circles under his eyes. He rubbed his eyes with the back of his hand and blinked rapidly, struggling to gain focus on Diane, Bridget, and Marlee. "Otherwise we'd have been here a lot sooner."

"Oh, no," said Diane, contrite for her outburst moments earlier. "What happened?"

"A victim was found along the road that runs on the east side of the mall. Looks like he froze to death," the officer reported.

"Do you know who it is?" Marlee asked.

"We can't release a name until family has been notified. I can tell you that it's someone who lives here in Elmwood," the officer reported.

"That's awful," Marlee said shaking her head, feeling instant compassion for the unknown victim's family and friends. "Another death in Elmwood."

Officers continued their investigation, which included collecting the shards of glass from the carpet and swabbing the surface to determine the accelerant. They determined the Molotov cocktail was flung through the window from the street, so there were no footprints in the yard or fingerprints on the windows. The best they could hope for was a fingerprint on one of the glass shards. It was 3:00 am and there were no lights on in the neighbors' homes, suggesting they had not observed who threw the homemade bomb. Officers decided to wait until a more suitable hour to interview the neighbors. Before leaving, an officer assisted Marlee tape cardboard over the broken window to hold out some of the cold air.

Marlee, Diane, and Bridget were unable to sleep after the police left. "What if whoever did this comes back?" Diane asked. She looked from side to side. It occurred to Marlee that Diane might be considering moving back to her own apartment where it was safer.

"I think whoever did this made their point. Either they were trying to scare us, which worked. Or they were trying to burn my house down, which failed. They know we'll be on high alert now, so I doubt they'd come back," said Marlee in an attempt to analyze the situation from the perspective of the perpetrator. She hoped she sounded more convincing than she felt.

"What now?" asked Bridget as she paced from one room to the next; at a loss for words and not sure what to do.

In the absence of a clear plan, the three women decided to make hot chocolate and look at the crime chart again. None of them expected to come up with solutions, but at least they could feel like they were doing something. After several mugs of hot chocolate, a breakfast of scrambled eggs and toast, and a thorough discussion of the death of Shane Seaboy and the mysterious details surrounding his murder, a loud thud was heard at the front door. The three women all jumped to their feet at the same time and Bridget struck a defensive kung-fu pose.

Marlee began to laugh when she realized the sound was just the daily newspaper being slid into the mail slot attached to her house. She walked toward the front door and lifted the small hatch leading to the mail chute and pulled out the newspaper. She flung the paper on the coffee table in the living room as she walked back toward the kitchen to continue looking at the crime chart. The newspaper unfurled when it landed on the coffee table and the headline caught Marlee's eye: "MSU Student Found Dead Near Mall."

I was just seventeen. A stupid kid. If I'd had any idea that getting involved with the eagle feather business would cause this much death and heart ache, I'd never started.

Chapter 25

"Oh my god, you guys!" Marlee yelled from the living room. "The guy who died a few hours ago was an MSU student!"

"What? Another death related to MSU? This is getting scarier and scarier! And we could've been killed last night too when the bomb came through the window!" Diane was pushed to her breaking point and there was no calming her.

Despite the early hour, Marlee called Bettina Crawford on her cell. Even though Bettina had been furious at Marlee when stormed out last night after the inquiry about Diego, Marlee knew Bettina would answer her questions about the death that morning in Elmwood. After the second ring, Bettina answered. "Bettina, I'm sorry to call you so early, but we just heard about an MSU student found dead. Do you know who it is?"

Marlee was silent while Bettina relayed the information and then hung up the phone. Her look was one of utter shock and confusion. "It was Collin Kolb," she said, sinking down on the overstuffed chair.

"No way! Did Bettina have any details other than he froze to death?" asked Bridget.

"The autopsy will be done later today, but for right now the death is being called suspicious. Collin reeked of alcohol and was dressed in just a t-shirt and shorts. No coat, no shoes, nothing else. The detectives on the scene suspect he drank a toxic amount of alcohol and then was taken out to the edge of town and left. Collin may have been unconscious when he was left there. At any rate, the fact that he probably drank a lot of alcohol and was outside in freezing weather dressed in summer clothes almost ensured that he'd die. The real mystery is if he was forced to drink alcohol or if he did it himself and how he ended up in a remote area out by the mall," said Marlee, thinking out loud.

"Why would someone kill Collin?" Bridget asked.

"You have to promise not to tell Bettina." Marlee said pausing until both Bridget and Diane nodded in assent. "When I went for a walk last night I went over to Collin's house to talk to him. He'd been beaten up. He was watching the football game with his roommates and said he couldn't get away until 9:00, so we arranged to meet at the library then. When I left again last night to go to campus it was to see Collin, not to get a book from my office. I waited for an hour and Collin never showed up."

"You lied to us!" Bridget yelled, hurt and anger both registering on her tired face.

"I knew something was up! It wasn't like you to just accept that you couldn't be involved in the investigation any more. I should've known you'd do something like that!" Diane shouted, stepping a bit closer to Marlee than was necessary.

"I'm sorry I lied, but I didn't want either of you to be involved anymore. Bettina said I was putting you both at risk, so I excluded you to keep you safe," Marlee said.

"Well, that's working out really well," Bridget snarled.

"Look, I said I'm sorry for lying. And I'm sorry I've involved you both in this whole thing," Marlee pleaded. "I just wanted to find out what happened to Shane Seaboy. I never dreamed there would be this kind of backlash toward us."

Bridget stormed off to the guest room, slamming the door behind her making the windowpanes rattle in the nearby bathroom. Diane just stared at Marlee with a wounded look. After her attempts at making amends fell flat, Marlee walked to her room and sat on the edge of her bed. It was after 6:00 am and she needed to be on campus for classes from 10:00 am until noon. Then she had a three-hour night class. Today was her busiest day of the week on campus, but she needed as much time as possible to figure out who killed Shane Seaboy and Collin Kolb. Time was of the essence. She also wanted to find out who was responsible for throwing the Molotov cocktail into her house and vandalizing the tires on her vehicle. Was one person responsible for all these acts of violence or were multiple people working together?

Marlee quickly showered and dressed. She knew what she needed to do and wanted to get out of the house before Bridget and Diane could confront her. She peeked into the living room and noticed that Diane was now asleep on the couch. Bridget was still in the guest room and had not made any noise since she went in. With any luck, she was asleep too.

Before dashing out the back door, Marlee penned a quick note and left it on the table. Her cousin and friend were already furious with her, so she doubted what she was about to do would yield consequences that were any more severe. She grabbed two twenty-ounce bottles of Diet Pepsi and a foil-wrapped pouch of strawberry Pop Tarts. Pippa was underfoot and meowing for attention. Marlee reached down and scratched her behind the ears, promising that when she returned Pippa would receive extra attention and plenty of kitty treats.

As Marlee drove on the main highway out of Elmwood, she detoured to the area where Collin Kolb's body was found. She saw two police cars and a Sheriff's SUV all parked in one spot along an isolated road, illuminated by the lights they had set up when securing the crime scene and searching for evidence. The young professor decided it would be in her best interest not to get too close to the investigation, since it would just raise questions. Plus, Bettina might be on the scene and she didn't want the police detective to interrogate her further.

It was before 8:00 am when Marlee rolled into Sisseton. The first stop was at a convenience store to get a cup of coffee and make a call to her department secretary, giving an excuse of being under the weather and unable to teach her classes that morning. Her next stop was Collette Many Lightnings' home in Agency Village. After making her usual drive around the block, she parked two houses down from Collette's, hoping she would not be seen by Collette, Tony, or Delphine. Marlee took quick steps across the snow covered yards of neighbors before reaching the Many Lightnings' home. She stood to the side of the door and used her fist to pound loudly until she heard a noise in the house.

The door opened and Tony Red Day Jr. stood in boxer shorts and a dirty white t-shirt. The heat from the house rolled out and Marlee welcomed the warmth on her chilled body. "What do you want?" Tony growled.

"Look, I just want to talk. I'm not here to cause any trouble." The lies rolled off Marlee's tongue so fast she did not even notice them anymore.

Tony stared at Marlee long and hard before stepping back into the house, leaving the door open. It may not have been an invitation, but Marlee took it as such, letting herself into the home and closing the door behind her. "Where's Delphine?" she asked, still curious as to the old woman's identity.

"Asleep," Tony said, motioning with his eyes toward the back of the house. "Why?"

"I heard Delphine Many Lightnings actually lives in Minneapolis now, but the lady we met the other day said that was her name. I'm wondering who's pretending to be Delphine. And why," Marlee said.

"You're crazier than a sack of monkeys!" Tony said. "Delphine!" he shouted toward a back room in the house. When there was no answer he pounded on a bedroom door and words were whispered.

"She'll be out in a minute. Why is this any of your business?" Tony asked, realizing that he was under no obligation to answer Marlee's questions or prove Delphine's identity.

Before Marlee could answer, a wheel chair rolled into the living room where Marlee and Tony stood. "What do you want?" croaked the old lady in a deep, raspy voice, made even more so since she'd just awakened. She wore the same flowered house dress and oversized cataract glasses Marlee had seen her in on the two previous occasions.

"Ma'am, are you Delphine Many Lightnings?" Marlee asked, leaning down so she was at eye level with the old woman. Marlee couldn't see the lady's eyes behind the ginormous glasses.

"I told you that last time you were here," Delphine

stated.

"I heard that Delphine moved to Minneapolis and her granddaughter, Collette, is the only one living here now," Marlee stated.

"I just moved back a few weeks ago. My diabetes caused trouble with my feet so I moved back here so Collette can take care of me," said the elderly lady, looking Marlee straight in the eye.

Marlee glanced around the living room, noticing a framed photograph. Front and center was the elderly woman before her, surrounded by people of varying ages. "When was this taken?" Marlee inquired.

"About five years ago. It was my sixtieth birthday party," the old woman stated without batting an eye.

"How do you get around if there's no wheelchair ramp on the house?" Marlee asked.

"There's a ramp on the back of the house," the old woman replied, furrowing her brows. "What's going on?"

Marlee felt a blush creep to her cheeks. She had been certain someone was using Delphine's name and impersonating her. "I'm sorry. I guess I thought you might be in some kind of danger or something," Marlee said, realizing she did not have much of a theory at that point. "Well, where's Collette at? I keep hearing about her, but she's never here when I come by," Marlee said, trying to regain some of the bluster she had when she entered the house.

"She musta went out while we were asleep. We were sleeping until you came barging in here with all your stupid questions," Tony said. Delphine lowered her head and rolled her chair into the kitchen.

Turning to Tony, Marlee asked, "Do you know Collin Kolb?"

"Sure, I know him. We went to high school together. He's a smart college boy now. Doesn't have any time for the likes of me," Tony said with bitterness.

"Did you know he was found dead early this morning?" Marlee asked, giving Tony a hard stare.

"What?" Tony asked, genuine surprise crossing his face.

"Police suspect he was heavily intoxicated and then dropped off on the edge of town wearing just summer clothes. He froze to death. Why would someone do this to him?" Marlee could tell by Tony's expression that he had not participated in the act, but thought he might hazard a guess as to who was involved.

"I... I... don't know," Tony stammered. She could almost see the wheels in Tony's head turning as he processed the information about Collin's death.

"See, here's the thing. I think you do know. I think you have a very good idea what happened to Collin and to Shane. I think you and Warren Keoke know all about it," Marlee said, acting much more confident than she felt. Especially after her faulty assumptions about Delphine Many Lightnings.

"Get the hell outta here and don't come back!" Tony yelled marching toward the door and holding it open. "I don't know anything about these guys dying."

As Marlee took her time walking toward the door, Tony grabbed her upper arm and pulled her toward the door and shoved her out on the step. "Get the fuck outta here. Go back to Elmwood," he said with a low, vicious tone and an icy stare.

Marlee turned on her heel and walked back to her car. She felt confident that the old woman really was Delphine Many Lightnings. Based on nothing other than her own instincts, Marlee felt that Tony had not been involved in Collin's death, but probably knew who was. She was still unsure as to his role, if any, in Shane Seaboy's murder.

Although the conversation with Tony Red Day and Delphine Many Lightnings had not provided answers to many of Marlee's questions, she remained optimistic. Her next stop was sure to break the case wide open, if it didn't get her killed.

And in an instant, everything can change. Suspicions are confirmed, lies are told, and threats are carried out.

Chapter 26

By the time the tires of Marlee's CR-V crunched across the hardened snow in Warren Keoke's driveway, she was beginning to put the pieces of the puzzle together. The bedraggled old dog who lay beside the trailer on her previous visit was nowhere to be seen. Marlee walked up to the door of the trailer and knocked. By the time the door finally opened, Marlee knew who was the mastermind in the sale of Indian artifacts. Now she just needed to put her plan into action.

"Hi, Warren. Or should I call you Diego?" Marlee asked with a smirk. The smirk was wiped of her face in an instant as Warren Keoke grabbed Marlee by the hair and dragged her into the trailer. He released his grip on her hair and shoved her against a wall, forcing a dream catcher crashing to the floor.

"Who do you think you're messing with? You're not very smart are you?" Warren growled.

"Look, I don't plan to turn you in or anything. I just

want information. I... uh... I know how to get some Native American artifacts. Maybe you could cut me in?" Marlee continued with her lies, almost buying into them herself.

"Yeah, right. Like I'd believe anything you have to say," Warren said, grabbing a cigarette and placing it in his mouth as he grabbed for a lighter. "Besides, I heard you used to be in law enforcement."

"Who's going to suspect a college professor who used to be a probation officer? It's the perfect cover. I'd been trying to find out more about the artifacts black market, but didn't know anybody who was involved. Then Shane Seaboy was killed and this whole thing fell into my lap. I know where there are uncovered tools and a spoon, along with a bunch of arrow heads. There were bones there too. Human bones. A lot of human bones," Marlee said with an air of calm.

"Where? Who?" Warren quizzed as he puffed on his menthol cigarette.

"Not so fast. If I tell you about my connections then you won't need me. You need to answer some of my questions first before I tell you anything else." Marlee held her ground. She knew this might be her one and only opportunity to get to the truth. Warren stared at her, thinking about his next move. Finally, he nodded.

"How did you get involved in this whole thing? And why don't the cops know you're Diego?" Marlee began.

"Ryan Campbell was the one who got everything going. He's a white guy from Minneapolis and was hooked into a market to sell eagle feathers and bones. The problem was that he didn't have a direct source for Native American artifacts. He dated Geneva Sanders when she lived over in The Cities. She brought him back to meet her parents. She introduced Ryan to Shane and I when he and Geneva were uptown one night. Then Ryan had his connection to a rez and his business grew," Warren said stubbing out his cigarette butt in a half-eaten dish of apple sauce.

Warren lit up another smoke and continued. "After I was brought into the operation, I figured I could run it, not just be Ryan's assistant. I needed to get Ryan out of the way. I made sure we got caught and that Ryan got most of the blame so he'd get a longer prison sentence. I also threw out a lot of clues about Diego being the mastermind of the whole operation with connections throughout the world. Basically, I learned all about the business from Ryan, hooked up with all of his connections, and got him out of the way. He's got several years yet to serve in prison because he was charged for stealing and marketing a lot more artifacts than me, Shane, or Chris. The rest of us just got charged with sale of a few eagle feathers, which has less of a penalty." Warren paused to take another drag from his cigarette.

"Why didn't somebody turn you in since you're Diego?" asked Marlee, curious as to why so many people in a small, concentrated community would conspire to keep a secret.

"Because everybody knew either they or one of their family members would suffer if they talked. Even people in law enforcement around here know but they keep their mouths shut so nothing happens to their families," Warren said with a smirk, proud of how he had the whole Lake Traverse reservation following his orders. "If enough people get beaten up, killed, or just disappear, then everybody gets the message loud and clear."

"How's Tony Red Day, Jr. involved in all of this?" Marlee asked, unable to understand Tony's role in the operation, yet knowing he was somehow involved.

"Tony works for me, but I made sure his name stayed out of it during the investigation. I didn't want him to go to prison. I needed somebody to stay behind and keep an eye on my girlfriend and the business. I couldn't have anybody moving in on my woman or my operation while I was in prison for seven months," Warren said.

"Who's your girlfriend?"

"Collette Many Lightnings," Warren replied. "You didn't know?"

"No, I thought she was Tony's new girlfriend," Marlee said.

"Nope. Tony hangs out over at her place when Verla kicks him out. Plus, he keeps tabs on Collette and the operation when I'm out of town and when I was in prison. Her place is sort of our home base. We hadn't planned on Delphine coming back, but it's alright. She understands how things are," Warren reported.

"You mean you've threatened her," Marlee accused.

"*Persuaded* is a nicer word," Warren said.

"So why did you kill Shane Seaboy?" Marlee dug in to the heart of the matter.

"I didn't kill him. Ashton Dumarce did. Shane found out that Tony was beating Verla, so he threatened to go to law enforcement and incriminate Tony in the eagle feather case. That would get Tony sent to prison and Shane could try to get back together with Verla. He's loved her since high school. The problem is that I couldn't have the FBI nosing around in the old investigation. I thought they might find out I was really Diego and get sent to prison for life. That's why I sent Tony to beat Shane up real good so he wouldn't be talking," said Warren.

"So when Tony and Shane got into a fight that's why Tony said, 'you shoulda kept your mouth shut,'" Marlee said.

"Right. During the fight both Tony and Shane were

ready to explode. Anyway, the fight between them at the party at Collin and Ashton's place was broken up. Tony was supposed to beat Shane unconscious, but that didn't happen so Ashton took over. He was back and forth between the party at his house and some kind of football banquet on campus. Ashton hit Shane in the head with some type of metal pipe he found," Warren said.

"Are you the one who sabotaged the tires on my car and threw a Molotov cocktail into my house?" Marlee asked.

"Ashton Dumarce did both of them," Warren said.

"How about Collin Kolb? Did you have Ashton kill him?" Marlee asked.

"Ashton was just supposed to teach Collin a lesson. He wasn't supposed to kill him," Warren said.

"Funny how all these people keep getting killed yet you say they were only to be roughed up," Marlee said.

"Some people need more encouragement than others."

"When did Collin find out what was going on?" Marlee asked.

"Collin was so busy playing basketball that he didn't know I was Diego or that Tony was working for me. He didn't even know his own roommate, Ashton, was working for me. In case you hadn't noticed, Collin's dumber than a box of rocks," Warren said.

"When did Ashton get involved?" Marlee quizzed.

"After I got back from prison. He was going to college on a football scholarship at MSU, but still needed extra money. We're cousins, so I cut him in on the artifact deal," stated Warren.

"So what did Ashton do to Collin?" Marlee asked.

"Ashton got Collin drunk and held him down and poured more alcohol down his throat with a funnel. Then Ashton drove Collin to the edge of town and told him to walk back home," Warren reported, looking Marlee straight in the eye.

"Collin wasn't wearing a coat or shoes. All he had on was a t-shirt and shorts. Of course he was going to freeze to death. You knew that and it's what you intended all along," Marlee accused.

Warren just raised his eyebrows and continued to stare at Marlee.

"And even though you didn't personally damage my tires or throw the bomb in my house, you ordered both of them to be done and you were hoping to kill me too," Marlee stated.

"I didn't think the loosened lug nuts or the slashed tire would kill you, but I was pretty sure you'd burn to death when your house started on fire from the Molotov cocktail," Warren said without a bit of remorse.

"Luckily a house guest started putting the fire out right away," Marlee said.

"You're one lucky lady," Warren said, his voice like ice water.

It dawned on Marlee that Warren was not buying into her ruse to join his illegal artifact business. She could see in Warren's eyes that he had no intention of cutting her in. In fact, he had no intention of letting her leave his home alive. He was just playing with her like a cat does with an injured mouse.

A noise in the back room startled Marlee, causing her to turn around. She never saw it coming. The next thing she knew, everything went black.

A friend in need is a pain in the ass.

Chapter 27

Warren's lean, wiry frame struggled to pull Marlee's plus-size body down the wheelchair ramp and into the trunk of his dilapidated old Buick. The dated vehicle was dark red with a blue passenger side door. Warren opened the trunk and heaved Marlee's unconscious body into the trunk, slammed the door, and ran back inside the trailer to grab a few items. Moments later he jumped in the car, wearing a tattered denim coat with fur lining, and drove toward the hills.

The oak-covered hills outside of Sisseton surrounded deep ravines known as coulees. The trees of Sica Hollow were spectacular in the fall. The burning reds, exploding oranges, and brilliant golds captured not just the eye, but also the soul of anyone who took in their beauty. Winter comes early in northern South Dakota and the Lake Traverse reservation is no exception. The leaves had relinquished their mighty colors and were now brown, most of them lying on the ground covered in a layer of snow.

Sica Hollow State Park was a major tourist attraction in the summer and fall, but not too many people visited during the cold months. There was not much to see; just barren trees standing watch on the snow-covered hills. This was exactly the environment Warren was looking for. No one came to Sica Hollow until late spring. By that time, the nosy professor's body would be badly decomposed and no one could connect her to him.

Within minutes of arrival, an engine roar could be heard and Marlee's CR-V cruised into the state park, parking the vehicle next to Warren's car. Tony Red Day, Jr. leapt out of the SUV, keys in hand.

"I hauled ass over to your place as soon as you called," Tony said as he approached Warren's vehicle. Warren remained in his car, window rolled down, smoking a cigarette. "I called Ashton's place, but his roommate said he was taking a test. Physiology or psychology. Something like that," Tony continued as he fished in his pocket for a cigarette of his own.

"We need to get rid of this bitch fast," Warren said. "Her friends will be out looking for her before too long."

"So she found out about everything?" Tony asked, puffing on a cancer stick.

"She knew enough to cause me serious problems. I told her the rest since I knew she wouldn't be around much longer. She came to me with some plan about cutting her in on the Indian artifact scheme and she'd hook me up with a supplier of human bones. She actually thought I was buying her bullshit." Warren shook his head in disbelief. He was not used to being treated like a chump.

"Is she dead already?" Tony asked.

"No, just knocked out. She should be conscious by

now. I'd rather have her walk into the coulees than us drag her. She weighs a ton!" Warren grumbled, stubbing out his cigarette in the car ashtray. He opened the car door and made it to the rear of the vehicle in four quick steps.

Warren opened the car trunk and found Marlee semi-conscious, lying amid a spare tire, various tools, and other miscellaneous items. Marlee blinked, her eyes adjusting to the light after being in complete darkness for the last twenty minutes. She tried to talk, but found that she couldn't form her thoughts into actual words.

"Get out!" Warren commanded. When Marlee's attempts at movement were not quick enough, Warren grabbed her by her left arm and began pulling on it with such a vengeance that Marlee thought her shoulder might become dislocated. She summoned every bit of strength to get out of the car trunk; not because she was anxious to see what Warren had in store for her, but because she wanted the strain on her arm to stop.

Marlee extracted herself from the trunk and landed on the cold, snow-covered parking lot at the state park. She used the car to pull herself up to a standing position. Since her legs were shaky and her balance was off, she held on to the vehicle for stability.

"Okay, Professor. We're going for a walk in the trees," Warren said, giving Marlee a shove away from the car.

Marlee stumbled and fell to the ground. "No... no..." she stammered trying to form the words to swear she would not reveal any of the information about their operation to law enforcement. Tony swung his booted foot back and kicked Marlee hard in her lower spine, reactivating the injury from her fall on campus the previous week. Bolts of pain shot through her back, down her legs, and up to the base of her neck. She scrambled to get back on her feet and was roughly assisted by Tony when he grabbed her arm and dragged her upward.

"I... I want in on this deal with you guys. I'm not telling anyone," Marlee said, regaining her voice but not her confidence. She knew it was a feeble attempt at saving herself from certain death at the hands of the criminal mastermind and his errand boy.

"You're really quite funny, Professor," Warren mockingly proclaimed. "It was amusing to watch you try to convince me that you would tell me how to find more human bones if I'd tell you all my secrets. Do you really think I'm that stupid? You must've thought I was buying your bullshit when I answered your questions." Warren was only inches from Marlee's face. She could smell the cigarette stench on his breath as she attempted to pull her face away from his.

Marlee knew no one was around to save her. She also knew she wouldn't be able to overtake both Warren and Tony in a fight. Fear, for the first time, gripped every cell in her body. Before she even realized what she was doing, Marlee was screaming louder than she ever imagined she could. Even as she did it, she knew it was no use.

"Shut up!" Warren snarled as he pulled a tire iron from the trunk of his car and slammed it shut. "There's no one else out here. Just us three at nine o'clock on a Monday morning in early December. The next time someone sees you, you'll look different. Much different." Warren grinned for the first time.

"Now walk!" Warren ordered, carrying the tire iron in one hand and giving Marlee a shove with the other. Tony followed behind looking around as if hearing a strange noise.

Marlee's throat was sore from screaming and she

was incapable of making any further loud vocal sounds. She put a hand in her coat pocket and touched a green, fleece glove. She inched it out of her coat pocket and let it drift to the ground. By this time she had accepted her fate, but hoped the glove might lead someone to finding her body and holding Warren and Tony accountable for her death.

Warren and Tony walked into the trees, with Marlee stumbling ahead of them. She knew she would suffer the same fate at Warren's hands that many others had undergone. Warren and Tony would take her far into the trees, beat her with the tire iron until she was dead, and then leave her body for the coyotes. If she was found at all, it would probably be just her bones and teeth, as her flesh would be consumed by scavengers and her clothing deteriorated by harsh weather conditions.

"Well, look at it this way," Warren said as the three walked deeper into the trees, not following any particular path. "Before long you'll just be a pile of bones and then we can pass them off to someone who doesn't know anything about aging of bones." A sinister laugh emitted from Warren's mouth, as his lips pursed against a newly lit cigarette. "I think I'll tell some of those new age dipshits that your bones are those of a Lakota princess who was killed during a battle with another tribe. They'll believe anything."

Marlee gasped as she subdued a sob. She would not let Warren and Tony see her cry. She knew her death was impending and would be brutal, but she would not show weakness by crying like a baby. Marlee thought about all she would be missing in the upcoming years. She had worked so hard to get her education and training for all her past careers and her current job as a college professor. And now all of that would be gone.

In desperation, Marlee shrieked one more time, as

loudly as she could muster. Warren swung the tire iron above his head and angled it toward the back of Marlee's skull. Before he could gain the momentum to strike her, there was a loud voice from the surrounding trees.

"Put down the tire iron NOW! We have guns trained on you and will shoot!" called out the deep, male voice.

Warren, holding his striking pose, glanced around to find the source of the voice. While distracted, Tony took the opportunity to kick Warren in the back of the knee, forcing him to the ground. Tony grabbed the tire iron, rolled Warren onto his back, and held the tire iron against Warren's throat. Warren kicked and struggled, but he was no match for Tony's heavier, more muscular build.

From behind a thatch of trees emerged A.J. Simms from the FBI and several police officers from the tribal police department. All had their guns drawn and were prepared to shoot. One of the officers handcuffed Warren and dragged him to his feet, rattling off a litany of charges that he would have to face. As the remaining officers holstered their weapons, more rustling could be heard from the trees. Bettina Crawford emerged and ran to Marlee, who was now leaning against a tree for support.

"I don't know whether to slap you or hug you," Bettina said with a mix of relief and anger.

"Well it took you long enough to get here. Some detective you are." Marlee's lame attempt at a joke did not serve to lighten the tension of anyone present.

"You knew I'd find you. Leaving a note at your house telling Diane and Bridget what you were doing and then driving by where Collin Kolb's body was found knowing full well that I'd be there and would see you," Bettina said.

"Yeah, I know it was dangerous, but I couldn't think

of any other way to find out information from Warren. I wanted to be sure somebody would show up to get me out of trouble, but I couldn't say anything beforehand because you said you'd shoot me." Marlee knew her account of Bettina's threats were exaggerated.

"I threatened to have you arrested, not shot," Bettina corrected, fighting back a small smile.

"So how did you guys find me out here at Sica Hollow? Did you watch Warren drag me into the trunk of his car and drive out here?" Marlee could not fathom why officers of the law would watch an ongoing crime, especially if there was a high likelihood she would die.

A.J. Simms stepped forward after finishing up a conversation with two of the tribal officers. "Tony Red Day, Jr. told us all about it."

"What? No, Tony is one of Warren's henchmen," Marlee corrected.

"Nope, he just started working as a confidential informant for us a few days ago. We were able to link him with the eagle feather case from a few years ago and approached him with a deal. If he would help us nab Diego, then we'd look at reducing his charges in the eagle feather case," A.J. reported.

"But how did Tony know I was at Warren's place? And how did he know Warren was bringing me out here?" Marlee asked, rubbing the back of her head where she was struck earlier. She was dizzy and her mind was groggy.

Tony, listening in on the conversation, chimed in, directing his comments at Marlee. "It didn't take a genius to figure out you were going to Warren's place after you talked to me and Delphine this morning. You said you knew Warren and I knew all about the deaths of Shane and Collin, so I figured you'd be going out to Warren's place to confront him. I called the FBI office in

Elmwood and they told me Simms was out here working on a case overnight. They patched me through to him and I told him what you said. Not long after I hung up, Warren called and said to get to his place right away. He told me to bring your car to Sica Hollow and we'd get rid of it after we got rid of you. Then I called Simms back and told him."

"So you actually helped save me?" asked Marlee.

Tony nodded his head, pleased with the work he had done.

"Then why in the hell did you kick me when I fell down?" Marlee growled, not forgetting the swift kick Tony gave her in the back.

"I didn't want Warren to get suspicious," Tony said, smiling then breaking out in a laugh.

"Very funny. By the way, we know you beat your girlfriend, Verla. I saw her with a black eye and a missing tooth, so don't act like you're some kind of super hero," Marlee snapped.

"I didn't do that. I've never laid a hand on that woman. Warren worked her over. Then he told Shane I did it. Shane and I've had bad blood for years now. Since high school. Warren knew Shane still wanted to hook up with Verla again and would fly off the handle if he thought I was beating her up. Warren told Shane lies about me and he told me that Shane and Verla were getting back together. Then he had Ashton Dumarce invite both of us to his party in Elmwood, knowing we'd both show up and there'd be trouble," Tony stated.

The bevy of law enforcement officers, Marlee, Bettina, Tony, and a handcuffed Warren all walked back to the parking lot. "C'mon, Tony. You've still got a lot to tell us about this whole thing," A.J. Simms said, pulling Tony toward his full-sized, black SUV. The tribal cops loaded Warren into the back of one of their police cruisers and drove to the tribal jail in Agency Village.

"Are you going to be alright?" a tribal officer asked Marlee. "We can take you to IHS to get checked out."

Marlee shook her head, which caused her to become even more dizzy. "No, I don't need to go to Indian Health Service. I'll be fine. Just need to get home and maybe have a nap. Who has my car keys?"

"I have them and I'll be driving you back to Elmwood. When we get there I'm taking you to see a doctor. No excuses," barked Bettina. Marlee knew better than to argue with her friend when she was this intent.

"Thanks, but I don't think I need medical attention. Just a nap," Marlee stated.

"Nope, to the doctor you will go," Bettina insisted and that was the end of the discussion.

Debts must be paid. Consequences are due. At least, that's how I think the world works.

Chapter 28

After finding out she was not suffering from a concussion or any other negative after effects of the blow to the head, Marlee was driven home by Bettina. The detective acted as friend and prison warden as she mapped out the remainder of Marlee's day. "You're just going to take it easy. Go in your room and take a nap. I'll call the window replacement people about getting your living room window replaced. You don't have anywhere else you need to be today." Bettina bustled about the house until she was sure Marlee was settled in.

"Diane is at her apartment, but will be stopping by later. Bridget is out but will be back shortly. I'm dropping your car keys over at Diane's to make sure you don't drive off somewhere," Bettina said before she closed the front door. Even though she and Bettina talked the whole way home about the case and the various twists and turns it had taken, Marlee was restless and wanted to talk more about it with someone else.

Until Bridget returned home or Diane stopped by, she was alone with her thoughts.

Sitting upright in her bed, Marlee remembered another situation that began even before Shane Seaboy's death and her investigation into the ongoing Native American artifact scheme. Walking to the living room, she grabbed the phone and moved to the overstuffed chair in the corner. Plopping down on the plush cushion, she placed a call to Eva Gooding at the MSU bookstore.

"Eva, any leads on who took the presents and other stuff donated for the gift tree? Has Tia done anything else suspicious?" Marlee asked, wanting an update on the newly-hired single mother who was one of the people who had access to the presents.

"It's solved! I figured it out on my own!" Eva exclaimed.

"What? Who was it? It was Tia, wasn't it?" Marlee was excited the matter had been solved, yet disappointed she had not been involved in the resolution.

"It was Rob. You know, the guy who's worked here longer than me," Eva said.

"Rob? Why would he steal all that stuff and then return nearly everything along with an apology note?" Marlee asked.

"He had been hitting on Tia and she rejected him. When she finally made it clear that under no circumstances would she ever go out with him, Rob decided to seek revenge and get her fired. He took all the gift tree items and, since they weren't wrapped, kept the clothes and toys that were age appropriate for Tia's two kids. He kept the money, gift cards, and food too, knowing that those were things Tia could also use. Then Rob wrote a note imitating Tia's handwriting. He was setting her up to be fired and arrested," Eva reported.

"Just because she rejected him? People get rejected

all the time. Rob's actions are way over the top," Marlee said.

"Yeah, I agree. He's a bastard," Eva said, not even stumbling over the bad word she had probably never uttered in her life before.

"Where's Rob now?"

"I called the police and they came and arrested him. He was terminated from his job this morning," Eva stated.

"How did you figure it out?" Marlee asked, impressed with Eva's detective skills.

"I was over at his desk this weekend and noticed a notebook so I thumbed through it. There was a note Tia had written Rob about some discrepancy with what was ordered for the bookstore and what had been paid for the goods. He had written the note over and over, trying to imitate her penmanship," Tia said. "So when he came in early this morning I confronted him and he lied about it for a while, but then finally confessed."

"Great work, Eva! Maybe we should start our own detective agency!" Marlee joked.

"No way! This was way too much drama for me," Eva said. "Oh, I let Tia know what really happened and she was relieved not to be under suspicion any more. She said to tell you she's waiting for an apology."

"From me? You accused her too!" Marlee recalled that both she and Eva had meeting with Tia in which the young woman was accused of the thefts.

"Yeah, but she likes me," Eva said with a giggle.

Diane came in the front door as Marlee finished up her phone conversation with Eva. "Heard you had a rough morning," Diane said, placing Marlee's key ring on the coffee table.

"That's an understatement," Marlee said, recounting her interactions with Warren Keoke and law enforcement arriving on the scene. "Thanks for calling Bettina when you read my note."

"Bridget and I were really mad at you, but we weren't going to let you get killed. We called Bettina right away and she swore and then said she was using the emergency lights on her vehicle to get to Sisseton as soon as possible," Diane said.

Diane was still furious with Marlee and not in the mood to discuss the intricacies of the Shane Seaboy murder, the ongoing eagle feather case, and the death of Collin Kolb. Things would be strained between the friends for a while, but Marlee hoped Diane would eventually forgive her.

After Diane's brief visit, Marlee scooped up her keys and walked out to her garage. She was still a bit wobbly on her feet, but felt she would be fine to drive the few blocks to campus. Driving proved to be simple. Parking was the problem. Marlee's depth perception was never that great, but the blow to her head and the stress of nearly being killed impeded her ability to line her vehicle up with the others parked in the Student Union lot. After several attempts, she decided it was good enough and made her way to her office.

Scobey Hall was a hotbed of excitement. Students were buzzing around finishing projects and papers since it was the last week before final exams. Professors were overwhelmed as students entered and exited their offices seeking assistance on final projects or begging for a better grade. On top of that, everyone knew about Collin Kolb's death and Ashton Dumarce's involvement in it.

Marlee walked into her office and eased down on her ancient chair with the creaky rollers. She needed to gather up some papers and go back home to prepare for class that night. It was Monday and she taught class from 6:00 to 9:00, although tonight's class would be a bit shorter since they had already discussed most of the material Marlee planned to cover that semester. She planned to hand back students' papers, prepare them for the final exam, and deal with any questions the students might have.

A sharp knock on Marlee's door startled her. She opened the door to a red-faced Dean Green. "McCabe, I know all about your activities here and over on the Indian reservation. I know you disregarded the directive that I gave you last week to stay out of the Seaboy investigation and I know you've been derelict in your teaching duties. You called in sick this morning because you were investigating. You've involved students in your schemes. I've started the paperwork for your suspension from Midwestern State University. You will finish out this week of teaching, next week of final exams, and submit the final course grades. After that, you'll be suspended until further notice. And if I get my way, you'll be out on your ass with no hope of ever teaching here again!" With that pronouncement, Dean Ira Green turned and stormed away, leaving a stunned Marlee to figure out what to do next.

BRENDA DONELAN

Afterward

The memorial service for Shane Seaboy was held on Wednesday. None of Shane's relatives were in attendance, but Geneva Sanders and her parents were there to pay their respects. A similar service was held for Collin Kolb two days later to a standing room only crowd. He had been a valued member of the MSU basketball team and most of the campus turned out to say farewell.

Warren Keoke, who was the real Diego, was arrested on charges of murder, aggravated assault, kidnapping, illegal trafficking in Native American human remains, grave robbing, burglary, and a host of other offenses. After presented with the massive amount of evidence against him, Warren accepted a plea agreement. He was sentenced to fifty years in federal prison. Ashton Dumarce was sentenced to life in prison for the murders of Shane Seaboy and Collin Kolb. Since the murders he committed were off the reservation and, thus not under federal jurisdiction, Ashton went through the state court system. With Warren and Ashton in prison, the link to the Lake Traverse Reservation was severed, forcing those who wanted to illegally obtain Native American artifacts to go elsewhere. The arrests had not stopped the artifact trade altogether, but it had been halted in the northeastern part of South Dakota. At least for a while.

In exchange for his cooperation, Tony Red Day Jr. received a reduced sentence in the eagle feather case he had been previously involved in. The judge ruled that Tony's assistance to law enforcement was essential in bringing Warren Keoke to justice. Tony was placed on probation and ordered to complete 500 hours of community service work at Agency Village. Marlee doubted he was the knight in shining armor that he portrayed himself to be. She felt his involvement in the past and current illegal dealings surrounding Warren Keoke were minimized since he acted as an informant for the FBI. Still, she owed her life to Tony. She would have been dead had Tony not contacted law enforcement right away when Warren called with the directive to bring Marlee's vehicle to Sica Hollow.

In a strange twist of events, Collette Many Lightnings was found dead. Tony reported to law enforcement that Warren became jealous when she was spending time with another man. They fought and he dumped her battered body in the coulees after beating her to death. Collette's killing served a main purpose; to reaffirm that anyone crossing Warren Keoke would face the same ending. The bodies of two other people from the Sisseton area were found in the same location where law enforcement found Collette's body. The teen males had been reported missing months ago. The FBI discovered the boys had been breaking into homes and stealing various items for Warren Keoke. When they decided they wanted to quit, Warren made sure they'd never talk.

Delphine Many Lightnings' story turned out to be just as she had reported. She came back to her old house so her granddaughter could help her since her health was failing. She'd lost the use of her legs due to diabetes and needed assistance. Delphine had been reluctant to let Warren's illegal schemes operate out of her house, but Warren made it clear what would happen if she did not cooperate. When Delphine suspected Collette had been killed, she knew better than to speak about it for fear she would be next. After Collette was killed, Warren made Tony go over to Delphine's house to take care of her.

Geneva Sanders resigned from MSU shortly after the memorial service for Shane Seaboy. She felt responsible for his involvement with the eagle feather operation and his subsequent death. When Geneva began dating Ryan Campbell in Minneapolis she had no idea of his involvement in trafficking Native American artifacts. After they dated for a few months, Geneva brought Ryan back home to meet her parents. She also introduced him to Shane Seaboy and one of his friends on that visit back to the Sisseton area. After Ryan, Shane, and the others were arrested and sent to prison, Geneva was racked with guilt. When Shane was released from prison he moved to Minneapolis and worked at a job Geneva obtained for him at a small grocery store. When Geneva was hired at MSU in Elmwood she was able to land Shane a job as a janitor there and help him find an apartment. Since his release from prison, Geneva considered Shane her responsibility. She felt it was the very least she could do after unwittingly involving him in Ryan Campbell's illegal operation.

Bridget McCabe finally went home, but was counting the days until she would return to Elmwood for her year-long teaching appointment at Marymount College. After she left, Marlee often found herself applying movie references to various real-life situations, just as Bridget had done *ad nauseum* when she stayed with Marlee.

Bettina Crawford and A.J. Simms, after working together to rescue Marlee from the hands of Warren Keoke, began dating. Marlee anxiously waited for Vince Chipperton to return from probation officer training so she could begin a regular stalking routine of him.

Marlee's suspension was reviewed by the administrative counsel at MSU and, although she was found to be in violation of a number of campus rules and regulations, she was told she would remain at the university at least until the end of the spring semester, which was May 2006. She had five months in which to turn around the dean's opinion of her.

Given Dean Green's outright hatred of her, it would be a tough road.

HOLIDAY HOMICIDE

Why did I get involved selling eagle feathers? Was it just for monetary gain? I'll admit, the money I earned was nice, but it wasn't the main reason I worked for Warren. It was because it gave me a sense of belonging. I hadn't felt like anybody even knew my name since I aged out of the foster care system and had to leave the Sanders'. Working for Warren and the others made me feel like a part of something. And I had a purpose. I didn't really like breaking into houses and stealing feathers and artifacts, but it wasn't the worst thing in the world. Little did I know that I would later experience the worst thing in the world... having my own people; my tribe; turn their backs on me.

The End

About The Author

Brenda Donelan is a life-long resident of South Dakota. She grew up on a cattle ranch in Stanley County, attended college in Brookings, and worked in Aberdeen as a probation officer and later as a college professor. Currently, she resides in Sioux Falls.

Day of the Dead is the first book in the University Mystery Series. She is currently working on the third book in the series, which will be published in 2015.

The author can be reached by email at brendadonelanauthor@gmail.com. For more information on Brenda Donelan, books in the University Mystery Series, and tour dates, check out her website at brendadonelan.com or find her on Facebook at Brenda Donelan–Author.